Praise for
SUSAN JOHNSON

"Her romances have strong, intelligent heroines, hard,
iron-willed men, plenty of sexual tension and sensuality
and lots of accurate history. Anyone who can put all
that in a book is one of the best!"—*Romantic Times*

"No one . . . can write such rousing love stories
while bringing in so much accurate historical detail.
Of course, no one can write such rousing
love stories, period."—*Rendezvous*

"Susan Johnson writes an extremely gripping
story. . . . With her knowledge of the period and her
exquisite sensual scenes, she is an exceptional writer."
—*Affaire de Coeur*

"Susan Johnson's descriptive talents are legendary and
well-deserved."—*Heartland Critiques*

"Fascinating . . . The author's style is a pleasure
to read."—*Los Angeles Herald Examiner*

SUSAN JOHNSON

Seduction in Mind

BANTAM BOOKS
New York Toronto London Sydney Auckland

SEDUCTION IN MIND
A Bantam Book / August 2001

ISBN 0-553-58254-2

Published simultaneously in the United States and Canada

Bantam Books are published by Bantam Books, a division of Random
House, Inc. Its trademark, consisting of the words "Bantam Books"
and the portrayal of a rooster, is Registered in U.S. Patent and Trademark Office and in other countries. Marca Registrada. Bantam
Books, 1540 Broadway, New York, New York 10036.

PRINTED IN THE UNITED STATES OF AMERICA
OPM   10 9 8 7 6 5 4 3 2 1

Dear Reader,

I'd just purchased a book on the Holland Park circle of artists and came on a description of a seductive lady wearing a dark blue dress. The imagery was intense; I could see her clearly. Alexandra Ionides suddenly came to life for me. She's not the lady in the description, of course; she's *my* lady in a blue dress and I wished to show everyone her world.

Sam Lennox was intrigued by her as well. In fact, he'd owned a painting of her long before he met her. But once he realized she lived in London, he was intent on knowing her better.

And he always got what he wanted.

Although the manner of that acquisition wasn't without obstacles.

Alexandra, you see, disliked men like Sam Lennox who only amused themselves in ladies' beds.

If you have any questions or comments, you can reach me at *www.susanjohnsonauthor.net*.

Happy reading,

Chapter 1

*I*t's the same luscious female," Lord Ranelagh murmured, surveying a painting of a scantily clad odalisque in the Royal Academy show. "I'd recognize those breasts anywhere."

"She had more clothes on in the painting you bought in Paris," the young Earl of Airlie said, his gaze intent on the splendid female form. "It looks as though she's become even more—er—emancipated."

Samuel Lennox, the Viscount Ranelagh, heir to an earldom of great fortune, rich in his own right, cast his friend a skeptical glance. "As if all models aren't bohemian by nature. More to the point—since Leighton's painted her, I wonder if the pretty vixen's in London?"

"Why not ask Leighton? Since the painting's not for sale, he might have a special interest in the model."

"Do you know him?"

"Not personally, but my cousin attends his musicals. I'll have George introduce us."

"Now?"

Edward McDonal frowned. "I thought we were going to the Marlborough Club."

"How long can it take to stop at Leighton's and find out her name? Besides, I want to buy the painting."

"There's a Not for Sale sign prominently displayed under the title," his friend pointed out.

A faint cynicism raised the viscount's dark brows. "Everything's for sale, Eddie. You know that."

An hour later, an imposing butler ushered them into Frederic Leighton's studio, despite the inconvenient hour and the artist's custom to receive by appointment only, despite the fact the artist was working frantically because he was fast losing the sun. The butler knew that Leighton, ever conscious of his wealth and position, particularly now that he'd been knighted, cultivated friendships with the aristocracy.

The room was enormous with rich cornices, piers, friezes of gold, marble, enamel, and mosaics, all color and movement, opulence and luxury. Elaborate bookshelves lined one wall, two huge Moorish arches soared overhead, stained glass windows of an Oriental design were set into the eastern wall, while the north windows under which the artist worked were tall, iron-framed, utilitarian.

Leighton turned from his easel as the men entered, and he greeted them with a smooth urbanity, casting aside his frenzied air with ease, recognizing George

Howard with a personal comment and his companions with grace.

Lord Ranelagh hardly took notice of their host, for his gaze was fixed on Leighton's current work—a female nude in a provocative pose, her diaphanous robe lifted over her head. "Very nice, Sir Leighton," he said with a faint nod in the direction of the easel. "The lady's coloring is particularly fine."

"As is the lady. I'm fortunate she dabbles in the arts."

"She lives in London?"

"Some of the time. I could introduce you if you like."

"No, you may not, Frederic. I'm here incognito for this scandalous painting." A lady's amused voice came from the right, and a moment later, Alexandra Ionides emerged from behind a tapestry screen. She was dressed in dark blue silk that set off her skin to perfection, the front of the gown still partially open, her silken flesh that had an alluring warmth about it, as though she'd been in the heat of the sun, quickly disappearing from sight as she closed three sparkling gemstone clasps.

"It's you," the viscount exclaimed softly.

Her eyes were huge, the deepest purple, and her surprise was genuine. "I beg your pardon?"

"Alex, allow me to introduce the Viscount Ranelagh," Leighton said. "My lord, Alexandra Ionides, the Dowager Countess St. Albans and Mrs. Coutts."[1]

"*Mrs.* Coutts?"

"I'm a widow. Both my husbands died." She always enjoyed saying that—for the reaction it caused, for the pleasure it gave her to watch people's faces.

"May I ask how they died?" the viscount inquired, speaking to her with a quiet intensity, as though they were alone in the cavernous room.

"Not in their beds, if that's what you're thinking." She knew of Ranelagh, of his reputation, and thought his question either flippant or cheeky.

"I meant . . . how difficult it must have been—how distressing. I'm a widower."

"I know." But she doubted he was distressed. The flighty, promiscuous Lady Ranelagh had died in a riding accident, and very opportunely, it was said; her husband was about to either kill her or divorce her.

"Alex and I were just about to sit down to champagne. Would you gentlemen care for a glass?" Leighton gestured toward an alcove decorated with various colorful divans. "I reward myself at the end of a workday," he added with a small, deprecating smile.

A bottle of champagne was already on ice atop a Moroccan-style table, and if Alexandra might have wished to refuse, Leighton had made it impossible. Ranelagh was more than willing, Eddie had never turned down a drink in his adult life, and George Howard, like so many men of his class, had considerable leisure time.

Sam made sure to seat himself beside Alex, a fact she took note of with mild disdain. She disliked men of Ranelagh's stamp who amused themselves in ladies' beds. It seemed a gross self-indulgence, when life offered so much outside the conventional world of aristocratic vice.

"Meeting you this afternoon almost makes me believe in fate," he said softly. "I came here to discover the identity of the exquisite model in Leighton's Academy painting, and here you are."

"Whereas I don't believe in fate at all, Lord Ranelagh, for I came here today with privacy in mind, and here you all are."

He smiled. "And you wish us all to Hades."

"How astute, my lord."

He'd never been offered his congé by a woman before, and rather than take offense, he was intrigued. Willing females he knew by the score. But one such as this . . . "Maybe if you came to know us—or me— better," he added in a low voice.

Their conversation was apart from the others, their divan offset slightly from the other bright-hued sofas, and the three men opposite them were deep in a heated discussion of the best routes through the Atlas Mountains.

"Let me make this clear, Lord Ranelagh, and I hope tactful as well. I've been married twice; I'm not a novice in the ways of the world. I take my independence very seriously and I'm averse, to put it in the most temperate terms, to men like you, my lord, who find amusement their raison d'être. So I won't be getting to know you better. But thank you for the offer."

Her hair was the most glorious deep auburn, piled atop her head in heavy silken waves, and he wished nothing more at the moment than to free the ruby pins holding it in place and watch it tumble onto her shoulders. "Perhaps some other time," he said, thinking he'd never seen such luscious golden peach skin, nor eyes like hers.

"There won't be another time, my lord."

"If I were a betting man—"

"But you are." Equal to his reputation as a libertine was his penchant for high-stakes betting. It was the talk of London at the moment, for he'd just won fifty thousand on the first race at Ascot yesterday.

He smiled. "It was merely an expression. Do I call you Mrs. Coutts or the dowager countess?"

"I prefer my maiden name."

"Then, Miss Ionides, what I was about to say was that if I were a betting man, I'd lay odds we were about to become good friends."

"You're too arrogant, Ranelagh. I'm not eighteen and easily infatuated by a handsome man, even one of your remarkable good looks."

"While I'm not only fascinated by a woman of your dazzling beauty, but intrigued with your unconventional attitude toward female nudity."

"Because I pose nude, you think me available?"

The merest smile appeared on his lips. "So blunt, Miss Ionides."

"You weren't interested in taking me to tea, I presume."

"We'll do whatever you like," he replied, the suggestion in his voice so subtle, his virtuosity couldn't be faulted. And that, of course, was the problem.

"You've more than enough ladies in your train, Ranelagh. You won't miss me."

"You're sure?" he pursued. "I can't change your mind?"

"Absolutely sure . . . and no," she declared firmly.

"A shame."

"Speak for yourself. I have a full and gratifying life. If you'll excuse me, Frederic," she said, addressing her host as she rose to her feet. "I have an appointment elsewhere."

The viscount had come to his feet. "May I offer you a ride to your appointment?"

She surveyed him slowly from head to toe, her gaze coming to rest after due deliberation on his amused countenance. "No, you may not."

"I'm crushed," he said, grinning.

"But not for long, I'm sure," she replied crisply, and waving at Leighton and the other men, she walked away.

Everyone followed her progress across the large room, and only when she'd disappeared through the high Moorish arch did conversation resume.

"She's astonishingly beautiful," George Howard said. "I can see why you have her pose for you."

"She *deigns* to pose for me," Leighton corrected his friend. "I'm only deeply grateful, because she models infrequently and according to whim. Although,

Alma-Tadema has intrigued her with his newest project." He offered the men a self-deprecating smile. "We're currently competing for her time."

"I'm surprised a woman of her magnificence isn't married again."

"She has notable wealth from both her family and husbands and she prefers her freedom," Leighton offered. "Or so she says."

"From that tone of voice, I'm surmising you've proposed," Eddie observed. "And been refused."

Leighton dipped his handsome leonine head in acknowledgment. "At least I'm in good company. Rumor has it she's turned down most everyone."

"Most?" Sam regarded the artist from beneath his long lashes, his lazy sprawl the picture of indolence.

"She has an occasional affair, I'm told."

"By whom?" Ranelagh's voice was very soft. "With whom?"

"Kemp seems to know. I believe he's acquainted with Alex's maid."

"With whom is she currently entertaining herself then, pray tell." The viscount moved from his lounging pose, his gaze suddenly intent.

"No one I know. A young art student for a time." He shrugged. "A banker she knew through her husband. A priest, someone said." He shook his head. "Only gossip, you understand. Alex keeps her private life private."

"And yet she's willing to pose nude—a blatantly public act."

"She's wealthy enough to do as she pleases . . . as you no doubt understand," Leighton noted with an urbane smile. "While a model is generally nameless anyway, particularly in cases like this, where a lady prefers a degree of anonymity."

"Like a Madame X."

Leighton shrugged again. "Something like that, I suppose. Although, keep in mind, Alex is also an artist in her own right. She views the nude form as quite separate from societal attitudes."

"Toward women," the viscount observed.

Leighton's expression was unreadable. "I wouldn't venture a guess on Alex's cultural politics."

"You're wasting your time, Sammy." Eddie waved his champagne glass toward the door through which Alex had exited. "She's not going to give you a tumble."

The viscount's dark brows rose faintly. "We'll see."

"That tone of voice always makes me nervous. The last time you said 'We'll see,' I ended up in a Turkish jail from which we were freed only because the British ambassador was a personal friend of the sultan's minister. And why you thought you could get through the phalanx of guards surrounding that harem, I'll never know."

"We almost made it."

"Almost nearly cost us our lives."

"You worry too much."

"While you don't worry at all."

"Of course I do. I was worried Lady Duffin's

husband was going to break down the door before we were finished last week."

"So that's why Charles won't speak to you anymore."

The viscount shrugged. "He never did anyway."

Chapter 2

Alexandra didn't have another appointment. Rather, she'd felt a desperate need to escape. Notwithstanding her disapproval of men like Ranelagh, something alarming had happened a few moments ago, and try as she might to disparage the viscount's blatant sexual magnetism and his infamous use of it, she'd found herself not only drawn to him but, more terrifying, tempted. She drew in a calming breath, her emotions in chaos, her nerves on edge, an unusual agitation gripping her senses. Not only were all the stories of the viscount's allure true, the man was fully aware of the effect he had on women—damn him.

Intent on repressing her alarming reaction to their meeting, she reminded herself he was just another man and she wasn't a missish young girl whose head could be turned by a seductive glance and a charming smile. Nor was she some tart who could be bluntly propositioned as though he had but to nod his handsome head and she would fall into his bed.

In spite of the fact that seductive power was his hallmark and he was notorious for inspiring carnal longing in legions of women, she didn't intend to be added to his harem of eager and willing females. She'd spent too many years struggling against conformity, trying to find a role outside the societal standards for women of her class, and she relished her hard-won independence. Surely, she was strong enough to resist a libertine no matter how sinfully handsome or celebrated his sexual expertise.

Regardless of the fact that she'd been celibate since a recent disastrous affair with a man who didn't understand the meaning of no.

Reason, perhaps, for her current agitation.

But after Leon, she'd vowed to be more prudent in her choices.

And Ranelagh would be not only imprudent but—if his conduct at Leighton's was any evidence—impudent as well.

Inexhaustible in bed, however, if rumor were true, a devilish voice inside her head reminded her.

She clasped her hands tightly in her lap, as though she might restrain her carnal urges with so slight a gesture. Impossible, of course, with the stark images of Ranelagh lodged in her brain—his tantalizing smile, the boldness of his glance, the overwhelming sense of power he evoked. He was tall, dark, breathtakingly handsome at close range, and all honed muscle and brute strength beneath the gloss of his fine tailoring. She'd never met such a man before, his presence one of sheer physical force. The purity of his finely modeled features only enhanced his image of physical perfection, while his brooding black eyes and sensual mouth suggested impassioned sensibilities beneath the consummate male animal.

And his hands were so *very* large—which meant—

Good God—she was carrying on like an infatuated adolescent.

Perhaps she should spend a few hours with young Harry and assuage her sexual urges, she tersely thought; he was always so grateful for her company. But boyish gratitude didn't hold much appeal when Ranelagh's virile maleness was in the forefront of her brain. Nor did young Harry's sweetness prevail over the unabashed impatience in Ranelagh's eyes.

"No!" she exclaimed, the sound of her voice shocking in the confined space of her carriage, as was the flagrant extent of her desire.

She really, *really* needed to talk to Rosalind. Her friend was always the voice of reason . . . or at least one of caution to her rash impulses.

Lady Ormand was entertaining at tea and Alex had to sit through a long, tedious hour before the last guest finally departed. "How do you stand it?" Alex exclaimed as the footman closed the door on the Viscountess Compton. "The conversation was solely of frocks and gowns. Do those women have a life beyond visiting their modiste?"

"Gwendolyn brought Emily and May today since they're in town, and you know how—"

"Shallow they are?"

Her friend smiled. "Indeed. But consider, you learned how to get Brussels lace for half price from Honitons."

"If I'd been listening after the first five minutes, I might have."

"I commend you for your courtesy, then. I doubt they noticed. So tell me, darling, what brought you here at such a dangerous time of day? I know how you dislike teatime."

"I needed your counsel or advice"—Alex paused— "or perhaps only a sympathetic ear." And she went on to explain the tale of her introduction to Ranelagh.

"You have to admit, he's the most heavenly man in London." Rosalind shrugged her dainty shoulders. "Or England, or the world, for that matter."

Alex offered her friend a sardonic glance. "Thank you for the discouragement."

"Forgive me, dear, but he *is* lovely."

"And he knows it and I don't wish to become an afternoon of amusement for him."

"Would you like it better if it were more than an afternoon?"

"No. I would prefer not thinking of him at all. He's arrogant and brazenly self-assured and no doubt has never been turned down by a woman in his life."

"So you're the first."

"I meant it facetiously."

"And you've come here to have me bolster your good judgment and caution you to reason."

"Exactly."

"And will that wise counsel suffice?"

Alex exhaled softly. "Perhaps if you're with me day and night," she muttered.

Rosalind's pale brows rose. "He's said to have that effect on women. In fact, Allison still trembles at the mention of his name, and her stories of his prowess are quite—unbelievable."

"And it annoys me immeasurably that I'm feeling as beguiled as all the mindless Allisons he amuses himself with—and don't look at me like that . . . you know Allison prides herself on *never* having read a book."

"While in contrast to Ranelagh's host of houris, you wish your intellect to be in control of your desires."

"I insist on it."

"Is it working?"

Alex shoved her teaspoon around on the embroidered linen cloth for a lengthy time before she looked up. "No."

"So the question becomes—what are you going to do?"

"I absolutely refuse to fall into his arms." She glared at her friend. "Do you understand? I won't."

"Fine. Are there matters of degree, then?"

"About what?"

"About falling into his arms. Would you fall, say, after a certain duration, or never in a million years?"

Alex shifted uncomfortably, tapped her fingers on the gilded chair arm, inhaled, exhaled, was silent for several moments more. "I'm not sure about the million years," she said finally.

"Ah." Rosalind scrutinized her friend with a benevolent gaze. "Then some measure of compromise will be required."

"How do you possibly compromise with a man like that? Women have been flinging themselves at him his entire life."

"But you haven't."

"Not yet."

Rosalind leaned back on the settee, her expression amused. "That would be a first, wouldn't it? But as I see it, you and Ranelagh are very much alike." At Alex's instant pique, she added, "Honestly, darling, you have to admit, men have been flinging themselves at you with similar abandon ever since you left the schoolroom. Not that you've taken up with many of them, but they've certainly tried. So, do you think you simply dislike Ranelagh's audacity? Or would you prefer he beg?"

"I would prefer not having met him. I don't like feeling this way . . . as though I were simultaneously breathless with longing and in peril."

"Then refuse him."

"I intend to. I'm probably making too much of a casual meeting anyway. Ranelagh, no doubt, propositions women every day."

"No doubt. Are you feeling better now that you've reconciled sense and sensibility?"

Alex laughed quietly. "Marginally, at least. He *is* spectacularly male, unfortunately."

"And you've been avoiding men since Leon insisted you marry him not long ago."

"Which is the problem, I tell myself. Ranelagh's handsomeness is only incidental to my frustrated sexual urges."

"Certainly frustration *could* be a consideration," Rosalind said kindly.

"At the moment, I should be entirely too busy to be frustrated," Alex returned. "Both Leighton and Alma-Tadema have appealed to my goodwill, and in a weak moment I agreed to pose for them—when my schedule is already overcommitted." She glanced at the clock. "Which reminds me, I must be at Alma-Tadema's by six. Larry's working on a painting in which evening shadows are required."

"A painting that will garner all the usual praise of both his skills and your beauty. At times, I envy you your freedom. Sidney would never let me be so modern, even though everyone is nominally discreet."

"You're not as insistent as I, darling."

"Nor independently wealthy."

Alex grinned. "I won't argue the advantages of my fortune. I'm well aware I'm allowed liberties that only wealth bestows. And there are advantages as well to being an artist. One's eccentricities are looked upon with a certain tolerance."

"And it pleases you to pose nude."

"On occasion. If I like the artist and the work. I paint nudes as well. What artist wouldn't?" She rose with a smile. "Thank you for letting me talk. I'm feeling quite in control of my feelings once again. And Larry always has all the latest gossip. My evening should be amusing."

Chapter 3

"You're boring the hell out of me," Eddie grumbled, reaching for the brandy bottle at his elbow.

Sam looked up from his putt. "Go to the Marlborough Club yourself."

"I might." Refilling his glass, the earl lifted it in salute. "As soon as I finish this bottle."

"After you finish that bottle, you'll be passed out on my couch," the viscount said, watching the ball roll into the cup on the putting green he'd had installed in his conservatory.

"You don't miss a night out as a rule," Eddie remonstrated. "Did the merry widow's refusal incapacitate you?"

"*Au contraire,*" Ranelagh replied, positioning another ball with his golf club. "I'm feeling first rate. And I expect she's in high mettle as well."

"She turned you down, Sam."

"But she didn't want to." He softly swung his club, striking the ball with exquisite restraint.

"And you can tell."

The viscount half smiled. "I could feel it."

"So sure . . ."

"Yes."

"And you're saving yourself for her now?"

"Dammit, Eddie, if you want to go, go. I don't feel like fucking anyone right now, and I drank enough last night to last me a week."

"Since when haven't you felt like fucking someone?" his friend asked, his gaze measured.

"What the hell are you insinuating?"

"That you fancy the voluptuous Miss Ionides with more than your usual casual disregard."

"After meeting her for ten minutes?" Ranelagh snorted. "You're drunk."

"And you're putting golf balls at seven o'clock when you're never even home at seven."

Sam tossed his club aside. "Let's go."

"Are you going out like that?"

The viscount offered his friend a narrowed glance. "None of the girls at Hattie's will care."

"True," Eddie muttered, heaving himself up from the leather-covered couch. "But don't do that to me again. It scares the hell out of me."

Sam was shrugging into his jacket. "Do what?"

"Change the pattern of our dissolute lives. If you can be touched by cupid's arrow, then no man's safe. And that's bloody frightening."

"Rest assured that after Penelope, I'm forever immune to cupid's arrow," Sam drawled. "Marriage doesn't suit me. As for love—I haven't a clue."

"I'll drink to that," Eddie toasted, snatching up the brandy bottle as Sam moved toward the door.

But by chance, their route took them past the studio of Sir Lawrence Alma-Tadema, an artist as celebrated as Leighton, and a small carriage parked at the curb caught Sam's eye. He recognized it from Leighton's. Knocking for his driver to stop, he turned to Eddie. "I'll meet you at Hattie's in a few minutes."

"Why are you getting out here?"

"I need some air."

"Why?"

Sam was already swinging down from his carriage. "No special reason," he said, pushing the door shut. "I'll see you in ten minutes." Glancing up, he gave instructions to his driver.

"You're sure now?" Eddie looked perplexed.

"You'll be entertained at Hattie's with or without me, but I should be there shortly."

"You're acting very strangely tonight."

"You're drunk," Sam replied pleasantly, and nodded to his driver.

The carriage pulled away.

Chapter 4

But Eddie was right, Sam realized as he stood on the curb before the commanding entrance to Alma-Tadema's pseudo-Pompeian palace. He was strangely out of sorts tonight, or curiously ruminative, or, more precisely, in rut for the tantalizing little bitch who had turned him down that afternoon. And he wondered for a moment if his vanity was involved, if he wanted her simply because she'd said no.

But he wasn't so crass, nor was he vain. Although he had no explanation for his motivation other than lust. Or none he could comfortably accept. So lust it was that made him stop—and propelled him toward the door.

Alma-Tadema was feted in society; they'd met before, but Sam had never crossed the threshold of his home. Taking note of the dearth of other carriages, he wondered if the artist's wife was out of town and he might be intruding on a tête-à-tête. His consideration was fleeting, however. He really didn't care.

Unconsciously straightening his cravat, he walked to the huge double doors, lifted the polished brass lion's-head knocker, and let it drop.

A young servant girl came to the door. No one so pretentious as Leighton's Kemp was there to greet Alma-Tadema's guests. Her curtsy was unpolished, her face scrubbed and rosy, and Sam decided that in spite of his wealth, Sir Lawrence was considerably more natural a man than the head of the Royal Academy.

He asked to see her master, and when the maid inquired whom she should say was calling, Sam said, "If you don't mind, I'd like to surprise him." Offering her a warm smile, he placed a twenty-pound note on her palm, winked, and added, "Miss Ionides and I are friends."

She didn't hesitate; the sum represented several months' salary. "Right up the stairs, sir, and turn to your left," she directed, taking the hat and gloves Sam handed her. "His studio be those double doors at the end of the hall."

When Sam reached the doors, one of them was ajar, revealing a portion of the studio and a fascinating view that brought his erection surging to life. A golden twilight bathed the room, gilding the naked flesh of the woman who had consumed his thoughts. Miss Ionides was languorously disposed on a large sable rug that was draped over a running course of marble plinths. The backdrop represented the partial ruins of a Roman temple—Alma-Tadema's speciality in history painting, as was his virtuoso depiction of female flesh. An alabaster bowl of white lilies at the lady's feet was no doubt meant to be metaphorical, or perhaps paradoxical, because this was no innocent maiden lying before him.

Miss Ionides embodied a flamboyant wantonness. Lying partially on her side, her supple body was flexed faintly at the waist so the curve of her hip was thrown into provocative silhouette. Her head and one shoulder rested on a sumptuous pile of plum-colored brocade pillows, the small feather fan she held over her mons the only nod to modesty in the flagrantly sensual pose. The contrast of her warm, glowing flesh against the cool marble backdrop and the luxurious fur was riveting, as was the voluptuous splendor of her body. Her breasts were enormous and plump, dangling like delicious ripe fruit with the slightly forward twist of her torso, her waist was hands-span narrow—which enchanting thought added dimension to Sam's arousal. As for her slender, shapely legs, he reflected, his gaze traveling leisurely down her form, surely they were made to be wrapped around him.

He was so hard, he was aching, the eroticism so explicit and palpable, he was hard pressed not to stride up to her and carry her off like some marauding barbarian at the gates of Rome.

Suddenly aware he might not be the only man on the scene so inclined, Sam shot a glance at the artist, who was applying paint to the canvas with a decided ferocity. Moved to action by the sight, Sam shoved open the door and strode in. "Forgive me for intruding." His voice was too curt for true apology. "I have a message for Miss Ionides."

Masking her shock, Alex didn't know if she should be gratified or angry at Ranelagh's intrusion. Her second irrelevant thought was that he hadn't changed, as though it mattered a whit that he still wore his day clothes when she wore none. She sat up as Sir Lawrence moved to intercept Sam's progress.

"We're busy, sir," the artist said gruffly, standing solidly in Sam's way. "You must leave."

"This won't take long," Sam replied, coming to a stop, glancing at the man's crotch. Either Alma-Tadema had enormous restraint or was a eunuch, he decided. His affability restored, Sam's voice took on a new degree of courtesy. "My compliments on your painting of the lady, Sir Lawrence. Could I buy it?"

The artist hesitated, wondering if he'd imagined the rude glance. Sam's expression was completely benign. "I'm afraid it's already sold," he finally said, giving the viscount the benefit of the doubt.

"To whom?"

"Mr. Cassels."

"A shame. It's very beautiful."

"Alex is an exceptional lady."

"How so?" The words were suddenly abrupt, cool, all traces of amiability stripped away.

The painter squarely met the displeasure in Sam's gaze. "I don't see that it's your concern."

Both men were large, fit, and obviously disinclined to back down, Alex suspected, if their pugnacious poses were any indication. Since she had no wish to become the center of an embarrassing altercation, she said quickly, "Never mind, Larry. I'll speak with Ranelagh."

"You see?" Sam nodded a cool dismissal at his opponent.

Sir Lawrence cast a searching glance at Alex.

"I'm fine," she asserted. "Really."

As Sam approached the dais, Alex tried to curb the heat rising to her face. He seemed larger than she'd remembered, and disconcertingly more handsome. Forcibly tamping down the flush of excitement that gripped her senses, she said crisply, "You shouldn't be here, but since you are and since I prefer you not grapple with Larry, kindly state your business and be on your way."

It took him a fraction of a second to answer because the view at close range was glorious.

She'd considered covering herself with the fur rug when he'd walked in, but it seemed too exaggerated and dramatic a gesture. She wasn't some innocent maiden. She'd posed nude before and she was comfortable in her skin. "If you're done looking . . ." she said coolly.

Reminded of his manners, his gaze traveled to her eyes and he smiled. "I saw your carriage outside, and I was hoping you might be free tonight."

"I'm sorry, I'm not." Temperate, imperturbable words.

He gave her high points for poise. She might have been refusing an invitation to tea . . . and, more to the point, been fully clothed. But his equanimity had been honed in the school of debauch, and it was impossible so tame a circumstance would extinguish it.

"Tomorrow, then?" he said with an equivalent dispassion.

"I'm afraid I'm busy tomorrow as well."

"You're not actually *afraid,* are you?" Was it possible beneath the cool gaze?

She shook her head, and a fortune in diamonds swung from her earlobes. "I'm simply not interested."

"Could I convince you somehow"—his voice dropped a half octave—"to *become* interested?"

In the deepening shadows, the unadorned grace of his face and form almost took her breath away—her artist's eye in awe of such stark, sensual beauty. She'd been trying, with difficulty, not to take notice of his splendid looks and, more particularly, of his sizable erection lifting the soft wool of his trousers. "I believe we've had this conversation before, and my feelings haven't changed." She kept her tone neutral with effort. His arousal was fascinatingly large.

"I could contrive to mend my ways."

A rush of heat spiked through her body at his wicked smile. "You don't mean it, my lord. We both know that."

But a faint equivocation in her voice quickened his senses. Did she mean no or not? Or how much did she mean it? His nostrils flared as though he might catch scent of the truth. Then a singularly familiar fragrance drifted into his nostrils, and his understanding was no longer in question. He recognized the redolent perfume of female arousal. Glancing downward, his gaze settled on the juncture of her thighs.

Her auburn curls melted into the soft sable fur, and she was getting wet for him.

"What if I really did mean it?" he said, heated and low, his gaze returning to hers. "What then?"

The lust in his eyes excited her, stirred and thrilled her, when she should despise a man who made love only for sport.

But he moved a step closer, leaned in, and whispered in a velvety tone, "We'll do whatever you want to do . . . you set the limits—you give the orders."

For a reckless moment, she wanted to clutch the heavy black silk of his hair, pull him close, and kiss him hard—in prelude to what he so temptingly offered. Clenching her fists against the rash impulse, she said instead, "I don't want to give orders."

"Better yet."

She shivered faintly at the implication.

"If I were to touch you . . . there"—he gestured languidly at her mons, and she found herself gauging the length of his long, large fingers—"I guarantee you'll change your mind."

"If you dare," she said tersely, feeling as though she were suffocating, "you'll never touch me again."

Her phrasing gave him pause, her "again" tantalizing—a myriad of possibilities instantly reverberating through his brain. "Tell me where or when or how"—his smile was carnal and lush—"or we could leave now and you could . . . show me."

A clamorous ringing crash shattered the heated ferment.

Sam didn't turn his head. "It doesn't matter," he breathed.

But Alex looked, and like a sluice of icy water rushing in, the world intruded. Larry was reaching down to pick up the fallen container and scattered brushes from the puddle of linseed oil spreading over the floor.

Leaping to her feet, Alex shoved past Sam before she lost her resolve and jumped from the dais.

He could have stopped her if he'd wished, but no one could accuse him of being gauche. And he understood with a libertine's expertise, it was only a matter of time before the skittish Miss Ionides yielded. Watching her stride away, Sam admired her beauty and nerve, not to mention the silken sway of her hips.

She was going to be one hot little piece, he thought pleasantly.

When she disappeared from sight, the studio was eerily silent.

Moving toward Alma-Tadema, Sam issued a well-mannered and self-possessed smile, as though he'd not just tried to seduce the artist's model. "Do you think Cassels might be talked into selling your painting to me?" he inquired, the cultivated world of the aristocracy in every smooth syllable.

Alma-Tadema shrugged. "Who knows?" Alex had escaped; he could be urbane as well.

Sam's mouth curved into a rueful smile. "You dropped those brushes on purpose, didn't you?"

The painter's expression was bland. "You'll have to do your courting on your own time, my lord."

"You're her champion, I presume." Sam's gaze narrowed as he approached the man. "Or are you more?"

"That would be for Alex to say."

"Your wife doesn't mind?"

"I'd say ask her, but you probably would. And I'm not obliged to suffer rudeness in my own home."

Sam sighed. "My apologies. Miss Ionides has put me out of countenance."

"You and a good many other men. You're not alone, if that's any consolation."

"It's not," Sam replied curtly.

Sir Lawrence smiled for the first time. "My condolences."

"Amusing, I'm sure." Sam bowed stiffly. "I'll bid you good night. My compliments on your talent. The painting of Miss Ionides is superb."

And he intended to own it just as soon as he found Cassels.

But much later, as the first light of day fringed the horizon, Lord Ranelagh walked away from Hattie Martin's luxurious brothel pervaded with a deep sense of dissatisfaction. What had previously passed for pleasure seemed wearisome now, a jaded sense of sameness enervated his soul, and sullen and moody, even the glorious sunrise failed to please him.

Walking home through the quiet streets, he was

plagued with thoughts of the bewitching Miss Ionides, wondering where she'd slept or, like he, not slept— which rankling thought further lowered his spirits. And by the time he'd reached his town house, he'd run through a mental list of any number of men who might be her lovers, the image of her delectable body in the arms of another man inexplicably disagreeable.

It shouldn't be. He should be immune to the nature of her liaisons. He hadn't even met the damned woman a day ago and there was no earthly reason he should care who the hell she slept with.

He snapped at the hall porter when he entered his house, immediately apologized at the man's stricken expression, and after making some banal excuse, pressed ten guineas into the servant's hand. When he walked into his bedroom a few moments later, he waved a restraining hand at his valet, who came awake with a start and jumped to his feet. "Go back to sleep, Rory. I can undress myself. In fact, take the day off. I won't be needing you."

His young manservant immediately evinced concern. The viscount was accustomed to being waited on, his family's fortune having insulated him from the mundane details of living.

Recognizing his valet's hesitation, Sam said, "I'll be fine."

"You're sure?"

"Why not take Molly for a walk in the park," the viscount suggested, knowing of Rory's affection for the downstairs maid. "She may have the day off as well."

"Thank you, sir!"

"Go, now." Sam waved him off. "All I want to do is sleep."

In a more perfect world he might have slept, considering he'd been up for twenty-four hours; but Miss Ionides was putting period to the perfection of his world *and* to his peace of mind. He tossed and turned for more than an hour before throwing aside the blanket and stalking over to a small table holding two decanters of liquor. Pouring himself a considerable amount of cognac, he dropped into an upholstered chair and, sliding into a sprawl, contemplated the injustice of Miss Ionides being so damned desirable.

Half a bottle of cognac later, he'd decided he'd simply have to fuck her and put an end to his lust and her damnable allure. He further decided his powerful craving was just the result of his not having what he wanted—her. And once he made love to the delectable Miss Ionides, that craving would be assuaged. Familiarity breeding contempt, as they say, had been the common pattern of his sexual amusements. In his experience, one woman was very much like another once the game was over.

But this particular game of seduction was just beginning, and glancing out the window, he took note of the position of the sun in the sky. The races would be starting soon at Ascot, the entire week scheduled with prestigious races, the Season bringing all of society to the track.

Including Miss Ionides, if he didn't miss his guess.

Rising from his chair, he walked to the bellpull and rang for a servant. He needed a bath.

His butler walked into his bedroom a second later, not in response to his summons—with a message instead.

"There's someone to see you, sir."

Owens's tone was such that Sam's gaze turned wary. "Who?"

"Your mother, my lord."

"At this damned hour?" Already bad-tempered and moody after his dissatisfying night, the last person Sam cared to see was his mother. "Does she know I'm home?"

"She saw your hat and gloves on the console table."

The viscount swore. "I don't suppose you could tell her I was sleeping?"

"She ordered me to wake you, sir."

The viscount swore again. "Don't send her up." His voice was brusque. "I'll come down."

"She's in the breakfast room, sir, having her breakfast."

"While she's ruined mine," Sam said.

The butler glanced at the glass of cognac the viscount held in his hand, his expression bland. "A shame, sir, but she wouldn't be deterred."

"Is she ever?"

It wasn't a question that required an answer, or certainly not one by a servant.

"Tell her I'll be down in ten minutes," Sam said curtly.

When the viscount entered the breakfast room a half hour later, bathed, dressed, and more tranquil for the three additional drinks he had imbibed, he was able to say "Good morning, Mother" with a modicum of courtesy.

"Your chef burned my toast," his mother noted irritably.

"I'll have him fired on the spot."

"I see your caustic sense of humor is undiminished."

"You're up early," he replied, not about to trade insults. He and his parents agreed on very little; they saw each other less. And if his mother was calling on him at what was for her the crack of dawn, she brought trouble for certain. He remained standing.

"I came to remind you of our dinner party tonight."

"I'm sorry. Did my secretary send an acceptance?"

"Of course he didn't, and that's why I'm here. Clarissa Thornton will be there with her parents, and I wish you to attend. The earl and countess always ask for you, and their land borders our Yorkshire estates."

"And their daughter is angling for a husband."

"You needn't be so crass, Samuel. Is it a crime for a beautiful young woman to wish to marry well?"

"Just so long as it's not to me."

"The Thornton family goes back well before the Norman invasion. Their bloodlines are as pure as ours. No taint of industry stains their heritage, nor does the stench of new money—"

"You may stop, Mother. I've heard the lecture a thousand times more than I wish, and the taint of industry or new money doesn't concern me. Nor does Clarissa Thornton." His smile was tight in spite of the fact that he was well sedated with cognac. "Is that clear enough?"

The Countess of Milburn sat up straighter, her blue gaze cool. "I told your father you would be obstinate as usual."

"You should have listened to him and saved yourself a trip to Park Lane so early in the morning."

"Your marriage to Penelope has left you bitter."

"Your persistent efforts to marry me off then and now have left me bitter, Mother. Kindly stop interfering in my life. Penelope was a disastrous mistake I have no intention of repeating."

"You shouldn't have been so cruel to her, and she would have been perfectly content."

A tick appeared high on his cheekbone and he restrained his temper with difficulty. "In the interests of peace in the family—however strained—let's not discuss Penelope. You know nothing about the matter."

"I know perfectly well what her mother told me. You treated her abominably."

"No, I did not," he said, his voice taut.

"She loved you to distraction."

"No, she did not." The tick was more pronounced.

"You don't know how to treat a woman with respect."

He was doing his damnedest just then. "I have an appointment, Mother. If you'll excuse me. Owens will bring you fresh toast if you wish."

"I don't wish fresh toast. I wish you to come to dinner tonight."

"I'm sorry, Mother. It's impossible."

"Have you no thought of an heir," she inquired heatedly, her eyes snapping with irritation, her slender shoulders quivering ever so slightly with her indignation.

"Marcus has sons."

"The Lennoxes have always inherited by direct bloodlines."

"Then maybe it's time for a change. Good day, Mother." And he walked from the room before he said something inexcusable.

His temper must have been evident on his face, for the servants moved out of his way as he stalked down the corridor. Fucking Clarissa Thornton! What the hell was his mother thinking? As if he were interested in another empty-headed schoolgirl intent on marrying a wealthy man.

And as though his heated emotions required surcease, the very unschoolgirllike sensuality of Miss Ionides appeared in his thoughts. He smiled. What a perfect antidote to his mother's annoying visit. He could be at the racetrack within the hour.

Chapter 5

The day was balmy with a light breeze, the sunshine brilliant, the field of thoroughbreds choice. It was the kind of afternoon to put anyone in good humor. And once he found Miss Ionides, Sam thought as he walked into the royal enclosure, he just might attain that state.

He'd missed the first race, having been waylaid by his steward, who'd required numerous signatures on numerous documents, most of which could have safely waited until tomorrow with anyone but Patrick. But Patrick McGuff ran Sam's estates with a fine-tuned precision and for his expertise, however compulsive, Sam willingly suffered an occasional inconvenience.

His headache was almost gone—several cups of very black coffee along with a quick breakfast had restored his energy after his sleepless night—and now all he had to do was find Miss Ionides and convince her to leave with him. Nothing too daunting, he facetiously thought, remembering her pointed rejections yesterday. But he remembered, as well, the look behind the look in her eyes, the one that responded to him with an instant susceptibility. And she wasn't a novice after two husbands and considerable lovers. She knew what she was feeling.

When he found her, however, she was surrounded by a flock of admirers, and she refused to acknowledge his presence. He stood apart for a time, enjoying the view—she looked especially fine in cream georgette and a small flowered hat—enjoying her obvious discomfort as well. She'd taken note of him despite her studied indifference. But when he finally approached her sometime later, his voice was deliberately bland. "Could you spare a few moments, Miss Ionides? I could use some help deciding which horse to bet on in the next race."

The Spanish ambassador's son, who had been the most solicitous of her admirers, looked at Sam and snorted. "Might you like some advice on the ladies as well, Ranelagh?" Sam's record of wins at the track was unparalleled.

"I wasn't talking to you, Jorges, but if I were, I wouldn't be asking for advice on either horses or ladies."

"I'm afraid I can't help you, Lord Ranelagh," Alex interjected, fixing her gaze on Sam's forehead because her pulse rate had quickened the instant he'd walked into the enclosure and only sheer will had maintained her composure under his surveillance. "I rarely bet on the horses."

"Perhaps we could learn together, then"—he smiled—"about the merits of thoroughbreds."

How beautifully he smiled, how at ease he was in pursuit. "Thank you, but I'm really not interested." Her voice was brusque because she'd barely slept last night for thoughts of him, and his assurance was galling. Furthermore, he looked as though he'd not slept either, his eyes shadowed with fatigue, and she wasn't naive enough to think he'd lost sleep over her.

"She's not interested, Sam," the Prince of Wales noted jovially, turning from his conversation with Lord Rothschild. "Now, there's a first, eh, my boy? And I don't blame you, Alex," he added, grinning. "Sam's not to be trusted with a pretty lady."

"I'm well aware of that, Your Majesty. As is everyone in London."

Wales laughed as Sam's gaze narrowed. "There, you see, your reputation has preceded you."

"You might mention to Miss Ionides that I contribute generously to charity," Sam drawled. "Several of yours, as I recall," he remarked pointedly, one brow raised faintly at the heir to the throne.

"Oh, ho! So it's blackmail and chastisement for my directness," the prince noted cheerfully. "Would you be placated, Alex, by a charitable nature?"

"Charitable in a great many ways, Miss Ionides," Sam interposed smoothly.

She knew what he meant; everyone within hearing knew what he meant, and she kept her voice temperate with effort. "I'm sure you are, Lord Ranelagh, and I commend you on your benevolence, but as I mentioned yesterday, I have a very busy life."

"There. You see, Sam? Just as I said. Now, come," the prince declared, taking Sam by the arm, "come entertain Lillie with your racing expertise. She wishes to parlay her money into a windfall, and if anyone can help her, you can. Excuse us." Familiar with having his wishes obeyed, Wales took Sam with him, and the viscount spent the next hour helping Lillie Langtry, the prince's paramour, bet on sure winners.

But even the Prince of Wales couldn't long prevail on Sam's good nature, and after the fourth race, which brought Lillie another generous return on her investment, Sam made his bow.

"All good wishes on your pursuit." Lillie gazed in Alex's direction. "But as a woman of great wealth, Miss Ionides is in a position to determine her own course in life."

"The advantage of having money," Sam replied lazily, taking note of Alex's mildly distracted air. "Although it allows a certain degree of impulsiveness as well."

"While there are those of us with neither luxury," Lillie murmured.

He couldn't with courtesy agree. "If Miss Ionides refuses me again," he said instead, "I'll be back to add to your winnings."

"Sam, dear, you were more than generous with your discerning eye for winning horseflesh. And I have plenty of time to feather my nest."

"Make sure Wales pays for your company, darling. He can afford it."

Lillie glanced at the prince, who was in conversation with several of his cronies. "I'm doing well," she said quietly.

"Better, at any rate." The viscount knew of the Jersey Lily's impoverished background as the daughter of a clergyman.

"Yes, much. And thank you for all the wins today."

"My pleasure." Sam grinned. "And now we'll see if Jorges has sufficiently bored Miss Ionides."

"Along with all the others," Lillie added with a nod of her head at the throng of men surrounding Alex.

"She looks weary of smiling, don't you think?"

"She does, rather. And you feel you can alter that stoic smile?" Her query was playful.

"Of course I can. If only the lady would overlook the burden of my reputation."

"She plays at amour occasionally herself, it's said."

"So why not with me?"

Lillie's eyes sparkled. "Why not indeed, when you have so much to offer."

But Sam was cautious in his approach this time, standing at the fringe of the throng for a short period, listening to the conversation, watching Alex's response, trying to gauge the extent of her boredom against the protocol of leaving before the prince. Personally, he cared little for Wales's sense of consequence, but Miss Ionides had given him the impression she proceeded with less rashness.

He entered the conversation when Princess Louise began discussing Edgar Boehm's newest sculpture.[2] A sculptor herself as well as Boehm's lover, the princess was waxing eloquent on the portrait he'd recently completed of her mother's servant, John Brown.[3]

"Did the John Brown sculpture appear at the Academy show?" Sam asked.

"Yes. It received much acclaim," Princess Louise proudly replied, always a spirited advocate of her lover's work.

Sam smiled. "As did your work, Princess, I hear. *The Times* said your Daphne was a triumph."

"They were kind in their praise," she noted modestly. "Have you seen the show, Lord Ranelagh?"

"Only quickly, I'm afraid."

"Then you must go again. Even Mama has gone twice."

"Perhaps I might. Has anyone been lucky at the track today?"

Immediately, a collective sigh of relief seemed to emanate from the group, and several people quickly responded. Everyone was aware of the princess's unhappy marriage to the Marquess of Lorne, who was homosexual, so her interest in Boehm was understandable, but the possibility of inadvertently speaking out of turn on either subject always made for a certain awkwardness. Racing was so much more comfortable a topic. As the conversation became animated, Sam was able to approach Alex with apparent casualness.

"You should have been a diplomat, Lord Ranelagh," Alex observed, Sam's finesse worthy of praise. "Everyone finds it difficult to discuss Boehm with the princess."

"You included?"

"Of course. One must agree with her or bear her displeasure, and while the man has talent—" She shrugged.

"It's his other talents that charm the princess."

"No doubt."

"Speaking of such talents," he said, smiling.

She surveyed him, a half-smile barely curving her mouth. "You're persistent at least."

"Did you think I wouldn't be?"

"I didn't think of you at all, my lord," she replied, perjuring herself in self-defense.

"While you quite effectively ruined my peace of mind and my night."

"You spent the night alone, then?" she noted archly, recognizing the weariness of debauch when she saw it.

He hesitated.

"I dislike men who lie."

His teeth flashed white in a smile. "How do you feel about evasion?"

"So you weren't alone, as if I didn't know."

"Were you?"

"No."

He was surprised at the degree of his annoyance. "Did you enjoy yourself?" he drawled.

"Did you?"

"No," he said brusquely, unsure why he chose to be honest. "I didn't."

"My condolences, then. My three-year-old nephew and I enjoyed ourselves immensely. He likes when I read him stories about animals that talk."

"You're a bloody little bitch," he said, but his smile matched the amusement in her eyes.

"That's no concern of yours, is it?"

"I could make it my concern."

"You can't without my leave."

"Why is that?"

Her large eyes seemed to grow larger. "Do you always assert your authority, Lord Ranelagh?"

"Rarely."

"Don't even think of doing it with me."

He smiled. "Am I supposed to be intimidated?"

"Cautioned perhaps. I don't take kindly to coercion."

"You might like it. St. Albans and Coutts were older, weren't they?"

"This conversation is over," she said tartly.

"I only meant in play, Miss Ionides. Think about it."

"Go to bloody hell," she said in an undertone, and walked away.

* * *

He should have been more tactful, and if it had been anyone else, he probably would have been. But she provoked him—an oddity in a woman—and if he were inclined to introspection, he might say her pronounced independence served as some benighted challenge. But he wasn't introspective, nor was he easily daunted when lured by such flagrant sensuality. Nor was he unaware of the contradiction between her words and her heated gaze.

A shame she wouldn't allow herself to do what she wished to do.

A shame he wasn't more patient.

Damn his conceit, Alex reflected hotly, her long-legged stride indication of her anger. Ladies didn't stride, or at least they didn't in these cursed tight skirts, she furiously thought, easing into a more sedate gait, searching the crowded enclosure for a quiet corner in which to compose herself. Whenever she was in Ranelagh's presence, she found herself exasperated by his unabashed cheekiness, disturbed by his brazen virility, reminded as well—the disconcerting voice inside her head whispered—that his extraordinary talents in bed were the stuff of legend.

Damn gossip.

Damn his blasted beauty.

Damn Leon, who had contributed to her unusual celibacy—the practical reason, she assured herself, of her too-ardent attraction to the viscount.

She really *would* have to go and see young Harry, she decided. Considering her ungovernable desires, it was the only sensible course—once she could see her way clear of all these people. Finding a deserted area near the box rail, she pretended to watch the racing horses below. On the other hand, her contrary voice persisted, she could take Ranelagh up on his blunt invitation, join him in bed, and be done with it.

Perhaps his reputation was highly overrated and unjustified, the result of hearsay and tittle-tattle. She drew in a sustaining breath and contemplated the possibility with satisfaction. Wouldn't that be fine. And she'd take great pleasure in telling him so afterward.

Afterward . . .

Good God . . . was she actually considering it?

The cheers erupting around her went unattended as she weighed the dramatic consequences. Could she, *would* she . . . would he be boorish—or not? What if he actually lived up to his exalted reputation? Where would that leave her? Discarded like all the rest, for he'd not been a pattern card of constancy since his disastrous marriage. Or before it, for that matter.

"Don't be angry with Sam. He's really very nice."

Alex turned to find Lillie Langtry smiling at her.

She grimaced faintly. "Did he send you?"

The tall, beautiful redhead glanced at the group of men around the Prince of Wales, Sam among them. "He doesn't need advocates." Her eyes gleamed with amusement. "Or at least not until now. And he would think me interfering if he knew what I was saying. But the darling boy is smitten with you."

"He said that?"

Lillie smiled again. "Of course not. I doubt the word's in his vocabulary. It's my perception only. I thought you'd like to know."

Alex offered the Prince of Wales's mistress a small smile. "Thank you, but whether Ranelagh is smitten or not, or whether he's nice or not isn't under debate. I find his reputation too daunting."

"You don't mean all that gossip about his wife? She was a hussy through and through in spite of her blue blood. She made his life miserable."

"Some might say he deserved it."

"But then, I know better. He was faithful to her— at first."

"You see."

"You misunderstand, Miss Ionides. He was faithful until he found his wife with one of his gardeners scarce a month after the wedding. And when she died, she was with one of her lovers."

"My Lord."

"Exactly. And I could tell you more. Suffice it to say, he acted the gentleman far longer than most men would have. Do you feel better now?"

"Enlightened certainly. But it isn't only gossip about his marriage. He was notorious both before and after."

"He hasn't found the right woman yet."

"Not from lack of looking . . ."

"With all the women in pursuit, Miss Ionides, he doesn't have to look. Now, you could prove an antidote to that pattern of sameness."

She didn't pretend not to understand. "Even were I inclined to serve as antidote to the sameness of his life, it wouldn't be for long, I'm sure. The transience of his connections is legend."

"You're interested in permanence? Are you looking for a third husband?"

Alex immediately waved her hand in denial. "No, no. I'm quite content alone. On the other hand, I don't wish to find myself added to the viscount's list of casual conquests."

Lillie's brows rose. "But then, there's no guarantees in amour, Miss Ionides. Who of us know how long we'll be amused? When you ended your affair with Mr. Baring, you broke his heart, he said."

A pink flush rose on Alex's cheeks. "I'm sorry to hear that."

"Surely you must have known. Harold isn't a Lothario by nature."

"I'm embarrassed to say, you've made your point, Miss Langtry."

"While I didn't in the least wish to embarrass you." She patted Alex's arm. "I'm just asking you to keep an open mind about Sam. You'd enjoy him immensely."

Alex's gaze held a new directness. "Do you speak from personal experience?"

"Does it matter?"

"Perhaps."

"The answer is no. Is that better?"

Alex grinned. "It shouldn't be, but it is."

"Good. Then I wish you much pleasure."

After Miss Langtry left, Alex smiled to herself. Ranelagh had actually been faithful to his wife. A charming quality she'd not thought possible in a man of his stamp. Perhaps she'd misjudged him. Or perhaps she was simply looking for a reason to have misjudged him. . . .

"I'm sorry."

The voice at her ear was without guile and soft with apology, and when she looked up, she saw Ranelagh as penitent, his expression so wholly innocent, she wondered for a moment if she should give him high marks for acting.

"I could send you my card tomorrow and flowers—something small and not too personal. A book perhaps . . . do you like Ruskin?"

"You don't look the type, Ranelagh, to observe the conventions."

"I could if you wish."

"Why?"

He shrugged infinitesimally. "Reparation—a peace offering for having offended you?"

"Are you and Miss Langtry accomplices this afternoon?"

"What did she say?"

"She extolled your virtues."

He grinned. "I didn't know I had any."

"So I told her."

"And she disagreed? Perhaps she's trying to repay me for my help in placing her winning bets. But she needn't have. I can speak for myself."

"I don't doubt you can."

"From that tone of voice I perceive you still have reservations."

"I do."

"About?"

"Your reputation for dalliance."

"You have one as well and I'm not taking offense."

"We hardly compare, Ranelagh."

"I'd be happy to discuss that matter of degree in any locale you choose."

"What if I said my parents' drawing room tomorrow morning?"

He swallowed before he spoke, but his tone was unruffled when he said, "That would be fine."

"You don't mind meeting my parents?"

"If you wish me to, I will. Don't, however, expect a reciprocal meeting with my parents. We don't get along."

Alex grinned. "Oh, dear, when I was so hoping to meet your mother."

A hint of amusement gleamed in his eye. "I can see you're going to be a great deal of trouble."

"If I allow it."

"Yes, ma'am," he agreed with such deference, she surveyed him with a measuring glance.

"Are you always so amiable?"

"Always."

And she felt a flutter where she didn't wish to feel such a flutter. "I should turn you off."

"Don't." His voice was husky and low, his dark gaze half-lidded.

She felt a mild heat begin to warm her blood, a familiar, tantalizing, insistent heat too long ignored. But her dilemma was compounded by their audience, the viscount's disquieting assurance, and her disinclination to join the large company of women discarded by the man towering above her. "Would you like to take me to the Academy exhibition?" she abruptly asked, her invitation a means of pleasing herself without plunging in completely—a compromise, as it were, between principle and irrepressible feeling.

"Now?"

"Do you have something else to do?"

Several something-elses—most having to do with beds and the naked Miss Ionides—but sensible of the delicacy of the moment, he smiled and said, "I've nothing I'd rather do. I'll make our excuses to Bertie."

"I'll come with you."

"You're sure?"

"I see you're anticipating some vulgar male response from Bertie. We're going to the exhibition, my lord, that's all. And if either you or Bertie think otherwise, I'll be there to clarify my position."

"He's not always . . . shall we say, well mannered."

"I know Bertie very well. And if he's not courteous with me, I'll point out his deficiency."

"How *well* do you know Bertie?"

"How well I know him is none of your business."

He shouldn't care, but curiously, he found he did. "You're highly provoking, Miss Ionides."

"And?" Her gaze was the most ravishing purple, and edgy.

His nostrils flared, but his smile an instant later was enchanting. "And I look forward to understanding you better."

"Understanding?" The single word was uttered softly, insinuation in every syllable.

Sam held out his arm. "Let's get the hell out of here." He was back on familiar ground.

Chapter 6

❧❧

$\mathcal{I}$n short order, they were seated side by side in Sam's carriage while the driver navigated the crowded road from Ascot. The viscount was in superb good humor with the object of his pursuit in proximity. Alex was more conflicted, her emotions in flux, and even as she experienced intoxicating desire, she still debated whether she would act on it.

The viscount, more focused, only contemplated the logistics of time and his nearby race box. "Do you actually want to go to the exhibition?" Well bred and courteous, he could have been asking her to partner him in croquet.

She didn't answer at first, struggling against her perception of the viscount and his profligacies, wondering how many times he'd done this before, chiding herself for caring, reminding herself she was a liberated woman unconcerned with prudish propriety. Was she not capable of making a decision based on her own wishes and needs?

"If you're unsure . . . about—" Sam started to ask.

"Going to bed with you?"

His brows rose. "I was going to say about the exhibition hours."

"The show's open until nine."

"Ah . . . plenty of time, then," he said affably.

"For what, my lord?"

"Don't get prickly, darling. For whatever you wish."

"I'm not your darling. You already have dozens of those. And I don't do this as a rule and I'm uncertain if I will now, and Lord almighty, Ranelagh, I don't know what I'm doing here. I just met you yesterday."

"If it's any consolation, I told myself the same thing when I couldn't sleep last night—" Her piercing glance stopped him.

"Don't bamboozle me; I didn't keep you from anything last night."

"*Au contraire,* Miss Ionides. It was a matter of saving face. And I shouldn't have gone."

"Really." Leaning into the corner of the seat, she pursed her mouth and contemplated the folly of believing she'd disturbed Ranelagh's debauch. Even for a night.

Sprawling in the opposite corner, he stretched out his long legs, offered her a surly look, and said, "Really. And I'm wondering why I'm even admitting to such foolishness. I don't know you."

"It's lust, I suppose."

He shook his head. "Lust I know. This isn't precisely it. And that's the problem."

"Does it have to be a problem? Surely, we're both adults."

"So a fuck is a fuck," he said gruffly.

She smiled. "Am I supposed to be shocked?"

He smiled back. "Later maybe."

She acknowledged his remark with a faint lift of her brows. "So our problems are swept aside?"

"I can do so if you can."

"Actually, I'm not sure I'm so cavalier. I've had much less practice."

"Any woman who poses nude for the world to see is beyond cavalier, Miss Ionides. I'd say you're capable of dealing with most anything."

"Including you?"

"I certainly hope so," he answered. "Now, are we going to the exhibition first or afterward?"

"Will there be time . . . afterward?" Her voice was calm despite the provocation in her query.

"Not if I can help it." He smiled. "I was being tactful."

Her gaze was examining. "Are you really as good as they say?"

"If you're ready, why don't we see? You have my permission to grade me."

"I don't need your permission."

"But you need something else I have."

His grin was infuriatingly cheeky. "Damn you, yes, and I wish I didn't."

He shrugged. "I dislike the intensity of my feelings as well."

She suddenly laughed at their mutual equivocation of everything save desire. "This should be interesting at least."

"I promise to do better than interesting." His voice was exquisitely soft.

"That will be for me to decide," she said lightly.

"If we weren't almost to my race box, I'd show you right now and you could let me know."

She shook her head. "I prefer my studio."

"I don't think so."

"What if I insist?"

His smile was pure seduction. "Insist away."

"Because I'll capitulate to your allure in the end."

"Because we're almost to Fair Grange, and I'll make love to you now instead of an hour from now."

"How convincing you can be." She enjoyed the game, noting how astonishingly beautiful he was at close range.

"You look like a practical woman."

"Or one in heat."

He grinned. "I'm on my best behavior, Miss Ionides. I hope you appreciate it."

"And I hope that good behavior continues once we're in bed. I'm selfish of my pleasure."

His gaze was insolent. "I haven't had any complaints."

"Then I won't be wasting my time."

"I hardly think so. I have more experience than priests or young boys."

Her brows rose. "Are you monitoring my acquaintances, my lord?"

"Lovers, I think, is the proper word."

"I doubt I'd have time to list all of yours, and with that thought in mind, I'm going to insist we go to my studio."

"You like to be in control?"

"Generally."

"That must be why you concentrate on inexperienced men."

"If you'd like to begin comparing the qualities of our sex partners, might I point out you were friendly with Countess Marley and Lady Walker, I believe. And several more in their style."

"Touché." The ladies all had been stereotypically beautiful but simple.

"So if you'd be so kind as to give your driver my address . . ."

Tipping his head faintly, he conceded, and conveyed Alex's direction to his driver.

Sam brought up the subject of painting on the journey into the City because he was intent on being well behaved and thought it prudent to discuss something of interest to the lady. She obviously wasn't inclined to wanton conduct, or at least not in the carriage, so he gallantly asked questions about her work and listened politely to her answers. He didn't mention the Gérôme painting of her he owned, in case she would take issue with the reasons he owned it.

And maybe Lillie was right. Maybe Miss Ionides could afford to be different. Certainly, she was unconventional, a quality rare in the females of his class. She had almost a mannish independence, a characteristic both intriguing and disconcerting. But any reservations he might have of her unorthodox nature were more than offset by her glorious sensuality.

She shouldn't be so shallow as to fall under the spell of Ranelagh's quintessential charm and dark handsomeness, Alex thought, trying not to stare at him. If she chose to bed him, it should be for reasons other than mere physical attraction. She'd always considered herself an intelligent woman, unmoved by the superficiality of the beau monde, and now she was allowing herself to be charmed by the most profligate libertine in London because she found him over-whelmingly attractive. Such a response didn't bear close scrutiny, and she deliberately set aside her unsettling thoughts.

Hadn't she always prided herself on living her life as she chose?

Hadn't she railed against the binding strictures that limited female options?

So she was physically attracted. What was the harm in that? She found herself relaxing at the obviousness of the answer, and when she said "You can't really care much about painting, Ranelagh; why don't you tell me instead of your racers," her smile was open and warm.

"Feeling better, are we?"

"I've put all my demons to rest. I don't suppose you have any."

"Honestly, no. And I *enjoy* hearing of your work. I've never known a woman painter before. Does your family approve?"

"As much as I require. They're rather more traditional than I. Does your family approve of you?"

His mouth twisted in a parody of a smile. "They gave up any thought of approval long ago. They're conservative in their ways, so I suppose we've agreed to disagree."

She knew an uncle's legacy had made him a wealthy man, so he wasn't subject to his family's whims. "You don't see much of your family, then?"

"My brother and I are close. The best of friends, actually, and he has children, should I not remarry."

Without thinking, she said, "The death of your wife must have been a shock."

His gaze narrowed and a chill invaded his eyes. "Would you like condolences on the deaths of your husbands?"

Instantly recalling the scandalous events of his marriage, she apologized. "Forgive me. I spoke out of turn."

"As did I." He'd regained his composure, the sudden coolness gone. "I'm sure the deaths of your husbands were a great sorrow."

"Yes, they were. Both were men of character."

"My wife was handpicked by my parents." He grimaced slightly. "Another reason we don't get along."

"Surely you weren't forced."

"Let's just say I gave in to the ten-thousandth lecture on family duty." His expression went utterly blank for a moment, and then he slowly exhaled, and glancing out the window, noted, "We're almost there."

Chapter 7

He was tellingly quiet as the carriage came to rest, and when he helped her alight, she could feel his constraint. After speaking briefly to his driver, he returned to her side.

"He'll wait if you don't object to my carriage at your curb."

"No, not at all," she replied, wondering if he'd changed his mind, if her gauche remark concerning his wife had terminated his interest. "The neighbors keep their distance."

He glanced to the left and right, taking in the sizable property surrounding her studio. "Have you been here long?"

"Two years. Would you like to see the studio?" And she waited with a degree of apprehension for his answer.

"Very much, and I apologize for my surliness. I must be tired."

She smiled. "And now I'll be surly about the cause of your tiredness—without reason, of course."

He laughed. "I'm constantly amazed by my reaction to you."

"While I want you and don't want you in equal measure."

"Our principles will be tested, then. I dislike intense emotion of any kind."

"In amour, you mean."

While he hesitated over how to answer so pointed a question, she took his hand and drew him toward the ornate gate.

"You needn't reply, Ranelagh." His silence had been answer enough, but she wasn't a moonstruck young maid with unrealistic expectations.

"I find myself apologizing again." He'd found it uncomfortable to lie when normally dissimilation in these matters was second nature.

"No need. I prefer honesty to glib phrases. And who knows, we may find we don't suit at all."

Reaching out, he unlatched the gate and pushed it open. "Not likely." He leaned forward to kiss her gently.

She'd not expected such tenderness, nor had she expected the rush of heat that delicate kiss could generate. It was no more than a butterfly kiss, courteous and restrained, one a brother might bestow on a sister, or a cousin on a cousin, but the aftermath shimmered through her body with a flooding warmth, and she wondered how she would respond to his lovemaking when so simple a gesture shook her.

"How do you do it, Ranelagh?"

"I was about to ask the same of you." Kisses were generally too tame to bring him to instant rut.

She glanced down at his blatant erection stretching his trousers. "We seem to be in accord."

"Not completely . . ." His smile was impudent.

"We should go inside."

"It might be wise." His hand tightened on hers.

She smiled. "You wouldn't be so brash."

His brows rose. "Normally, no, but then, you tantalize me in the most exceptional way. And you *did* say the neighbors keep away."

"If I'm dealing with such impetuosity," she said, smiling, drawing her hand from his, "I'll hurry us inside." And putting actions to words, she quickly moved down the flagstone walk to the door.

The building was new, as were most structures in the exclusive Holland Park area.[4] Imaginative new architects were building significant examples of domestic architecture around the original Jacobean mansion at the center of the property. Philip Webb, George Aitchison, William Burges, Richard Norman Shaw, and J. J. Stevenson were all doing their part to contribute to the stature and prominence of the colony of eminent artists and middle-class industrialists, merchants, and bankers who were profiting by the rapidly expanding economy.

Alex's studio was of red brick, and like so many of the new structures had wide and comfortable windows, high-pitched roofs of tile, a gabled facade, and ivy-covered walls that gave it the homey, lived-in look of a country parsonage. And as if a further decorative touch were in order, someone had left a large bouquet of larkspur on the front step.

Harry had been by, Alex realized. He picked bouquets for her from the public parks despite her remonstrances.

"You have an admirer."

"Like you, Ranelagh, more than one," she said, picking up the bouquet.

"Aren't you going to look at the card?"

Cradling the flowers in her arm, she opened the cobalt-blue door. "I doubt it's anyone you know." And Harry's love notes were always lengthy. "Please, come in." Stepping over the threshold, she suddenly stopped. Harry was coming toward her down the hallway.

"Do you like my flowers?" he called out.

"Your admirer has made himself at home, it seems."

Taking note of Ranelagh, Harry's tone turned petulant. "I thought you were going to the races."

"He keeps close watch on you," the viscount drawled.

"And why shouldn't I?" Harry replied heatedly, bristling like a puppy as he stopped before them. "I know her and you don't."

With an insolent gaze Sam surveyed the young man. "If you'd leave, we could become better acquainted."

"Alex, don't!"

"Harry, for heaven's sake. What do you think you're doing?"

"Why don't you get the hell out," Sam said.

"I beg your pardon." Alex shot a scathing look at Ranelagh.

"Do you want him to stay?" A sudden coolness had entered Sam's tone.

"Whether I do or not is my decision, not yours, my lord."

"Well, make up your mind."

Who did he think he was to give ultimatums. "Thank you for the ride home," she said crisply. "I wish you good day."

Sam offered her a stiff bow. "Your servant, ma'am." He turned and walked away.

"How could you, Alex," Harry decried. "Ranelagh is the most libertine man in all of London."

"When I wish your advice, Harry, I'll be sure to ask for it." Her voice was sharp. "And I'll thank you to stay out of my home unless invited. I don't appreciate you interfering in my life."

"He's not good for you, Alex."

"I think I'm old enough to make my own decisions, Harry. Now, if you'd kindly leave."

"I'm sorry, truly I am. Please, don't be angry with me. I'm so very sorry. Let me put those flowers in water for you." He plucked the bouquet from her arms and rushed down the hall before she could take issue. "I just wanted to make sure you liked the flowers. . . ."

She watched him disappear into her kitchen and sighed softly. So much for her first foray into the world of impulsive behavior. Ranelagh, apparently, required a tractable female. A shame, she reflected with a modicum of regret. He was devilishly attractive. She uttered another small sigh—of resignation; now she had to find a way to politely send Harry on his way.

It took considerable courtesy, because Harry was so intent on pleasing her, she didn't want to hurt his feelings—a long-standing problem in their friendship, or whatever term best described the nature of their involvement. She agreed, finally, to walk him back to his studio, recognizing she could better oust him without bruising his feelings if she spent some time with him.

It was warm and sunny, a perfect summer day, and in the course of their stroll down the several streets that separated their studios, Alex found herself reconciled to the abrupt departure of Lord Ranelagh. He really wasn't her style of man anyway. Harry was right. And she'd definitely violated all her usual principles in allowing herself to be seduced by his charm. Perhaps Harry's appearance had been in the way of fate and she'd been saved from disaster.

A few yards from Harry's, they met Chloe Addison watering her flowers and were cajoled into coming inside to see her newest painting. Shortly after, Walter Newly stopped by and then Peter Randel, at which point Chloe opened a bottle of wine. The discussions on art took on an increasingly heated tone as the bottle emptied and another was opened—not an unusual circumstance in the coterie of young artists who all had distinctly personal views. But their vigorous debates were without rancor, the analyzing and dissecting of the newest movements and personalities in their field undertaken in a spirit of friendship. Alex always enjoyed the camaraderie and as an added benefit, in the company of others she didn't have to concern herself with Harry's possessiveness.

Pandias Ionides could tell his wife was in a pet as she came down the walk from Alexandra's studio. Sitting in their carriage, he sighed, knowing he would have to use his considerable diplomatic skills to assuage her.

"She's not here!" Euterpe exclaimed, waving away the groom who had come forward to help her into the carriage. "I went in through the terrace doors," she continued heatedly, taking her husband's hand as he leaned forward to assist her into the carriage, "which Alex *insists* on leaving open"—she dropped into the seat opposite her husband with a wrathful snort— "when I've warned her *time* and *time* again what might *happen* to a young woman alone in London!"

Pandias was Greek consul in London and a man of cosmopolitan background, and he was pleased he'd raised a daughter with such modern views, because anyone looking to the future understood the world was rapidly changing. His wife, however, clung to tradition, and his role had always been that of peacemaker between mother and daughter. "I'm sure she just stepped out for a moment," he soothed. "Or perhaps she's at her Melbury Road house."

"Of course she isn't! She hasn't stayed there since John Coutts died. And don't take that cajoling tone with me, Pandias. You know very well she's quite likely with that scoundrel Ranelagh, because Tula saw them at Ascot and she saw them leave together! Where did I go wrong?" she wailed, her lament one of long standing in regard to their daughter, who had twice married outside the Greek community. "You know she could marry Constantine Spartalis tomorrow, or Vassilis, who's loved her forever! But no, she insists on living like some bohemian, painting pictures where it's impossible to recognize a tree from a flower—and she never comes home and stays for more than a few hours! You have to find her, Pandias! And warn off that libertine Ranelagh! Why aren't we moving? We have to find her!"

The head of the Ionides family knocked on the carriage roof to order his driver on and then leaned forward and took his wife's hands in his. "I'll make some inquiries," he said softly, stroking the backs of her hands. "I'll find Alex, and I'll see that she comes to our next Sunday open house."

"And I don't want her speaking to that rake Ranelagh again," his wife insisted, leaning back in the seat, her anger beginning to subside now that her husband had agreed to intervene.

"I'll do what I can, dear, but Alex doesn't always

listen. And after two husbands, I can't very well tell her how to live."

"You're too lenient, Pandias. She should have been made to marry one of our own. She should have babies now; she's thirty years old. I had all our children by the time I was her age." Her dark eyes took on a melancholy expression. "I just don't want her hurt. You know what Ranelagh's like. The whole world knows."

"I'll talk to her, I promise. But, darling, she's probably out with friends. Just because Tula saw Alex and Ranelagh leave Ascot together doesn't mean they're together now."

"For heaven's sake, Pandias, use your brain," she bristled. "Alex has spent her entire life doing exactly as she pleases—marrying two old men like she did, focusing all her energy on them and now on her painting. It's as though she displeases me on purpose!"

There were great similarities in the untrammeled nature of mother and daughter, but Pandias prudently kept his counsel. "Consider how her charities please you, darling. The schools for Greek immigrant children she finances are favorites of yours."

"Hmpf . . . at least those old men were good for something."

"Everyone can't marry at twenty like we did."

She sighed. "You were the handsomest man in Athens."

"And you the most beautiful woman. You still are,

darling." A tall, slender woman, she bore her age well. "Now, don't you worry."

"Tell me she'll be fine, Pandias." Euterpe Ionides's eyes filled with tears. "She's our baby."

"She's strong like her mother." He patted his wife's hand. "Our baby girl will be just fine."

Chapter 8

❧

"I didn't dare go inside," Sam said with a smile, rising from the steps fronting Alex's cobalt-blue door. "Although you leave your studio open. Did you satisfy your young swain? You've been gone quite a while."

"I can't see how it's any business of yours." Alex had come to rest a small distance away, not sure she wanted to deal with a man who could make her pulse race on sight, not sure she shouldn't be angry with him for his earlier brusqueness, particularly unsure what he meant by "satisfy."

"I apologize. It isn't my business. I have a peace offering." He slipped a slender leather-bound volume from his jacket pocket and held it out to her. "Ruskin. People either like him or hate him."

"I find him long on theory and short on experience."

Sam slipped the book back into his pocket. "I'll

have to think of something else you might like, then."
His voice was rich with insinuation.

Taking issue with his cheekiness, she asked crisply,
"Why are you here?"

His impudence vanished and it took him a moment
to reply. "I'm not sure," he said finally. "Maybe the
same reason your cheeks are flushed."

She swept her hands upward and briefly pressed
her palms to her cheeks as though gauging her fevered
sensibilities.

"I'm sorry," he said, "I intended to be obliging, but
you're highly provocative. I don't suppose I could just
carry you inside and make love to you and we could
decide why we're feeling this way later?"

A carnal flame spiked through her senses, but her
voice when she spoke trembled only slightly. "I'm
afraid not."

"Are you still angry?"

"Like you, I'm not sure."

"I should have controlled my temper."

"Perhaps I as well."

"I *do* want to stay."

For how long, she wished to ask even as she understood how completely irrational her response.

"And in order to accomplish that, I'm quite willing
to—"

"Perform good deeds for me?"

"Exactly." With difficulty he kept from smiling. "I
couldn't have said it better."

There was no point in pretending she didn't want
to make love to him. She had from the first moment

she'd met him, and if he was willing to show such deference, perhaps it would be counterproductive to be churlish. And it *had* been a while since Leon. "Do come in, Ranelagh," she said, her mouth lifting in the faintest of smiles. "I apologize for my temper as well."

He stepped aside as she approached the entrance, then leaned forward to push the door open once she turned the knob. "I'm pleased you came back," he said.

"I feel the same way—about you." Her brows rose. "Although I'll probably live to regret it . . ."

"I doubt it."

"The voice of experience?" she observed sardonically.

Following her in, he shut the door. "Just a feeling I have."

She was walking before him, her gait sure, almost brisk, and he wondered for a moment how many other men had followed her like this—wanting what he wanted.

The hall carpet was museum quality—he'd not had time to notice before—the pine paneling a lustrous honey color in the afternoon light, the paintings on the walls small landscapes and London scenes in the airy impressionist style he'd first seen at Durand-Ruel a few years earlier. So she wasn't Leighton's protégée in matters of style, he thought, strangely cheered by this revelation. When she was posing nude for the artist, he'd assumed other things. Not that artistic differences meant they couldn't sleep together. Nor did it mean he viewed Leighton as a rival if they did. When women were only transient amusements, rivalry wasn't an issue.

But if the viscount had been more perspicacious, he might have realized his consideration of the issue, however briefly, was in itself novel.

Alex's only debate at this point was whether she could restrain her urges sufficiently to appear the lady. "Please, pour yourself a drink. I'll be right back," she said half over her shoulder as she entered the main room of her studio. "The liquor table's over by the terrace door."

Coming to rest at the entrance to the large room, Sam took in the enormous space with a discerning gaze. As a collector of sorts, he'd been in numerous studios, and while Alex's was luxurious, it had a charming intimacy despite its size. Furniture was arranged in groupings on colorful carpets, vases of flowers were scattered about, the gas lamps had hand-painted shades, an occasional bit of clothing was draped over a piece of furniture. Her paintings were stacked everywhere, a large unfinished canvas of a summer garden was on her easel. Her talent was considerable. For a brief moment he didn't know if that further indication of her superior qualities offended him or not. He'd never known a woman so far removed from average.

"What do you think?"

Her voice came from behind him, and as he turned from the easel, he saw her in the doorway of what looked like a kitchen. "You're damned good."

"Is that a problem?"

He smiled. "Forgive me. My masculine biases are showing. Your technique is masterful. You're a woman of great talent."

"There, you see, Ranelagh. I'm broadening your horizons."

"Perhaps I can do the same for you," he replied pleasantly.

"Oh, you're definitely outside my normal scope."

"I meant you might have predisposed ideas as well."

"About you."

"About men."

"About men like you."

He grinned. "I rest my case."

She smiled back. "I forgot. You have charitable impulses as well."

"Among other things. I expect you have a life beyond the superficial too."

"Would you like to hear about it?"

His smile formed slowly. "I'd love to—in about an hour or so."

"And I'd love to tell you—in an hour or so."

"You can't be accused of being shy."

"If you wish shyness, you've come to the wrong place."

His gaze slowly surveyed her. "I think we're both in the right place," he said. "And I'm not really in the mood for a drink."

"So I should hurry."

"If you don't think me too demanding."

"There are moments when 'demanding' appeals, my lord," she said softly.

"I'll be sure to remember that," he said equally softly. "And your work is better than most I've seen in Paris. I just wanted to say that . . . now."

"Are you planning on leaving quickly?"

"Not at all. The way I feel, you might find it difficult to push me out the door."

"So I'm not alone in my rapacious lust."

He shook his head. "I'm there."

"But exceedingly polite."

His grin was boyish. "I'm trying."

"Don't you usually?"

"Nothing about this is usual, Miss Ionides. I hope you understand that."

"I didn't. I don't. I'm not sure I believe you, but thank you nonetheless for so charming a sentiment."

"If you're basing your perceptions of me on my reputation, I don't believe 'charming' is in the description anywhere."

"*I* find it charming, and in the end, my lord, that's all that matters."

"Please . . . my name's Sam."

"And mine is Alex."

"And now that we're suitably introduced . . . Alex," he said soft and low. "Might I help you off with your gown?"

"I didn't realize you were such a stickler for protocol," she declared.

"Hardly. I'd just prefer less talk and more . . ."

"Sex?"

"If you don't mind."

"If I minded . . . Sam . . . you wouldn't be here right now."

He opened his mouth to speak, thought better of it, and closed his mouth.

She chuckled, understanding the reason for his restraint. "How gallant you can be."

He tipped his head gently toward her. "I have my moments."

Her gaze traveled slowly down his well-formed body and settled on his obvious arousal. "Because of your erection."

"Do lady painters use that word?"

"This one does. And yours is very fine and the thought of feeling you inside me is tantalizing in the extreme."

Her words added dimension to his rigid length, and he found it necessary to take a small breath before speaking. "I'd suggest doing whatever it is you still wish to do quickly, or you're going to find yourself backed up against the wall and fucked standing up."

It was her turn to require the sustaining breath before speaking, the image he evoked intensifying the throbbing between her legs. "I'd prefer a bed the first time."

The implications in the words *first time* sent a heated rush through his senses. "Clothed or unclothed. You've about a minute to decide."

She moved from the doorway. "Unclothed," she said, and walking to a tapestry screen set in the corner of the studio, she added as she disappeared behind it, "Come and see me in a minute."

He rapidly counted to twenty and, impatient, followed her. Walking around the screen depicting Leda and the Swan against a vivid scarlet background—an appropriate subject in his current ramming-speed frame of mind—he came to an abrupt stop. The screen hid the entrance to her bedroom, and from the size of the bed dominating the small room, he'd say the lady he was about to fuck knew what she was doing. It wasn't the bed of a tyro, nor of a lady for that matter, if he subscribed to the conventional meaning of the word. The bed would be more appropriate in a seraglio, its headboard and canopy ornately carved and elaborately gilded, the entire structure swathed in diaphanous tulle and even though those silken draperies were white, it wasn't a virgin's bed.

"People tend to have that reaction to my bed."

"People?" A low, faint growl underscored the word.

"I have women friends too."

"And what the hell does that mean?"

"What would you like it to mean?"

He exhaled slowly. "You're enjoying yourself, aren't you?" She was partially undressed, standing to the left of the door, her gown at her feet, her chemise and drawers lace-trimmed silk and pristine white.

"You forget, I live outside the aristocratic world by choice."

"Not always. Not this afternoon at the races."

"Mostly I do," she corrected herself. "Because I

wish to separate myself as much as possible from people who ask the kind of questions you just asked. And
if I wish to have women friends who are more than
friends, I will, as will I cultivate the kind of men
friends I wish. I hope that's clear . . . Sam."

"As a bell . . . Alex."

"Then I'll meet you in bed."

It wasn't as though he made love only to deferential women. The range of females in his life ran the
gamut. And he was the least likely man to demand
submission. But this splendid woman, this image of
incarnate femaleness, was so blatantly challenging, he
found himself responding to her with a kind of
brutish authority, as though some contest of wills
were about to commence.

"If you don't mind," she said with a smile, taking
note of the sudden rigidity of his stance.

"I'm trying to maintain my equilibrium, and don't
say people always say that."

"I wouldn't think of it."

"Good." Kicking off his shoes, he began unbutton-
ing his coat because he was going to fuck her regardless of the modicum of contention she provoked,
regardless of the fact that she evoked so extraordinary a lust, he should be wary, or that he found it necessary to tamp down the violence she inspired.

A small, heated silence ensued as they undressed,
both struggling with the tumult of their emotions,
both driven by ungovernable desires, both unfamiliar
with such loss of control.

And then Alex swore softly, unable to untangle a

knot in the ribbon threaded through her chemise neckline.

Sam dropped his shirt on the floor. "Let me do that."

"Are you sure you want to?" She had her own provocations to deal with.

"I'm sure," he insisted, crossing the short distance between them. "And I don't want to fight."

"At least not until after," she replied crisply.

He was standing very close. "We don't have to do this."

His powerfully muscled chest, nude, inches away, only added to her discomposure. "Speak for yourself. I wasn't out last night. Or the previous night for that matter." She grimaced. "Actually, it's been a fortnight now that I think about it, which accounts for—"

"Then it's not my chivalry." He smiled.

Her gaze dropped to the rampant bulge in his trousers. "Not unless *that* goes with chivalry."

"It does."

She found herself smiling back. "Definitely chivalry, then. And I'm feeling as though I might attack you soon, when I've been trying to restrain myself since—"

"Yesterday."

"Yes. Satisfied? Since the moment I saw you at Leighton's."

"I thought so."

"You needn't sound so smug."

"I'm not smug, just pleased."

"Then you may please me now as well."

"Now? Here?"

She shot him a stern look. "I'm not giving up my bed. Untie this knot."

"Is that an order?"

"It is."

He grunted softly, an almost inaudible sound.

"You don't take orders."

"No."

"You feel your authority is at risk?"

"Strangely, yes."

"We're just going to make love, not meet on the field of battle."

His mouth quirked faintly. "With you, I'm not sure."

She offered him a sportive look. "Should I be concerned?"

"You *are* all alone," he noted teasingly.

"And you are"—she reached out and ran her palm down his erection—"very large. . . ."

He drew in a constrained breath. "You probably shouldn't do that if you want to get to your bed—"

"Do this?" She drew her fingertips up the length of his engorged penis, the soft wool of his trousers warm to her touch.

"Be careful, darling. At this point I can't guarantee politesse."

"If I were looking for politesse, I wouldn't have invited you in."

"That's it," he said, scooping her up into his arms.

"And if you feel the need to give any more orders," he added, striding toward the bed, "you're going to have to do it lying on your back."

"Hurry," she whispered, twining her arms around his broad shoulders.

He quickly looked down.

"That wasn't an order," she breathed, her eyes half closed. "Just—please . . ."

Her breathy plea jolted through his body, his own covetousness at fever pitch and moving swiftly, he deposited her on the bed, stripped off her drawers, and tossed them aside. Wrenching open the buttons on his trousers, he undressed in seconds, lowered himself between her open thighs, and plunged in without foreplay or preliminaries, without so much as a kiss, because she was clutching at his shoulders and rising to meet him and so damned wet, he was sliding into her yielding flesh without resistance. Whimpering, she arched up to meet him, impatient, needy, the supple strength of her thighs in counterpoint to his driving invasion. And when he was fully submerged, when he was buried to the hilt, she blissfully sighed. Gratified, he moved slightly upward so she would feel the pressure more intensely.

"Oh, God, oh, God . . ."

And it felt as though her breathy cry were vibrating through every pulsing nerve in his body. There was no accounting for the inexplicable feeling, for the tremulous, breath-held sensation, and he understood in those seconds that a fuck was no longer a fuck. That he wished to feel this again—that he would. And if the strength of Miss Ionides's grip—everywhere—was any indication, she was going to eat him alive.

Or he her, because this astonishing pleasure was unique in his much-explored sexual universe.

Wishing to experience the momentous rapture once again, he withdrew against her protest, and driving back in caught his breath against the awesome pleasure. "Christ," he whispered, and holding himself hard against her womb, he absorbed the shimmering ecstasy while she panted beneath him. Impaled, stretched taut, enchantment rolled over her in heated waves. And then he pressed forward that exquisite distance more, and she screamed.

Neither was capable of restraint after that, and in the grip of such fierce desire they moved in a greedy, fevered flux and flow, rocking the seraglio bed, exploring the extremity and dimension of their need, avaricious—famished—frenzied.

She discovered he was as good as rumor maintained—better, in fact, and beyond his practiced skills and expertise, he had all the natural gifts—breadth, width, length—to bring a woman extraordinary pleasure.

But her fleeting moment of appreciation was interrupted by his next powerful downstroke and any further reflection was swamped by glorious sensation, by the hovering imminency of orgasm. The explosive pleasure broke, shocking, violent, so intense it rocked her senses, burned through her body, inundated her soul with glowing rapture—was beyond anything she'd ever known. And blissful moments later, panting, flushed, her senses still reeling, she marginally lifted her lashes and met the viscount's faint smile.

"Tell me when it's my turn," he whispered.

She was about to speak, but he moved just then and she caught her breath, a delirious splendor riveting her attention. And when he glided a fraction deeper, she cried out, ravishing sensation jolting down every nerve and pulsing tissue.

"No," she breathed, overwrought, overwhelmed.

"Yes," he said almost as softly, and sliding his hands under her bottom, he lifted her into his next downstroke.

She screamed—the sound filling the canopied bed, the room, echoing through the high-ceilinged studio. And she came again in a wild, agonizing convulsion that brought tears to her eyes.

He kissed away her tears afterward, murmuring sweet love words along the dampness of her lashes, down her cheeks, across her parted lips, and her body warmed to his caresses as he knew it would. Whether it was chivalry or politesse or a novel degree of affection for the lady in his arms, he indulged her easily incited senses with both patience and gallantry three times more before he allowed himself his own indulgence and withdrew to come on her stomach.

The afternoon sun was low in the sky, a lemony light pervading the room, bathing their sweat-sheened bodies. Contentment was palpable in the air.

"This must be an enchanted bed," Sam whispered, brushing her cheek with a kiss.

She smiled up at him. "Now it is."

"The world has taken on a cloudless charm." His gaze was warm, close.

"All because—"

"I saw you in Leighton's painting at Grosvenor House."

"I was going to say . . . I invited you in."

"Definitely because of that," he agreed, lightly running his fingertip over the curve of her lush bottom lip. "And because I had to have you."

"And I you."

He smiled. "After I overcame your reservations."

She shook her head gently. "When I no longer could resist."

"That I understand," he simply said. "Because I'm not leaving anytime soon. Don't go away." Rolling off her, he leaned on his elbows and surveyed the room, looking for a towel.

"Over there." Half raising her hand, she pointed toward the door to her bathroom.

"I hope you can read my mind. I wouldn't want to think this was so routine, you—"

"If it were routine, darling, I'd have the towels close by."

"Excellent answer. You're eligible for a prize."

"I hope you can read *my* mind," she noted playfully, "in terms of prizes."

He was already halfway across the room. "No problem there."

"Good. Bring extra towels."

"I don't suppose it would do any good to mention that men don't like women who tell them what to do."

"If you don't mind being told that women abhor dictatorial men."

"I'd say you need some schooling in the finer points of courtship," he observed playfully. "Aren't women supposed to be pleasant and agreeable?"

"I doubt what just transpired was courtship. Unless the word has taken on a new meaning since last I heard?"

"I meant it in the broadest sense." Looking back, he wet his finger with his tongue and ticked off an imaginary mark. "Another demerit, Miss Ionides, to add to your list. You may not receive your reward if you're not more complaisant."

"Perhaps I can think of some way to please you," she purred.

He disappeared into the bathroom and reappeared quickly, carrying several towels. "See, you're learning already."

Her small moue was enticing. "If you weren't so well endowed, my lord, I wouldn't be inclined to listen to you at all. However . . ."

"I am—with all due modesty." His gaze was amused.

"Lucky me."

"Lucky us," he said. "But if I offend you with my teasing," he added with a new gravity, "let me know. I don't wish to offend you."

"Don't worry, darling. I have no trouble speaking up."

He liked the sound of *darling* when she uttered it, the endearment gentle to his ear. And their benevolent mood may have continued indefinitely had not a man's face at the window brought him to a standstill. Tossing her a towel, he gruffly muttered, "Jesus God, he's back."

She turned, following the direction of his gaze, and found herself looking into Harry's soulful eyes. Suppressing the exclamation that came to her lips, she quickly swiped the towel over her stomach and, rising from the bed, wrapped the sheet around her. "Excuse me."

"Will you be gone long?" A contentious note rang in his words.

"No, but if it's a problem for you, you're excused."

"Maybe he brought you more flowers."

With Harry, one never knew. "I'll be right back."

"Fucking hurry."

She turned at the fiat in his tone. "I beg your pardon?"

He glowered for a fleeting moment and then said with exquisite restraint, "I'd appreciate if you'd return as soon as possible."

Chapter 9

*W*hat are you *doing?*" Harry lamented, gazing at her with his puppy-dog eyes as she walked up to him in the garden.

"I might ask the same of you." Alex sighed, the summer light illuminating the youthful beauty of Harry's face, his pale golden hair, the dew-fresh texture of his skin. "Darling," she said in a kinder tone, "you can't do this. You know I see other people."

"I wish you didn't."

"But I do and I will and I made all that perfectly clear from the beginning."

"I adore you, Alex . . . I can't sleep—I can't paint . . ."

"Don't talk like that, Harry. You're too good a painter not to concentrate on your work."

"Come and see me. Then I'll work."

"Don't you dare do that to me. I'm not taking responsibility for your career." Having spent enough years subordinating her own wishes to those of others, she turned to leave.

"I'm sorry." The young man grasped her arm. "Alex, please . . . I'm sorry. Tell me you'll come and see me again."

Tall and coltish at twenty, he towered over her, but the misery in his eyes was plain to see. She was overcome with guilt. "I'll come over on Friday, but promise me you'll work."

"I will . . . absolutely." Swiftly bending, he kissed her and as quickly said, "I'm sorry . . . I couldn't resist. I'll finish the Brighton seascape by Friday and you may have it."

"You'll sell it to Beecher. He's been waiting for it for months."

"Yes, ma'am," he said with a grin, his spirits restored. "Whatever you say. And I'll have flowers for you on Friday because the roses in Hyde Park are in full bloom."

She smiled at him. "You're a cheeky brat and I forbid you to steal any more flowers."

"Didn't you like the larkspur? I did a small pastel sketch of them before I brought them over. You may have that if you won't take the Brighton painting."

"Harry, darling. Sell the pastel too. You can use the money for new paints, and Beecher will buy anything you have."

Pushing his hair behind his ears in a quick, brushing gesture, he smiled. "Now that I'm painting again."

"I'm going to have to find you a nice young lady

your own age, so you'll settle down and work," Alex declared.

"I don't want one. I want you."

"But I can't always be there to inspire your painting mood. Now, be a darling and go home. I have company."

"Ranelagh came back, didn't he? You know, he's not your type, Alex. He's notorious."

"Thank you for the advice, you wet-behind-the-ears pup."

"At least he won't stay long. He never does, they say. And then you'll have more time for me," he observed cheerfully.

"You're full of pleasantries today," she remarked, although she was pleased at his altered mood.

"You'll see. While I'll be faithful forever because I love you with all my heart."

"I don't want you to love me with all your heart. I've told you before, I want you to find other amusements, Harry. I'm too old for you."

"Of course you're not." But he had no intention of arguing now that she'd agreed to see him again. "Do you want me to cook dinner on Friday?"

"You work. I'll bring something."

"Just you is enough." He quickly kissed her again and then turned with a wave and, whistling, walked away.

"No more flowers?" Sam asked as Alex reentered the bedroom.

"Harry says you're notorious and won't stay long and he was quite cheerful when he left."

"You must have promised him something."

The man was prescient and she hesitated, debating how truthful to be.

He recognized the moment of evasion and obligingly changed the subject. "He's young. Where did you find him?"

"He found me. You don't approve?"

He shrugged. "It depends how young, I suppose, although it's none of my business."

"That's true."

"As long as we won't be interrupted again, it's not a problem." He'd had time in her absence to come to his senses.

"I doubt we will, although, as you say, Harry's young—and rash." She smiled at him. "Not altogether a youthful trait."

"My reckless behavior doesn't include voyeurism."

"Really . . . never?" She'd heard of the tableaux vivants in the brothels.

"I recognize a leading remark when I hear it—but I'm too involved"—his smile was lush with suggestion—"in my own affairs to worry about others."

"Like now."

"If you're still in the mood after your adoring swain."

"Adoration has its disadvantages."

"So I've discovered."

"We've become blasé, it seems," she said with a small smile. "Do you ever wish for the naïveté of adolescence? Or perhaps a man like you was never naive."

"Like me?" He grinned. "What the hell does that mean?"

"I can't picture you in an adoring mood."

"Just because I don't have long blond hair and calf's eyes?"

"No, because you're too jaded and cynical."

"But not worth dismissing for all that," he said, one dark brow raised in conjecture.

"No," she replied softly. "Even for all that."

His smile was distinctly uncynical. In fact, it was gloriously inviting. "I'm glad."

"These feelings we have—I have—"

"We have," he countered. "Have brought us here against our best judgment."

"And kept us here when we both know if we were thinking clearly, we'd walk away."

"While we could."

She looked at him for a salient moment. "Surely, it's not that dramatic."

He shrugged. "I can't leave, and I told myself I should when you were outside with that damned child."

"I told him I'd see him on Friday."

"I know. He wouldn't have left otherwise."

"You've done this before."

"Probably," he said.

"And does it work?" He was importuned ceaselessly, she suspected.

"Sometimes."

"And when it doesn't?"

"You switch to another plan."

"Do you continue switching, or are you rude eventually?"

"I'm not going to tell you. You have to do what you have to do."

"But none of that applies to us, because we're going to be adults about this."

"Fucking, you mean."

"Yes. And you didn't feel the need to dress, for which I'm grateful."

"I wasn't going anywhere."

"How cool you are. Does it take enormous practice?"

The amount of practice he'd had wouldn't be something she'd appreciate, so he answered with diplomacy. "My nannies beat good manners into me. Now, come here and we'll see about you having some more orgasms."

She moved toward him, wanting what he wanted, feeling famished when she never did, feeling as though he'd been away a month.

And when she came to rest before him, he slowly unwrapped the sheet covering her, let it slide to the floor, untangled the knot in her chemise ribbon, eased off the filmy garment, and drew her close with such aching slowness, she moaned softly as he bent low and touched her mouth with his. "Now then," he said a moment later, raising his head. "Are you going to insist on the bed again?"

Wondering how he could bring her to fever pitch

with a mere kiss, she drew in a calming breath. "At the moment, I'm not sure I'm capable of insisting on anything save speed."

He lifted her chin with a crooked finger. "We can do that. Is he gone?"

"Does it matter?"

"Not particularly."

A frisson of excitement flared through her senses at the casualness of his reply.

"Let's go outside and see."

"Like this?"

"What's left of the sun will feel good." He picked up the sheet from the carpet. "So your delicate skin isn't damaged."

"Or yours, and I'm not sure I can do this in daylight."

"I'll show you how." Taking her hand, he drew her out into the studio and through the terrace doors.

He moved with an uninhibited grace, at ease with his nakedness, and she regarded him from under her lashes as they moved outside. As an artist, she viewed the perfection of his form with both an objectivity and a keen eye for detail, and she wondered the degree of activity necessary to maintain the steel-hard muscle tone and the lithe grace of his limbs. He had the body of an athlete, broad-shouldered, lean-hipped, long-legged, and his hand holding hers was callused from riding.

"So you don't normally make love al fresco," he remarked casually, skirting a beautifully clipped boxwood.

"I don't even normally make love—only on occasion."

He shot a glance at her. "I would have thought your dance card full."

"I have other interests."

"I see," he said politely, moving down a grassy path alongside a trellis of flowering jasmine. "But not right now."

"You're much too smug, Ranelagh."

"Call me Sam." He smiled. "I feel I know you."

She stopped abruptly and tried to pull her hand away.

And when he turned to look at her, her temper showed.

"I've changed my mind."

He was instantly apologetic. "Forgive me. It was tactless and rude of me"—he suddenly smiled—"but I couldn't resist when you said 'I have other interests' in that decorous, prim tone. And at the risk of offending you further—why the hell did you marry two old men?"

She was every man's dream standing before him, gloriously naked, her voluptuous body as perfect in person as in the paintings she'd posed for, the auburn hair on her mons still wet from their lovemaking.

"You wouldn't understand."

She hadn't moved, but she'd not withdrawn her hand either. An encouraging sign, he thought. "Tell me anyway."

He seemed taller, standing on her grassy path—larger than life—more perhaps than she could comfortably deal with considering the scope of his wildness. But she wished to find out now that she had him . . . here, and while her feelings were chaotic and unsure, whether he wanted what she wanted. "Do you want to make love or not?"

"You don't wish to tell me."

"No." How could someone like Ranelagh ever understand?

"I'm sorry I asked . . . and I do want to make love." He dropped the sheet he was carrying and pulled her close. "I won't ask another question. I'm here only to serve you, ma'am. . . ."

His cheeky smile matched the impertinence of his remark, but she wanted him, cheeky or not, inquisitive or not, disreputable or not, for the sheer beauty of his lovemaking. She nodded, a moment of truth for herself perhaps, or perhaps only affirmation of his statement. "Good . . . because I enjoy the quality of your"—she glanced down at his beautifully formed erection—"service."

He took a small breath, the provocation in her words highly arousing. "Would the grass suit you, my lady?" His voice was soft, low, touched with a tantalizing deference, artless in its single-minded purpose.

"Perfectly."

"Is the sun warm enough?"

"Very."

"The scent of the flowers—is it adequate?"

"Completely."

"Then I should see if you're ready for me," he whispered.

She felt his words in the heated core of her body, in the fevered rhythm of her heart, and when she said "I've been ready for you since yesterday," her voice trembled at the last.

He smiled. "And I've been wanting to take out these hairpins since the first time I saw you at Leighton's," he told her, reaching up to lift one of the ruby pins from her tousled hair.

"You were much too arrogant at Leighton's and last night. I told myself I wouldn't do this," she said on a small caught breath as a tress of her hair tumbled onto her bare shoulder.

He reached for a second pin. "And here we are."

"Lost to all shame."

He stood arrested for a flashing moment, the jeweled pin between his fingertips.

She smiled. "I didn't mean it literally."

He looked relieved.

And she laughed. "So you're aware of respectability."

Amusement flickered in his eyes. "Only from a distance."

"You were actually worried."

"Not worried, thinking," he replied, pulling out the second pin. "Such moral integrity is offputting."

"You mean you wouldn't be able to perform?"

He chuckled. "No, I didn't mean that."

"Because you always do."

Pulling out two more pins, he shrugged faintly. "I'm not about to answer that."

"As long as you perform for me, I'm content."

He tossed the pins in his hand onto the sheet and ran his fingers through her loosened hair. "No problem there," he assured her. Sliding his hand under her chin, he lifted her face. "How many times do you want it?"

The grass was cool on her back even through the sheet, and she trembled as he gently eased her thighs open. He was kneeling between her legs, his broad shoulders blocking out the sun, his lean torso limned by the light, and there was no explanation for the intense, fevered lust she felt. Nothing in all her past that would serve as a reference—not one lover, not one husband, not a hero from the pages of a book had ever made her feel such mindless desire. It was as if he exuded some potent allure, or cast a magical spell and, mesmerized, she was in thrall.

But he had more than bewitching allure, she realized, gazing at the enormity of his upthrust erection lying flat against his stomach. And she ached with longing to feel him deep inside her.

There was no question of his sexual accomplishments, nor of the reason he was so much in demand. Neither could she begrudge the legions of ladies in his wake. Like them, she'd been given the benefit of his virtuoso talents.

And like them, she wanted more.

He seemed to understand, or perhaps his emotions were in accord, for he entered her short moments later with a soft apology for his impatience, gliding in with a silken friction that touched her to the quick, overwhelmed her senses, gave credence to the phrase *lost to all reason*. And when at last he filled her completely, when she felt as though she couldn't breathe for the size of him, when ravishing sensation strummed outward from her tautly stretched tissue and pulsed through her body, she sobbed from the sheer, sublime, overwrought pleasure.

"Don't cry," he whispered, terrified he'd hurt her.

"I'm—not . . ." she sobbed, her hands hard on his back.

And then he understood and put away his brief apprehension and did what he did so well—what made him vaunted, pursued, cherished by females far and wide. He made love to her as though she were the first in his heart—in the world—taking care to please her, knowing how to please her, going slowly when she wished it and not slow at all when she wanted more. And when she came that first time—quickly, as she had before—and melted around him, the sun on his back and the heat of ardor merged in an uncommon feeling even he was forced to recognize as rare.

"You don't have to be so polite," she breathed, knowing he'd withheld his orgasm.

"It's not politeness." His voice was low, hushed, the warmth of his breath caressing her cheek. "It's a fucking game. . . ."

She could feel him hard inside her, the smallest of tremors beginning again, rippling, shimmering up her stretched tissue. "I'm pleased you came back. . . ."

"Not as pleased as I." He kissed the tender flesh behind her ear.

"I haven't had a playmate before."

He smiled at his good fortune when it shouldn't have mattered, when he'd had playmates galore. "I haven't either," he whispered, understanding he spoke more truth than lie. She fit perfectly, they fit perfectly, the notion of play had taken on a degree of pleasure hitherto unknown—the fluid rhythm of his lower body a gratifying case in point—and hedonist that he was, he wasn't about to let her go. "I'll be staying . . ." he said, sliding in deeper, holding himself hard against her womb.

"I'll . . . let . . . you." Breathy pauses punctuated her words, her fingers tightened on his back.

"Much obliged," he drawled softly.

But she didn't hear him, or if she did, the impudence in his tone didn't matter with another orgasm beginning to overwhelm her. And her soft cry a moment later drifted up into the bank of yellow roses tumbling overhead.

After a time, the scent of crushed grass rose in the balmy air—and the aroma of sex, and were it possible, the fragrance of bliss would have mingled as well in the sweet-smelling air.

She was insatiable, he thought, indoors and out, and he wondered if she'd truly been without a man at all. From a personal point of view he wouldn't have thought it possible, but after her fifth climax he was no longer so sure. Although, perhaps the lady was just hot-blooded.

No matter the reasons for her demanding sexuality, the mutual ravishment couldn't be faulted, and much later, when he considered his gentlemanly duties sufficiently performed, he finally allowed himself release.

Gazing up at him, she smiled sweetly and said "Thank you. I've really enjoyed myself" as though it were over.

"No need to thank me yet, I'm not finished." And grabbing a corner of the sheet, he wiped the come from her stomach, rolled away, and lay spread-eagle under the sun, content. "This is much better than being polite to the Prince of Wales all afternoon. . . ."

"Your politeness to me can't be faulted," she replied, a small drollery in her tone.

Turning his head, he offered her a lazy smile. "But then, I'm having fun too."

"Fun?"

"Isn't it?"

Quicksilver, she rearranged a lifetime of perceptions. "Does anyone ever disagree?"

A transient pause brought the trill of birdsong suddenly to the fore.

"I've never actually—"

"Talked to a woman?"

He rolled upward into a seated position, the play of his abdominal muscles dramatic. "I'm not so sure I like your insinuation," he said, frowning faintly.

"Answer my question."

He exhaled softly. "If you must know, most women aren't interested in talking."

"Or you don't give them time."

"There're better things to do."

"What if I wanted to talk?"

A sportive grin lifted his mouth. "What do you mean 'what if'?"

"I mean really talk."

Leaning back on his hands, he tipped his head. "Talk away."

"You'll listen?"

"I've plenty of time."

A small silence fell while Alex mentally scrambled to find a suitable topic.

"There. You see?"

"I dislike smug men."

"Do you dislike men who can make you come another dozen times?" His gaze flicked downward to his erection and then back again to her.

"That's *exceedingly* smug, Ranelagh."

"Answer my question," he said as she had only moments before.

"I suppose I don't," she noted grudgingly.

"You *suppose?*"

Her glance fluttered to his rampant erection and as quickly away.

"Why let this go to waste?" He looked up at the sun as though gauging the time.

"Is your schedule busy?" Taut, thin-skinned, not wishing to feel so needy and overwhelmed, she sat up quickly. "Don't let me keep you."

His laugh was beguiling. "I don't have a schedule, and if I did, I'd change it to stay here with you."

She found her temper subsiding under the charm of his reply.

"I'll have to mind my manners," he observed playfully. "Your temper is damnably quick."

"I'm sorry."

His eyes widened in feigned astonishment. "Have I finally done something right?"

"You've done any number of glorious things right, as if you didn't know," she said with a sudden grin. "And perhaps we really *shouldn't* waste our time."

"Are we done talking, then?" His voice was smooth as silk.

She nodded.

"Thank you, ma'am." Leaning over, he lifted her onto his lap, minutely adjusted her as though it mattered where their bare flesh met.

His power was awesome—the startling width of his shoulders, the solid, honed muscles of his chest and arms, the iron-hard thighs beneath her. "You're very strong," she said on a caught breath, feeling exceedingly small against his body.

"The better to handle you, my sweet."

"Even if I don't wish to be handled?"

"Even then," he replied quietly, swinging her around so she was straddling his thighs.

She touched the dark curve of one brow with her fingertip. "Should I take offense?" Their eyes were almost on a level, desire mirrored in their depths.

"You probably should," he whispered, lifting her bottom with one hand, guiding his erection to her damp cleft with the other. "If you didn't want this cock I'm putting—"

She sighed softly as he thrust upward.

"Here," he breathed, pressing her hips firmly downward.

She purred, a low, pleasurable sound, and clung to his broad shoulders, giving herself up to the rush of pleasure, no longer questioning his power to incite, only reveling in the wondrous feeling. Every cell, every nerve, was alive with delirious sensation, the world distant and ordinary, delectable rapture coiling in the pit of her stomach and in her brain, in the heated silk of her skin, most exquisitely where he rested deep inside her.

As he gently raised her, she resisted.

"There . . . there," he whispered, forcing her upward. "I'm coming back." And he held her suspended on the very crest of his erection.

"Now," she insisted, struggling against his strength.

"Soon . . ." His breath brushed the jewel-hard tip of one nipple. "If you behave," he promised, drawing the taut bud into his mouth.

She should repudiate his authority; she shouldn't be so in thrall, but at that instant his mouth closed on her nipple, a racing heat melted downward to the pulsing core of her body, and covetous lust inundated her brain. "Please . . . please—oh, God, please . . ."

"Are you begging me?" he asked against her skin, pausing in his sucking.

"Yes, yes, whatever you say . . . please. . . ."

Such sexual largesse was too much for even the most practiced libertine, and the concept of casual play gave way to a more avaricious hunger. Precipitously, she was impaled on his engorged penis, his large hands spanning her hips, holding her motionless while she panted in ecstasy. Struck by his own irrepressible sense of engagement, he decided there must be a God after all—why else would he be here with this particular woman in this particular garden, feeling these staggering sensations or, more pertinently, why was he feeling as insatiable as she? The question was briefly disconcerting; he was never insatiable. But male impulse quickly took over, obliterating intellectual preoccupations. Leaning back on his elbows, he focused on her delectable offer to do anything. Which thought brought a new dimension to his erection.

She moaned, a full, lush sound.

He briefly shut his eyes against the need for restraint, and then he said, his voice husky with passion, "Ride me, Miss Ionides. Show me what you can do."

It was the voice of authority however softly put, and were she less insensate with desire, she might have responded differently—slapped him for his effrontery perhaps, or lashed him with her tongue. As it was, she was too much in rut to experience anything but a stabbing rush of longing, and she complied, because she desperately needed what he could give her.

He watched her raise and lower herself, once, twice, three times, while an unnerving tumult coursed through his brain. Her large breasts quivered as she moved, he noted with a reckless lack of detachment.

Her cheeks were flushed, her flamboyant eyes half-hidden behind her lowered lashes, and he wondered why he felt such a headlong need to master her.

Her fevered gaze met his as she slid downward again and traced her forefinger down his chest with just enough force to leave a mark on his bronzed skin. "Who's winning?" she whispered as if she could read his mind.

He brushed her hand away, the stinging path left by her nail as provoking as her gaze. "It depends on who wants to come the most," he muttered, not sure of the answer for the first time in his life.

She drew in a sharp breath. "Bastard."

"Bitch." But the word was dulcet and low, without rancor. "Sweet, fucking bitch . . ."

He abruptly took over then, because he suddenly couldn't wait any more than he could pretend this game was like the others.

It wasn't.

She wasn't.

It wasn't even a fucking game anymore.

He wanted her as much as she wanted him—maybe more—because he knew his eagerness and impatience had nothing to do with any possible celibacy. Quickly rolling her onto her back, he covered her, engulfed her, drove into her welcoming heat with an unnecessary ferocity, as though he could possess her and obliterate his own chaotic feelings by brute strength alone.

She was literally panting in his arms, his own breathing equally labored, when voices intruded from beyond the jasmine hedge and rose trellis and a conversation about watering hydrangeas brought her rigid in his arms. Not about to stop this side of death, he quickly covered her mouth with his, inhaled her soft cry of alarm, and tightening his grip on her hips continued his hard-driving rhythm until she no longer cared about the neighbors' discussion or no longer heard it. She was clinging to him now as if he were her last hope or her best hope or her own personal savior, and when she came, she bit down hard on his lip, sank her nails into his back, and silently died away in his arms.

No more than a second after her climax ended, he followed her to his own blissful fulfillment and, braced above her, panting, he tried to catch his breath.

"I might have to move away after this," she whispered, the neighbors' voices having drifted away. "Oh, dear—you're bleeding!"

"It's nothing." He licked away the blood on his lower lip. "And consider, I learned not to overwater hydrangeas."

She laughed. "And I learned not to make love in my garden."

"No one even knew we were here."

"Nevertheless, you're corrupting my sense of propriety."

One dark brow rose. "It's a bit late for complaints, isn't it?"

She blushed a deeper shade of pink. "I don't know what's come over me. You've quite turned my head."

A number of replies having to do with turning various parts of her body sprang to mind, but interested in continuing their pleasurable acquaintance, he only smiled. "Then I should beg your pardon and say please consider me your servant in all things, ma'am."

Her purple eyes sparkled. "Do you mean it?"

"Have I been somehow obtuse in pleasing you?"

She had the grace to look embarrassed. "No, and never, and I apologize profusely."

"No need to apologize. Just tell me what you want."

She blushed again.

"Or I could tell you," he said.

She took a small breath and said so low he could scarcely hear no matter they were only inches apart, "Or we could tell each other . . ."

His heart skipped a beat. "What a good idea," he replied gently.

Much later, when the sun was almost set, when there was no longer any question of who wanted whom, or how much or how often, they lay side by side, both in full measure replete and content.

A rare feeling for a man of Ranelagh's restless temperament.

As rare for Alex, who had filled her days of late with a multitude of well-ordered, useful efficiencies.

Lying on his back, his eyes were shut, his hand

lightly touching hers. "Do you still want to go to the exhibition?"

Sprawled beside him, Alex turned her head. "Do you?"

His eyes opened and he glanced at her. "I asked first." Inexplicably, he felt like an adolescent with his first lover. He wished to show her off, wanted everyone to know that she was his, that the flush on her cheeks was because of him. But when she didn't immediately answer, he said, "If you'd rather not."

"No, I'd like to."

He rolled over and kissed her, and smiled from mere inches away. "Do you know when I last lay in the sun like this?"

She looked amused. "I'd rather you didn't tell me."

"I meant myself, alone"—he smiled—"content like this."

She reached up and touched the dip of his brow. "In that case, tell me."

"I was twelve and at the beach in Brighton, or near the beach, lying on the grass. I was completely alone—no servants, no family." He grinned. "That's probably why I was content." He shrugged. "Anyway, it's been a long time. So I thank you."

"My list is long in terms of thanking you." Her voice was very soft. "I won't forget this. . . ."

"Consider me available to refresh your memory anytime," he drawled.

"How kind of you," she teased.

"Kindness has nothing to do with it. Now, before I

lose control again, which I never do, by the way—like lying in the sun—why don't we dress and you can point out your paintings at the show."

They dressed, but leisurely as it turned out, because Sam was particularly good at putting on her silk stockings, Alex discovered, and then inevitably, taking them off again. Until as twilight fell, they agreed that if they didn't dress themselves, it would soon be too late to go to the gallery.

Chapter 10

They arrived at Grosvenor House just as the doors were closing, but Alex knew the attendant. "You just go along in, Miss Ionides," he said. "I'll wait to lock up when you leave."

"Another admirer, I see," Sam remarked with a smile.

"I've known Charlie since childhood. He was the first to congratulate me when I was accepted by the jury and my first painting was hung three years ago."

"When did you start painting?"

"Seriously? About five years ago."

"When you were still married. Did your husband mind?"

She shook her head. "John encouraged me. We went to Paris together and visited all the studios. He was a great collector."

John Coutts had owned one of the prominent West End banks. Sam suspected he was capable of buying a painting or two, but he was struck instead with his benevolence toward his wife's career. Most wealthy men preferred their beautiful young wives concentrate exclusively on them. "Did you see the first impressionist show in Paris in 'sixty-nine?"

She nodded. "And those in 'seventy-four and 'seventy-six and all the exhibitions at Durand-Ruel as well. I know most of the artists."

"Do you have a favorite?"

"Manet, I think, for the intensity of his color and his interesting perspective. Although, perhaps, he's more conservative than some."

"Your work has a lighter palette than his."

She smiled up at him. "It depends on my mood, darling."

He pulled her to a stop in the middle of the broad bank of stairs and kissed her because he found not only her smile appealing, but the fact that she was smiling at him. And when he released her mouth after a lengthy interval, he said, "I find my mood much improved in your presence."

"What a coincidence. I do as well. And if you'll pose for me sometime, I'll have the best of both worlds—good spirits and sex personified right before my eyes."

"Or anywhere else you might like it."

"We could discuss that later tonight—that anywhere."

His expression went blank for a moment.

"Oh, dear," she said, but without alarm, because she was feeling confident of her appeal.

"Sorry, force of habit." He grinned. "I'm available tonight."

"I rather thought you might be."

"Hussy."

"But you want me."

"No question there."

"And while your ego doesn't require any further encouragement, I freely admit, at the moment, I can't live without you . . . it . . . that—you know, darling, what you have that I want."

"Don't be shy about asking."

"In about a half hour, I'll do more than ask," she said, undeterred by his teasing. "But right now I want to show you my favorite pieces."

They'd reached the first floor by that time, and she proceeded to take him to each of her favorite paintings, where she explained with great enthusiasm why she liked them.

"Show me yours now," he proposed when he'd had the tour of favorites. "I thought you weren't shy."

"There's a difference between shyness and modesty."

"I don't require either. Nor do you strike me as particularly modest"—his brows rose in sardonic appraisal—"if I recall."

"I expect only glowing accolades, then."

He grinned. "Would I offend a woman of your inestimable charms?" But neither benevolence nor courtesy were required, for her two paintings were magnificent. And he told her so.

"Do you really like them?"

He was reminded of a prideful mother with her children. "I do, and the jury did as well, for they've hung your work in prominent positions."

"That's what Charlie told me as well."

He was surprised at her hesitancy. She hadn't displayed that characteristic before. "You have to know you're extremely good. And I was about to say *for a woman,* but you know what I mean."

She nodded, as aware as he of the prejudices toward female accomplishments in anything construed as a male domain. "I haven't been painting very long and so many of these artists have spent a lifetime in their endeavors."

"This is one field where perseverance is no indication of genius. And if you won't take offense because he's your friend, Leighton is a case in point. He's capable but not brilliant. While you are. Also, keep in mind, your landscapes aren't quite as academic as the jury would like, and they accepted you anyway. That's quite a coup, darling."

"I'm finding you more and more a man of exceptional taste."

"I'm serious. You're very, very good."

"Thank you," she said quietly. "I get more than my share of advice from many of the established male painters."

"And it annoys you."

She nodded. "Sometimes."

"I hope you don't pay any attention to it."

"Not usually, but"—she shrugged—"it can be disconcerting."

"Ignore them." He smiled. "And that's an order."

"Yes, sir, and I shall deliver my orders to you in the privacy of my boudoir."

"A charming prospect, but on the way we'll stop at my house and you can look at my collection. I could use your expertise."

"My goodness, Ranelagh," she remarked playfully. "Can't you do better than that old line?"

"I'm serious. And I can have my way with you," he drawled silkily, "without showing you my paintings."

She offered him a coy look. "A gentleman would never—"

"I don't aspire to that status. . . ."

"I see," she said with dramatic primness.

He laughed out loud, and sweeping her up into his arms, ran down the corridor and raced down the stairs with a reckless disregard for safety. And when they reached the ground floor, he set her on her feet and kissed her. "It wouldn't do for me to carry you out the door in sight of Charlie et al."

"Maybe I don't care."

"Then I'll be prudent for both of us." He was well aware of his reputation, and while he might squire Miss Ionides about without ruining her reputation, he didn't wish to compromise her to the world. "Now lay your hand on my arm like a woman of fashion, and we'll say good night to Charlie like well-behaved adults."

"But I'll have you later for myself." She smiled up at him as she placed her hand on his offered arm. "When you're not so well behaved."

"Try to keep me away," he challenged her.

"I might just a little," she teased.

"And I might spank your sweet little bottom just a little."

"Ummm . . . that sounds divine."

"Your house or mine?" His dark gaze was heated.

"What will your servants say?"

"You're not serious."

"Of course I'm serious. Or do you take all your lovers home?"

For a brief moment he thought she was joking, and when he realized she wasn't, it took him a moment more to come to terms with the enormity of his invitation.

"You're having second thoughts, aren't you?"

"No," he said politely, but his tone indicated otherwise.

"You're allowed your reservations, darling. My expectations don't go beyond the pleasure of your very expert lovemaking. I don't want anything more."

For a minute he took offense, because he didn't want her to be so cavalier about something that was astonishingly rare for him. But as quickly, he realized she was right, and if he didn't come to his senses tonight or tomorrow, he would eventually. He wasn't looking for permanence, only sex.

And apparently, so was she.

Chapter 11

$\mathscr{H}$is house on Park Lane was very new. Alex recognized Wyatt's hand in the design, the architect one of the bright young talents who were able to effectively combine traditional elements and creativity without either suffering from the union.

"I didn't know this was your house," Alex said as the carriage came to rest before the porticoed entrance. "Although I saw the designs when Martin was beginning the preliminary drawings. He comes to my studio occasionally." And at Sam's sudden piercing glance, she added, "For my Sunday literary afternoons."

"Now, why would he do that?"

"Please. Martin is happily married. His wife is a good friend of mine."

"I didn't know he was married."

"Because you met him in your library with your steward and secretary and they took care of all the details once you gave your approval to his design."

"I can see I'm going to have to improve my image with you."

She smiled. "Not completely. In many ways, you're quite exceptional."

"Thank God."

"God doesn't have anything to do with it."

"Sometimes he seems to make his presence known," he noted waggishly.

"You needn't remind me."

"I didn't know anyone could blush so much."

"Hush," she warned, glancing at the carriage window that framed a footman's head.

"They don't hear anything."

She glared at him. "Of course they do."

At that, the door opened and Sam helped her out with courtesy and deference and only one surreptitious wink. He spoke of the weather with circumspect blandness as they moved up the paved walk to the entrance, and had not the beautiful dark-haired woman dressed in an exceptionally scanty costume more appropriate to the harem not jumped from the bushes and leaped at Sam, their approach to Ranelagh House would have been uneventful.

As it was, Alex screamed.

Sam swore.

And the young beauty shrieked, "You swine! You despicable cur! You filthy son of a—" Sam's hand stopped the remainder of her diatribe, and curbing her flailing arms with a wrestling hold, he handed her over to his footmen, who'd come at a run.

"You can't get away with this! I'll hound you! I'll

see that you pay! I'll see you in court! You can't desert me. . . ." Her cries trailed off as she was hauled around the corner of the house.

"Perhaps this isn't a good time," Alex said into the sudden silence.

Sam looked at her blankly for a moment, as though he'd forgotten she was with him and exhaling softly, he said, "No . . . it's fine."

"I don't think so. Shouldn't you speak to the woman?"

"God no," he said with feeling.

"She's obviously distrait." Alex's expression was cool.

"It's not what you think."

"Really. I had the impression she knew you."

"Jesus, don't look at me like that. I'm not the devil incarnate." He softly sighed. "In fact, Farida's a more likely candidate."

"A male viewpoint, no doubt."

"Do we have to talk about this?"

"No, of course not. We can ignore it. I'm sure you ignore former lovers with great regularity."

"I don't have to tell you anything," he said gruffly.

"No, you don't."

"But you're going to talk in that disapproving, snippy tone forever, aren't you, if I can't explain this away."

"Explaining this away, as you so quaintly put it, isn't my major concern. The woman seemed genuinely distressed. I think you should see to her."

"I already have, countless times. Look," he said,

resentful and defensive. "I gave her a house and a very large bank draft and paid her gambling debts. And that's all I'm going to do."

Alex's gaze widened. "Good Lord, is there a child involved?"

He gave her a withering look. "What kind of fool do you think I am?"

Oddly, she was relieved, when it shouldn't have mattered in the least what his relationship was with the scantily dressed young woman. "I see," she said, as though the bland phrase would mask the disarray of her thoughts.

"This was unfortunate." For a fleeting moment he looked afflicted. "Come inside . . . please?"

"I'm not sure."

"I don't want you to think me callous. But this mess isn't your mess." He shrugged. "And escape is high on my list of priorities at the moment."

"The woman has money?"

"Plenty."

"And a house?"

"A rather nice one. And she lives with her brother, if you're concerned she's alone and defenseless." He snorted. "Not likely, that."

"So she's not destitute and at the mercy of the world."

"Rather the opposite. The world's at her mercy."

Alex couldn't help but smile at the irony of the situation. "Apparently, she's dissatisfied with you."

"She's dissatisfied she's lost my financing."

"My goodness. So they don't all want your charming body."

"Apparently not," he replied dryly. "Are you finished being amused at my expense?"

"She must be very good."

He shrugged.

"Perhaps I should ask for lessons?"

"Stay away from her. And you don't need lessons. You're quite accomplished enough, thank you."

"You say that as though it were vexing."

He scowled at her. "Don't start. I'm not in the mood."

"What are you in the mood for?"

Her tone was so lush with promise, he questioned his hearing. Either she was more wanton than he thought or more understanding. But unsure on such short acquaintance, he carefully said, "I'm in the mood for escape—with you. I've an apartment near the City if you'd like to see it. It's private."

"She doesn't know of it, you mean."

"That's what I mean."

"Dare you trust me not to stalk you there later?"

"You're much too busy beating off your suitors. I doubt you'd have time to pine over me."

"We could go back to my studio."

"Farida's unpredictable. It's better if she doesn't know where you live."

"Is she dangerous?"

He hesitated. "She could be."

"You've had problems?"

"Could we talk about something else? She's been one of the major mistakes in my life."

"Sam!" she protested. "You can't imply some sort of nefarious activity is involved and then expect me to suppress my curiosity."

"I'll tell you at the apartment."

"Do you have food there? I'm hungry."

"I have a chef there."

"Then, how can I refuse?"

"How indeed?" He felt immeasurably cheered, Farida's rampage banished from his mind. "I have a small collection of watercolors there as well."

"Good God, Ranelagh. I yield to your numerous allures."

He held out his hand. "And I thank you for your understanding."

His apartment was just off the Strand in a building that had once housed an Elizabethan grandee. He owned the entire complex, but his quarters were on the main floor, six large rooms he kept for his private retreat. Had she known he'd never even brought a friend there, not to mention a lover, she would have been honored. There was an array of servants at his beck and call as well as the chef, who was summoned to the drawing room to discuss dinner with them.

Candles had been lit; Sam hadn't had gaslight brought into his apartment by design, and the early twilight lent an air of calm and peace to the large, paneled room.

Claude was beside himself with joy that he could demonstrate his considerable skills to more than his employer on the rare occasions Sam was in residence, and his Gallic sensibilities were entranced at the prospect of serving so lovely a lady. When Alex spoke to him in flawless French, his eyes literally filled with tears. There was nothing too good for the beautiful mademoiselle after that. When Claude finally left after bowing himself out of the room, Sam offered Alex a soft round of applause.

"You've charmed him completely."

"He's very sweet. And apparently you never give him the opportunity to fully express himself. He doesn't like to cook your steaks."

"He's paid handsomely to cook my steaks."

"Which is why he stays."

"In addition to the fact that he has an English wife."

"Nevertheless, he's pleased to be allowed some creativity tonight."

While the dinner menu had been discussed, Sam had drunk two cognacs and quietly observed the remarkable Miss Ionides with delight. Her charms were diverse, catholic, and undeniably natural. She was capable of most anything, it seemed, and he felt fortunate to have her company this evening. And not necessarily in the usual sexual context, he reflected, recognizing the rarity of his feelings. He was actually looking forward to dining and conversing with her, not to mention enjoying her beauty across his candlelit table.

If he weren't such a pragmatist, he might consider his benign sensibilities as impressionably romantic.

Chapter 12

❧❧

"I was dismissed like some lowly lackey and run off his property," Farida spat out. "Damn his arrogant hide!"

"Come to bed, Fari. Ranelagh's made us rich enough. Don't be greedy."

"I'm not greedy, Mahmud, when the man's worth ten million. He can afford to give us more and not even miss it."

Her brother curled his fine mouth in a grimace and stretched his lithe brown body. "We should sell this grand house and go back to Egypt. It's always damp here in England and the sun never shines."

Farida stood at the end of the bed and glared at her brother. "We'll go back once I have the fortune I want. And we'll live in Cairo near the Azbakiyah Gardens, where the British nabobs live—"

"Not unless you're serving their wallah wives," he pointed out, less prone to daydreams than his sister. "Only the Europeans live there."

"Then we'll have our mansion somewhere else."

"We can do that now. We don't need more of Ranelagh's money."

"You've always thought too small, Mahmud."

His gaze turned sullen. "While you've lain with anyone who has ten piastres to offer you."

"And look what we have, thanks to me. Darling, consider"—her tone turned coaxing—"if I can make Ranelagh pay, you'll have all the desert ponies you wish."

"I want only the ones Hasim stole from us."

"And you'll have them. I promise."

"When?" Moody and sullen, he gazed at her, his handsome face a male duplicate of hers, brother and sister a stunning matched pair who had advantageously used their beauty for profit.

"Soon. The barrister said we can file a breach of promise suit, and there's always Ranelagh's Egyptian collection. Think what we could get for it on the art market." She moved around the end of the bed and sat down beside him. "I missed you today," she whispered, leaning over to kiss his sulky mouth.

"I waited for you all afternoon." His fingers tangled in her hair and he pulled her closer.

"I'm here now . . . ," she murmured, stroking his rising erection.

Chapter 13

ave you ever thought about having children?" Alex asked.

Sam and Alex were looking at a series of watercolors painted by Ingres during his Italian sojourn. They had paused in front of one of small children at play in the shade of an olive tree, the dappled sun illuminating their plump, rosy faces. After a superb dinner and several glasses of wine, Alex found their cherubic looks even more endearing.

Under normal circumstances the viscount would have been alarmed at such a question, but he felt an odd tenderness toward the speaker and he only said, "No, have you?"

"I would have liked children," Alex replied, "but . . ." Reluctant to discuss the idiosyncrasies of her marriages, her voice trailed off.

"It didn't work out."

"No."

"Penelope said she was too young to have children." Even as he spoke, he questioned his sanity. He'd never discussed his wife with anyone.

Alex smiled faintly. "St. Albans said he was too old."

"And Coutts?"

The color rose on her cheeks. "It was a personal matter."

"Ah." He took her hand. "You haven't seen my Turner watercolors yet," he said, mannerly and urbane. From the girls at Hattie's he'd heard Coutts was impotent. "They're so fragile, I have them stored in drawers." He drew her toward a large cabinet in the center of his study.

His well-bred kindness further commended him, when she was already more enchanted than she wished. She tried to repress the affection he inspired. "I first saw Turner's work when I was very young," she told him, forcing herself to speak with composure. "And I thought I was looking at dream landscapes."

"These river views especially remind me of dreams." Sam carefully lifted two sheets from a drawer and set them on the broad cabinet top. "He's been a favorite of mine for years. I bought my first Turner when I was fifteen." He glanced at her empty glass. "Would you like more cognac?"

"I shouldn't." She smiled. "But I will if you will."

Taking his glass from her, he grinned. "If you insist."

"I don't usually drink so much, but it's so peaceful here and the company is superb," she said with a smile, "and I seem to be in the mood for lethargy."

He looked up from pouring. "Are you going to fall asleep on me?"

"*On* you?"

"Now, there's a concept. Maybe we can look at the rest of the watercolors later." Setting down the bottle and glass, he pushed the cabinet drawer shut.

"If you don't think me too presumptuous."

"Not at all. I'm capable of saying no if I wish."

"Have you ever?"

"Do you think I haven't?"

"Answer the question." She was curious.

"What happens if I do?"

She tipped her head faintly. "You get a reward."

"Ah, then . . . yes, I have," he replied smoothly.

"Liar."

He looked amused. "I was just ordered to answer. You didn't say you wanted the truth."

"And we both know the truth," she declared. "Which makes this all very bizarre—my being here." She was resting her arms on the high cabinet top in a comfortable lounging pose, the wide sleeves of her gown falling away at her elbows.

"Why? It's a perfectly benign evening." But he knew what she meant by bizarre, because not only had he never had anyone to his Strand apartment, he hadn't dined alone with a lady since the early days of his ill-fated marriage. And she looked as though she belonged in his study in her softly draped gown designed in the Pre-Raphaelite mode—an Elizabethan lady to match his apartment.

"But I've never given in to impulse before—in terms of sex."

"Why not?" The pattern of his sexual life had been essentially based on impulse.

She lifted one shoulder slightly in the merest of deprecating shrugs. "Circumstances perhaps, or cultural pressures for women. Who knows?"

"So young Harry wasn't an impulse?"

"God, no. He was amazingly persistent."

Harry would bear watching, he noted silently, struck by a curious sense of possession. "Well, then this is a change for us both. You see, I've never actually had a lady in for dinner."

She smiled, warmed by his admission. "Did you enjoy it?"

"Profoundly. My compliments on the menu. The food was superb even if it wasn't steak."

"Didn't I tell you I'd expand your experience?"

"Speaking of experiences—let me show you my rooftop garden. And the stars. The lights of the City are less evident in this section of London. You may lie on me there."

"You enjoy this garden alone?"

"Always. It's peaceful and my life is too often—"

"Dissolute?" she offered.

"Filled with people, certainly," he remarked calmly, immune to censure, playful or not. "And not always those I wish to see."

"My studio offers me the same kind of solitude on occasion."

"When you can keep your suitors at bay."

"I suppose. We both can use the hermitage of your rooftop, it seems."

She hadn't disagreed with his assessment of her admirers, he noted with chagrin. But he knew better than to take issue with it, considering the manner of his own entertainments. "Then, I'll take the cognac bottle, you take our glasses, and follow me."

They were almost to the study door, when a servant knocked. After Sam bid him enter, his butler stood stiffly on the threshold. "There is a *person* here, my lord, with a note for the lady."

"For me?" Alex said, the words half suffocated in her throat.

"What kind of a person?" Sam inquired, the disdain in his butler's voice obvious. Who the hell knew of his apartment, he wondered, and, more particularly, of his guest?

"A rather rough sort of fellow, sir, with a decided limp. Should I have the footmen throw him out?"

"A limp?" Alex breathed, setting the glasses down before she dropped them.

Sam turned to her, taking in her pallor with a small frown. "You needn't see anyone," he said crisply. "Barclay, bring the lady a chair."

"I'm fine, really, there's no need . . ." Alex drew herself up straighter, as though readying herself for a confrontation. "Show the man in, Barclay. I believe my father sent him."

The viscount choked back his exclamation and nodded to his servant. Brief moments later, a small, wiry man of indeterminate age walked into the room with an awkward gait. He was dressed like a seaman in wide-legged trousers and a striped jersey, and the knit cap pulled low on his forehead hid the color of his hair.

"Good evenin', Miss Alex." The man saluted briefly, his deference plain. "Beggin' your pardon, miss, but your pa sent me."

"I understand, Loucas. You have a note, I believe." There was a possibility some emergency existed, but she rather doubted it. Her father's factotum didn't look agitated in the least.

"Yes, miss." He fumbled in his trouser pocket before extracting a small folded sheet of paper and handing it to her.

"Excuse me," she murmured, opening the seal. She spread the sheet and quickly perused the few lines. A blush began at her throat and slowly moved upward until her face was suffused with pink. Her father had politely informed her of her mother's visit to her studio, the reason for it, and her subsequent displeasure on not finding Alex there. Because he'd promised he'd make inquiries, he went on, he had to keep his word. He expressed his regret at intruding.

"My apologies," she said, turning to Sam, crumpling the note in her hand. "That will be all, Loucas, thank you."

"Yes, miss." With a sharp glance in Sam's direction, he left.

The moment the door closed on their visitor, Sam tossed the cognac bottle toward a settee and asked coolly, "Have we been under surveillance today?"

"No, but I'm absolutely mortified, and I don't blame you in the least for being annoyed." She grimaced. "It's my mother."

"How did she find you?" There was no conciliation in his tone or in his gaze.

"I don't know if you're aware, but my father is Greek consul in London and his merchant business, too, offers him, shall we say, a broad range of contacts in the City. At all levels of society," she quietly added.

"He has informers," Sam said curtly.

"I'm not sure *he* personally has any, but he has access to them."

"And he wished to find you."

"Actually, my mother did." She shrugged. "She worries, and he must placate her, and if it's any consolation, he apologized for his intrusion."

"Gratifying," Sam conceded, his gaze dubious.

"I do apologize most humbly."

Sam was silent, and her embarrassment deepened. She didn't know what more she could say. That this had never happened before? That her mother considered him unacceptable company for her daughter? That her mother wished her to marry a Greek shipping merchant and have a dozen children?

"Fuck." The soft expletive was pronounced with a distinct scowl.

This probably wasn't the time for levity, Alex

reflected, although it was tempting, and she suppressed the impulse to say *here or on the rooftop?* Instead, she said, "I'm sure you'd rather I leave now. I can find a hackney to take me home."

"Sit." He pointed to a chair.

His brusque tone stripped away any further thought of remorse, and she drew herself up to her full height. "I beg your pardon?"

His gaze seemed to refocus, and his voice when he spoke held its familiar warmth. "Please sit, darling. And forgive my gruffness. I was just wondering if perhaps we should reply to your father's note. Reassure him of your safety."

"Don't joke, Sam"—her voice took on a nervous edge—"you don't know my mother. She'll be on your doorstep in no time."

"We could invite her in for tea," he drawled, his good spirits returning as he realized he was dealing only with a domineering mother. That particular style of female was familiar to him.

"No, *we* could *not*! We *will* most certainly not! We—I . . . neither of us wants to see my mother over tea or otherwise." She could just imagine the scene. "My mother has very set notions of a woman's role, none of which I conform to. She's particularly offended that I'm her only child who hasn't given her grandchildren, and she reminds me of that deficit several hundred times a year."

"We could work on that," he teased.

"She would prefer a legitimate grandchild," Alex

replied tartly, "and I doubt that was a proposal of marriage I just heard."

"And if it were?" Even as he recognized the flippancy of his question, the matter of her answer intrigued him.

"I would refuse, of course, because I prefer a husband who understands what the word marriage means."

"Do I detect a modicum of censure?"

"If modicum means oceans full and mountains high, you'd be close."

"And yet your mother disapproved of your marriages, when both men were clearly stable and reputable."

"How did you know?"

He grinned. "A wild guess. And she disapproves of me, I expect, although, I admit, I'm in awe of the Ionides spy system. I met you just yesterday."

Alex grimaced. "Terrifying, isn't it?"

"It almost makes one consider locking the bedroom door and closing the draperies."

"I'd recommend it."

"So that leaves out the rooftop."

"Really, Sam, you needn't be polite. Loucas's appearance must have been unsettling."

For a man who'd performed sexually before spectators on occasion when the revels at Hattie's turned lewd, a servant delivering a note hardly bore notice. Now that the explanation was clear. "Is it unsettling for you?"

"Of course."

"How much?" And then he smiled and opened his arms and said very low, "Queen Elizabeth actually slept in my bed, and I was thinking you might like to try it out before you leave."

She didn't reply immediately, but the pleasure Sam offered was no longer an unknown, and the tantalizing possibilities in staying overwhelmed prudent behavior. "I suppose," she said, walking toward him, "lying in Queen Elizabeth's bed would be in the nature of a history lesson—an edifying experience."

"I could guarantee the edifying part." He ran his hands down her arms as she reached him. When their fingers touched and twined, he drew her close. "And I can't let you go."

"Nor do I wish to leave . . . although—"

"We'll worry about that in the morning," he whispered.

"I warn you, I'm an early riser."

"I wasn't planning on sleeping."

"Oh," she said on a caught breath.

He found himself charmed by the lovely Miss Ionides's naïveté.

Chapter 14

*H*is bedroom was small and plainly furnished with a tester bed, two chairs, a small table, and a bureau. The walls were covered in tapestries depicting the life of Ulysses, the bed hung with green cut-velvet in a design contemporary to the building. The fabric was new, as was the upholstery on the chairs. The only light was from two huge silver candelabra.

"In the interests of privacy," Sam said, walking over and pulling the draperies shut. "And I'm definitely interested in privacy," he whispered a moment later when he returned to take her into his arms.

"I'm not sure I can guarantee it," Alex said, smiling.

"Then we'll lock the door." He went to the door and turned the key in the lock, then tossed the key on the table. He approached her with a smile. "You're mine now until I let you go."

"Or you're mine," she replied lightly.

The idea of belonging to someone, even temporarily, struck him as odd; he'd been selfishly alone for so long. "I might be more than you can handle." He gave her a roguish wink.

She kicked off her silver kid slippers. "I think I'll manage."

"Let me help you."

"Manage you?"

"Undress."

"And then I'll help you—undress. I never have, you know." Her comment was spontaneous, part of the exuberance that filled her soul in this small, candlelit room where the Virgin Queen had once slept.

"Then I'll have to see that the occasion is memorable," he replied, keeping his voice sportive with effort when he felt instead a jolt of inexplicable pleasure. "We'll start with you." Leaning close, he unclasped one of the large pearl ear drops she wore.

She trembled at the delicacy of his touch, anticipation warming her senses. "I wanted to make love to you all evening," she admitted.

"While I didn't know how much longer I could play the gentleman." He unloosened the second earring and placed it with the first on the bureau top.

"Please don't any longer."

"It's been almost three hours—I'm damned proud of myself."

"Three and a half, and I'm not interested in pride." She was unbuckling the mother-of-pearl belt buckle at her waist, a note of haste in her voice.

Recognizing the tone, he turned her around by her

shoulders and quickly unhooked the back of her gown. As the belt and light summer garment fell to the carpet, she spun to him, threw her arms around his neck, and pressed into his body. "I think there's something wrong with me," she whispered. "I'm frantic to have you make love to me. . . . I'm never like this—never—frantic about anything, and I apologize. But if you don't mind, maybe we could undress you afterward. . . ."

The message was loud and clear despite her whispered accents. He doubted there was a man alive who would have minded. "I'm more than willing," he calmly said, scooping her up into his arms. Carrying her the few feet to the bed, he placed her on the green cut-velvet coverlet near the edge and quickly unfastening his trousers, moved between her legs. As he entered her without undressing, he was reminded of occasions at Hattie's when hasty sex was convenient, although Miss Ionides didn't precipitate the same kind of casual disregard. In fact . . . He brushed away the subsequent thought, not wanting to acknowledge the degree of affection she inspired.

His attention was quickly engaged in far more pleasurable activities as the fascinating Miss Ionides wrapped her legs around his waist. She pulled his head down so she could eat at his mouth while he plunged deep inside her. Between her contented groans and sleek, wet cunt, he was hard pressed to think at all. She came, then he did, then they did. It was an orchestration of timing that could have been accomplished only by a man of his expertise, because there were only half-seconds to spare between her climax and his withdrawal.

There was a brief period of time after that when they felt sated enough to finish their undressing. Hers required only the removal of her chemise, drawers, and stockings, which he did with dispatch. Her undressing of him was more convoluted, both in time and emotion. They both understood the rarity of the event.

He stood beside the bed while she kneeled on the mattress and eased his coat off his shoulders and down his arms. When she began to fold it, he took it from her and tossed it aside impatiently.

Forcing himself to stand still while she unbuttoned his shirt, he found himself counting the seconds it took for each button to be freed and thought surely she must be a witch to make him feel eager as an adolescent once again. It was ninety seconds before his shirt followed his coat onto the carpet—eighty-nine seconds too long in his current frame of mind. When Alex reached for the single button that was keeping his trousers in place, he stopped her hand. "This is taking too long." She was utterly naked kneeling beside him and much too close and much, much too voluptuous—like some fertility goddess made to be fucked by rampant cocks like his. He inhaled against the raging state of his arousal. "I'll do the rest myself."

His trousers slid down his legs and his silk underwear followed in quick succession. When he took her in his arms, he said as a sop to his previously nonexistent conscience, "I hope you don't mind."

"I'm ravenous—I'm crazed—look . . . I'm shaking." She lifted her hand the merest distance so he could see the tremor.

His glance was quick, dismissive, his own sensibilities on an irrepressible rampage. He tumbled her backward on the bed, followed her down, slid between her outstretched thighs, and wondered if anyone was keeping count.

"I'm sorry I'm so . . . demanding," she whispered, arching up to meet his downthrust.

"Don't be. I'm in the mood to fuck myself to death," he breathed, plunging into her silken cunt with an unquenchable frenzy.

"How nice . . ."

Her words were so damnably polite, his gaze swiveled downward, and he scrutinized her fleetingly.

"I mean I'm grateful," she purred, sliding her hands down his spine.

His glance slipped away. Now, there's a concept; she was grateful. He didn't think the word applied to himself. He was wild for her, inflamed and impatient, but that all had to do with lust, not gratitude. Whatever she was feeling, though, matched the rhythm of his lower body to perfection, and she could call it what she liked.

It was fucking at its very best.

Later that night, he lay in bed, watching her brush the tangles out of her hair. His teak-handled brush looked large in her hand, oversized, as did the bureau she stood before on tiptoe so she could see herself in the mirror propped on top. Her slender form seemed to glow in the candlelight, her skin almost luminous, and he was reminded of a Titian nude, where female flesh always seemed lit from within. Such recall brought with it the memory of her posing for Alma-Tadema and in its wake a flood of disconcerting emotion.

"Are you sleeping with Alma-Tadema?"

She turned at the roughness in his voice, offended that he felt he could inquire. "Why do you ask?"

"For obvious reasons. You were stark naked with him last night."

"And a naked woman implies only one thing?" she said, her voice sweet and mocking.

"Generally." Or in his experience, always.

"If you knew me better, you'd know not to ask, or if you knew me better, you wouldn't have to ask."

"I don't need riddles. Answer me."

Her shoulders straightened marginally. "Why should I?"

"Why not?" His brows rose in suggestive response. "I'd say we know each other fairly well."

"Because we've made love? Surely, you of all people understand, it's essentially a physical act."

"Not necessarily."

"Really . . ." Melodrama echoed in her drawl. "Has this been love, then, and not sex?"

"Very funny."

"Exactly. Now, darling," she purred, "let's make a

pact. You don't ask me about my friends and I won't ask you about yours."

He was surprised at the level of his affront. "You pose for all sorts of men and you won't tell me what else is involved in those relationships?"

"If it was any business of yours, I would. Of course, it isn't."

His temper quickened, but he chose not to question his bizarre need to know. That was no longer the point; her mocking challenge was the point. "You could pose for *me* and I could find out for myself."

"Why would I do that? You don't paint."

"Because I wish it." The world had been laid at his feet too long.

"Droits du seigneur are no longer in effect in England." Alex lifted her chin faintly. "Or haven't you heard?"

"It depends where you are."

She could almost feel the heat of his jealousy, and it pleased her on some primitive level far removed from any discernible good judgment. "Meaning what, my lord?" Her gaze held his as she set the brush down on the dresser.

The temperature of the room seemed to rise.

"Meaning I can make you do whatever I want."

"A rash statement even for you, Ranelagh."

He hadn't moved from his lounging pose. "I believe the door's locked."

"I know where the key is."

"I doubt you could reach it in time."

She tried.

She didn't.

The key dangled from his fingers a moment later, and he was smiling.

"You're fast."

"So I've been told." He wasn't even breathing hard.

"I wasn't talking about your sex life," she said. "And I *still* have no intention of taking orders from you."

"Maybe I could make it worth your while," he drawled, lazily swinging the key.

"What makes you think I'm interested?"

His mouth twitched into a faint smile. "Call it a premonition. Now, I'd like you to pose first on the table."

"And if I refuse?"

"I'd have to help you."

An ignoble heat warmed her senses, and she chastised herself for responding to such base authority. He had no right to play master, to order her around as though she were subordinate to his desires. "I don't like this kind of coercion, Ranelagh."

"But, darling, you *like* fucking. And once you've posed, I'll give you what all your artist maestros do." His smile was tight. "Your reward." Gently snapping his fingers, he pointed at the table. "Either get up there or I'll put you there."

She stood her ground. "It's none of your affair whom I pose for."

"I understand. I just thought I'd get my share."

"You don't deserve it," she replied coolly.

"But, darling, that's for me to decide—here . . . now . . . in my home—alone with you." He smiled, nodded toward the table. "Should I count to three?"

Her eyes snapped with indignation. "You're extremely annoying."

"One."

"I don't know what makes you think—"

"Two."

She thrust out her bottom lip in a pout and moved toward the table. "I suppose you must be humored."

He was utterly still, his face half in shadow. "It might be wise." He tossed the key on the bed.

"I'm not afraid of you, if that's what you think," she muttered, climbing up on the table.

"I don't think that at all," he said, his dark gaze trained on her as she sat down. "Spread your legs . . . like you do for Alma-Tadema and Leighton."

"Screw you." There was fury in her gaze.

"Do as you're told."

"We're done," she said briskly, beginning to slide off the table. "Play your games with someone else."

Her feet hadn't touched the floor when he was beside her, his fingers shackling her wrists, holding her in place on the table edge. Leaning close, his dark hair fell forward, framing his face, and his heavy-lidded eyes, redolent with lust, blatantly offered her sex. "*Please* spread your legs," he said quietly.

She struggled against his hold, moody, disquieted—by his tantalizing virility, by her inability to resist. "You have to apologize first," she said, terse, resentful.

"Tell me if you're sleeping with them."

"Apologize."

A taut silence fell.

The muscles in his shoulders rippled as his grip tightened, his fierce gaze bore into hers for a moment, and then, inhaling deeply, he looked away. A second passed, then two in this sexual standoff—a voiceless, muted contention. Somewhere a clock chimed, and as though some signal had been given, Sam slowly released his breath and met her gaze again. "I apologize," he said, his voice tight as a drum.

"In that case," she ground out, each word mutinous with malcontent, "no, I'm not."

"I don't know if I believe you."

Incredulous, she stared at him. "I beg your pardon?"

"Call me cynical," he said gruffly.

"Some people have principles," she replied hotly. "Some people are discriminating about their bed partners," she added, each word trenchant with affront. "Some people don't sleep with everyone who crosses their path, present company excepted, of course."

His sudden smile dazzled, like a glorious rainbow after the storm. "You don't say."

"I do—most emphatically." She refused to smile. "So I hope we're finished with your jealousy."

He jerked back, apprehension flaring in his eyes. "I'm not jealous."

Sensing that the equation of lust or fascination or whatever term best described their extraordinary attraction was suddenly more equable, Alex's mood altered. "Well then," she said amiably, her mouth curving in amusement, "that should make everything so much easier."

Not about to acknowledge anything so outré as jealousy, Sam dipped his head and spoke with similar casualness. "By way of explanation, when I saw you posing last night, I wanted to carry you off and make love to you for a thousand years or so. Nothing excessive, you understand," he said with a deprecating lift of his hand. "You just have that effect on me."

"I understand completely," she agreed, the degree of excess he incited beyond comprehension.

"Does that understanding extend to, say, a more physical harmony? I apologize in advance for my licentious impulses, but you're irresistible."

"You have a certain compelling charm as well," she told him, her gaze dropping to his seemingly indefatigable erection.

He'd seen that look a thousand times. But Miss Ionides was more of an enigma than most, so when he spoke he was conciliatory in the extreme. "Does that mean you might be willing to spread your legs for me?"

"When you ask so nicely . . ." She slowly opened her legs. "I'd be delighted."

"We'd both be delighted," he said with feeling. Leaning forward, he grasped her around the waist, lifted her to the center of the table, eased her thighs slightly wider with his palms. "Now, that's even more delightful," he approved, his gaze focused on her sweet, damp cleft. "Do you masturbate?"

"Good God, Ranelagh." Leaning back on her hands, she quirked one brow. "You certainly ask a lot of questions. Isn't it enough that we simply enjoy ourselves tonight?"

"Do you?"

She surveyed him for a critical moment. "Sometimes, if you must know."

"Would you like to now?"

"Why should I, when I have you?"

"Because then I could watch."

Her lashes half lowered over her eyes. "I thought you weren't a voyeur?"

"I was planning on participating."

His smile was intriguing, along with the rest of him. "So I'd have you to look forward to—afterward," she observed pleasantly.

"Without question."

"One can hardly refuse such gallantry."

He almost said something impertinent but caught himself in time. Miss Ionides didn't respond to orders, although she responded to just about anything else. In the interests of future satisfaction, he was polite. "That would be for you to decide."

She grinned. "You're not taking any chances, are you?"

"Not a one," he replied with a flashing smile. "And whenever you want to stop, you just let me know."

"Because you can go all night?"

"Because I'm interested in pleasing you," he said, unutterably well mannered.

She laughed. "You really are good, Ranelagh."

"We try, ma'am," he replied silkily.

"And with enormous success, I don't doubt."

He wasn't about to answer that. "Later on, let me know." He traced his fingertip up the warmth of her inner thigh, reaching out with his other hand to lift his hairbrush from the dresser top. "I'm always open to suggestions."

She was about to answer, when the pad of his finger touched the nub of her clitoris and a frisson of pleasure refocused her attention. With extreme delicacy, he caressed the silken tissue, over and around, up and down, in a slow, delectable massage, while she leaned back and felt the rapture travel upward and outward in rippling waves. He was painstakingly subtle, his fondling leisured, controlled, as though he understood the finite degrees of bewitchment and female arousal. As though he might have done this once or twice before and after a time, in answer to her softly undulating hips and breathy pleas, he slipped his fingers inside her honeyed warmth and explored the sweet paradise that kept his cock standing stiff.

In very short order, she was quivering under his hands, her swollen tissue weighty with blood, her senses aflame. Aching for consummation, for his primed cock and consummate skill, she turned more demanding. "I want you *now,*" she said as a spoiled heiress might.

He refused, although with infinite politeness. He knew better now. "Let's try this first," he suggested, taking up the teakwood hairbrush, twisting the handle and lifting it away.

"You said—you didn't—have women here." Her breath was gone, lost to lust.

"This is for hiding diamonds." He held out the teak handle so she could see its hollowed core. "It's African, and I *don't* have women here. It's virgin."

For a flashing moment, she debated his honesty, but frenzied, nearly dizzy for wanting him, her next ravenous pulse beat vanquished unnecessary thought.

"Why don't we see how you like something virgin." The faint curve of his mouth was more a grimace than a smile. "There's a novelty . . ." Not sure she was listening any longer, not sure himself why her sexual experience seemed to matter so, he turned his attention to an activity sure to please them both. Slipping the smooth wooden tip of the brush handle into her pouty slit, he slid the polished wood around the verge of her throbbing labia with exquisite finesse until she lifted her hips, reaching for more. "Not just yet," he whispered, smoothing his hand over her hip as though gentling a skittish filly. "I want you wetter. . . ."

"Sam!" Half-whimper, half-plea, she tried to brush his hand away.

"Hush, darling," he soothed, his voice velvety, holding her still. "Don't move and I'll give you more."

She instantly quieted, and his erection surged higher, submission a powerful aphrodisiac. He chided himself briefly for such uncharitable impulses, but she was lying before him in all her opulent womanhood, predaceous in her desires, and charity didn't stand a chance against primal lust.

He slid the makeshift dildo in a calculated two inches, and stopped. "More?" he inquired gently, driven by some inexplicable need for sovereignty over her.

Her lashes lifted, and the smoldering heat in her eyes was potent answer.

"You look ready," he whispered, spreading the swollen flesh of her labia with his fingers, pushing the teak handle two inches deeper.

She softly moaned as her tissue slowly yielded to the pressure of his invasion, gently arched her back at the delicious flood of rapture. He could deliver nirvana on cue, she blissfully thought, basking in a warm, gossamer ecstasy. "I might have to bring you home," she breathed. "You're so much better at this than I."

This wasn't the place to mention the extent of his practice. He bent to kiss her instead, brushing her lush mouth with his, burying the wooden handle the last providential measure into her welcoming flesh, inhaling her rapturous cry as he held it solidly in place. Then, lifting his mouth away, he gently ran his fingers over her labia, closing her pouty lips over the lodged handle.

She whimpered at the slight pressure of his fingers, her tissue stretched, filled, crammed to surfeit, the resulting jolt to her fevered senses almost too much to bear. But the continuing massage, no matter how delicate, drove the dildo deeper, brought her passions, raging and overwrought, near orgasmic, she rocked against the stunning delirium.

His palm was pressed hard against her wet cunt. She was eager, frenzied, hungry for sex, and for the first time in his life he felt an overwhelming urge to keep a woman. He didn't question his motives, self-indulgent too long; he only understood he wanted her—preferably in bondage to his whims. And all the fairy tales of women imprisoned in towers or cottages deep in the woods suddenly took on a licentious cast. The fact that he wished to keep her for himself alone, available and in rut, didn't bear close scrutiny, so he ground his hand against her flaming cunt instead, replacing disquieting thoughts with the familiar constant in his life—sex.

Her breathy scream exploded in the shadowed room, and she melted under his hand. Quickly catching her as she slipped backward, he gathered her in his arms, holding her close as her last shuddering spasms died away. He glanced at the clock, anticipating the remainder of the night with pleasure, fairy-tale images of the delectable Miss Ionides as his personal bond servant a decidedly lascivious fantasy. When she stirred in his arms a moment later, when her eyelids fluttered open, he said, "You can come again . . . soon . . . and then, if you're very good . . . next time—"

"I'll let you have sex with me," she whispered.

He leaned back, astonishment in his gaze. "You'll *let* me?"

Postcoital now, returned to the world, she smiled, sat up, and caught her breath. Her rising had stirred the dildo, stimulating already overstimulated nerves, and quickly reaching down, she moved to extract it.

He caught her hand. "I don't think you understand."

"*You* don't understand," she countered softly, shaking his hand off.

"What? About you wanting cock?"

"About this propensity of yours for supremacy."

"Or yours."

They gazed at each other for a charged moment, these two people familiar only with compliance.

"You don't stand a chance, sweetheart," he drawled gently. "Because you want to come again."

"And you don't?"

"Not with the same, shall we say, greediness."

"We can't all be libertines," she said with a sniff.

"Nor would I want you to be," he returned softly. "Except when your ready passion is conveniently mine."

"I don't find it currently convenient."

"I might disagree," he replied with despicable calmness.

"That's your prerogative, of course." She reached for the dildo again, only to find herself curtailed by Sam's firm grasp.

"Why don't we see?" Forcing her back down onto the table, he rested his hand directly above her mons. It was a light, skimming touch for a brief moment before he exerted a tempered pressure on an especially sensitive portion of her already oversensitized anatomy, bringing it into contact with the submerged dildo.

She tried not to gasp at the searing jolt, but he knew how prone that particular area was to arousal. He wasn't surprised at her sudden stillness. "Feeling a little something?" he asked impudently, massaging her susceptible flesh lightly into the unyielding dildo, watching with a knowing competence as she speedily came to fever point. This particular neat-handed skill was the result of a long-ago liaison with a celebrated French actress who had a fancy for young men, and it was always effective.

In fact it was a headlong rush to orgasm, and he took note of the unmistakable evidence of the lady's readiness in the creamy fluid issuing from her insatiable cunt. The liquid oozed in pearly rivulets down her thighs, and he was relatively sure there was no longer any question whether her passions were currently involved.

"Do you want to come?" he inquired with unabashed insolence. "All you have to do is ask."

She heard his voice through a wall of insensibility; sheer will lifted her lashes. "Go to hell."

He shouldn't care; he shouldn't insist. On an intellectual level, he disapproved of submission. "Tell me," he said.

He was leaning over her, the scent of his hair sweet in the air, his bronze skin even darker in the shadows, the powerful muscles of his arms taut as he waited for her answer. Thick black hair dusted his forearms and fingers, his virility mesmerizing. Her gaze dropped to the engorged beauty of his upthrust erection, and ultimate temptation lured and seduced. Perhaps he'd been right when he'd said she needed a man like him. Perhaps he was right about everything.

"What do I have to do to have *you?*" Her voice was strong, not needy, her gaze direct.

He raised his brows and flexed his wrist. "Instead of this?"

She shuddered at the riveting pleasure.

"Why not both?" he suggested softly.

"Together?" Shock registered in the blurted-out word.

"You decide."

"No . . . no," she said quickly, the look in his eyes wolfish, hungry. An instant later, she wondered if she'd imagined the wicked gleam, because his dark eyes were alight with laughter.

"You're sweet as candy underneath it all, aren't you?" he teased.

He was so damnably tempting—even his wickedness. "I don't know," she breathed, her sensibilities in chaos. "With the exception of wanting you, I don't know anything at all anymore."

He knew what she meant, but he'd been the object of pursuit too long. He was wary. "It doesn't matter." The phrase was ambiguous, as were his thoughts, but gentleman that he was, he slipped the dildo out.

"They say intellect is much overrated," she remarked, reading something different into his words, throwing caution to the wind in any event. Only ravenous desire mattered, Alex decided, pulling his head down for a kiss and making love to this man who made her forget everything but wanting him.

Meeting her passionate kiss with equal ardor, Sam decided the way he was feeling right now, he'd be more than satisfied to keep the bewitching Miss Ionides impaled on his erection for the foreseeable future and all the rest be damned. Grasping her hips, he hauled her bottom to the edge of the table, lifted her legs onto his shoulders and, bending forward, guided his erection to her alluring cunt and proceeded to execute his single-minded plan.

When he woke the next morning, he was momentarily startled to find a woman in his bed. For a dreadful moment he thought he was with Penelope again. The error immediately corrected itself in his brain, and more pleasant sensations came to the fore, along with lush memories of the previous night.

Alex was truly remarkable, unrestrained in her passion—and also in her demands, he recalled, smiling. The satisfying feel of her in his arms this morning was equally remarkable, for he preferred waking up alone. He'd have to find a larger bed, he thought, if they were to make use of his secret apartment. A moment of apprehension struck him at such an extraordinary consideration, and in the cold light of day, with his independence at stake, he decided the bed was perfectly fine. He wasn't ready to alter his life for a woman. Particularly not after having known Miss

Ionides, however remarkable her talents, for less than a day.

Unsettled by his thoughts, he unconsciously shifted his position. The slight movement brought Alex awake.

When she smiled at him, his reservations vanished, and when she stretched up to kiss him, he forgot all but the tantalizing promise in her smile.

"I recall someone like you making me very happy last night," she sighed. "Are you still available, or does duty call?"

"What did you have in mind?" he drawled.

"I was thinking about something sexual," she breathed.

His brows rose. "How sexual?"

"Surprise me. . . ."

He laughed. "I'm not sure I have any surprises left after last night."

"Something simple will be equally appreciated." She twisted her hips slightly, and her damp cleft slid up his thigh.

"As long as it's soon?" he said, smoothing his palm down her bottom, touching her slippery wetness with his fingertips.

"And long and hard . . . like this," she purred, lightly grasping his swelling erection.

He rolled over her a second later, plunged into her waiting sweetness, and bid the lady in his bed good morning with such extravagant lasciviousness, neither heard the sounds of the City waking outside. It was a tropical morning in Queen Elizabeth's bed; it was a dawn of obsession for two people who had until then been unaware of the concept; it was a private, sequestered world filled with dazzling pleasures.

Much later, when passions were quenched, when the level of satiation and contentment was sufficient to let in the outside world, when the chiming of the clock seemed to have become conspicuously shrill, they reluctantly rose from the bed and even more reluctantly dressed to face the events of the day.

Sam extended an impulsive invitation for breakfast, when he'd never actually shared his breakfast with a lover. Alex accepted, when she'd not been sure she could speak of mundane things after the glorious splendor she'd experienced. But they found they could converse like ordinary humans and that they both liked bacon more than eggs and not kippers at all. After three cups of coffee, they agreed as well that most of the problems of the world were entirely solvable.

When it came time for Alex to leave, Sam escorted her downstairs and helped her into his carriage. He had a meeting that morning; she had plans to work and appointments scheduled.

"You're sure you don't mind if I don't see you home," he said once again, not wishing to offend.

"I prefer you *not* see me home," she replied with a smile. "Just in case my family is parked on my doorstep."

"You know best." He leaned in and gently kissed her.

"Thank you for a most enjoyable . . . time," she

whispered. "You certainly know how to entertain a lady."

"And I consider myself the most fortunate of men," he replied graciously.

She smiled. "Adieu, then, Ranelagh."

"Sam."

"Sam," she repeated, and after a hushed moment glanced past him to the sidewalk.

Taking his cue, he moved back and shut the door.

She waved once and smiled.

He nodded at his driver.

And the carriage pulled away from the curb.

But rather than his normal relief at taking leave of a lover, a niggling discontent insinuated itself into his brain.

She hadn't once asked "When will I see you again" or "Won't you come over soon" or any of the familiar cajoling female phrases he was used to evading.

He was not only surprised but mildly annoyed.

And, more startling, disappointed.

For her part, Alex was wondering if she'd ever see him again. Realistic about the viscount, she wasn't unduly optimistic. Her view was purely rational, quite separate from the blissful happiness she was feeling. Ranelagh certainly knew how to leave a woman ardently aglow. But if he didn't call upon her, her life was entirely complete without a man. After two husbands, she was well past the point of *needing* a man in her life. And not from malcontent. Rather, she was enjoying the broad and diverse pleasures of her unmarried state.

As the carriage took her away from the beauty of last night, though, a small sigh escaped her.

If Ranelagh didn't call on her, she *would* miss his magnificent and inventive talents in bed, she thought selfishly.

Chapter 15

Euterpe Ionides came sailing through Alex's open terrace doors shortly before noon, her fashionable persimmon and white striped skirts trailing over the green slate entryway, her mouth set.

"You finally came back, I see." Her acerbic pronouncement was delivered in a biting staccato, the tattoo of her heels brisk on the stained wood of Alex's studio floor.

"In the future, kindly refrain from monitoring my activities, Mother," Alex said blandly, brushing a slash of pale rose on the canvas before her. "At thirty, I find it extremely embarrassing."

"I should think it better to be embarrassed than ruined," her mother said crisply, coming to rest behind Alex. She surveyed the painting on the easel with a critical eye. "Wouldn't it be nice, darling, if you painted lovely portraits like Letty Cassavettis."

"And wouldn't it be nice, Mother, if you spent more time at your needlework than you did bothering me."

"Letty sells every portrait *before* she paints it. She's a very good businesswoman. Is that yellow thing a gate or a chair?"

"It's Christ on the cross, Mother," Alex replied mockingly. "I'm painting him in a summer garden to make his suffering more palatable to the viewer."

Euterpe sniffed and pulled off her white kid gloves with a brisk snap. "Make your jokes at your old mother's expense, but I've seen much more of the world, and it wouldn't hurt you to heed my advice."

"And what advice would that be? On my painting or on my lack of children, or perhaps you'd like to know exactly how large Ranelagh's bed was."

Horrified, Euterpe stared at her daughter. "Now I'll have to have the priests say a thousand prayers for your soul."

"They can save their prayers for the starving beggars in the streets. Those poor souls need God's grace more than I."

"You may ridicule my concern all you wish, but mark my words, Ranelagh will ruin you and then leave you without so much as a good-bye. Look what happened to his wife!"

"She died while out with one of her lovers, Mother. Surely, you can't blame Sam for that."

"Sam, is it! Well, it certainly didn't take him long to bewitch you!" Her mother's eyes snapped with affront. "I suppose he has you curled around his little finger already! And don't look at me like that," she noted peevishly. "I know what men like Ranelagh do. And while your father may be too polite to chastise you, I have no such compunction and I tell you straight out, *Miss Bohemian Artist,*" she articulated with a withering sarcasm, "you'll rue the day you took up with a man of his notoriety! And if you don't care for your own reputation, think of your family's!"

Alex set down the brush she was holding and began wiping the paint from her hands. Clearly, she wasn't going to be allowed her privacy this morning, nor did she care to engage in a fruitless argument with her mother. "I have an appointment in the City. You're welcome to watch me dress if you wish."

"With *him,* I suppose!"

"No, with the superintendent of one of my schools. And for your information, Mother, I doubt I'll be seeing much of Ranelagh. We both have very busy lives."

"He's tossed you over already," her mother said testily, following Alex into the bedroom. "As if I didn't know his kind. You see, dear, what comes of allowing men liberties?" she reproved, picking up a blouse draped over a chair and walking toward the armoire. "They have no respect for you."

Alex sighed, having heard this lecture countless times, along with disapproving ones on her modeling, which she ignored as well. "I'm sure you're right, Mother."

"Of course I'm right," Mrs. Ionides decreed, hanging up the blouse. "A little mystery in a woman is alluring."

"I'll think about it, Mother." At the same time she thought about becoming a monk. . . .

"Don't you have any couturier gowns in here?"

Her mother was brushing through her array of garments, her mouth pursed in distaste. "Surely you can afford to dress a bit more stylishly, darling."

"I like my clothes. They're comfortable."

"If a lady wishes to appear to best advantage, comfort is not necessarily a first priority."

"Many ladies of the first rank wear the same styles I do." Alex preferred what was deemed "aesthetic dress." The gowns were natural-waisted, the sleeves comfortable and loose, the fabrics flowing with the rhythm of the body. They were worn without corsets or crinolines.

"Bluestocking women." Her mother pronounced the phrase like an epithet.

"Women who prefer not strangling their bodies in tightly laced corsets." Another ongoing argument with her mother.

"Hmpf," Euterpe muttered unsympathetically.

"I don't need a nineteen-inch waist because fashion dictates it."

Her mother turned away from the closet and gazed at her daughter. "You have a perfectly fine waist."

"I know, Mother."

"But I still don't like Ranelagh."

"You don't have to like him."

"And I disapprove of you seeing him."

"You made that clear." Alex smiled. "And who knows, Mama, you may be right after all. He may be long gone, in which case perhaps I shall be more inclined to listen to your advice in the future."

Euterpe didn't indulge her daughter's humor

enough to actually smile, but she said, "You know, your papa and I want only the best for you."

"I know."

"And we dearly hope you don't marry another man old enough to be your father."

Alex's eyes gleamed with amusement. "Ranelagh's only thirty-three."

"But not the marrying kind," her mother pointed out, her lips pursed in contempt.

"Are you coming with me to the Camden Street School?" Alex asked, because there was no rejoinder to such unalloyed truth.

"If you don't wear that awful crumpled white muslin."

Alex lay down the gown she held. "You pick one out, Mother."

Ten minutes later Alex and her mother set out for the meeting with the superintendent. The immigrant schools she supported were an undertaking on which she and her mother could always agree.

Sam's meeting with his brother and the golf course designers took place in his offices in the Adelphi, and before lunch they'd agreed on the exacting dimensions of each fairway on their five-hundred-acre estate. There was the pretty tree-girdled third and the scary blind drive over yawning cross-bunkers fifth. The first and fourth would be manicured around two natural pond sites. A dauntingly narrow driving corridor over a large fairway bunker confronted them on the second hole, while the remainder of the front nine was a succession of lovely holes along the western stone wall of the property and through the remnants of a mature forest. The tight, leafy back nine would meander around a series of small ponds and natural trout streams, which should prove a technical challenge, particularly on the gorgeous downhill par-five twelfth and the hazardous, short fourteenth.[5]

By early afternoon, consensus had been reached on combining the best of classic golf with the most brilliant of technical subtlety. The two young designers left with the plans under their arms and the approval necessary to begin excavating.

Sam and his brother, Marcus, enjoyed another drink from the bottle of brandy they'd opened to toast their new endeavor.

"You seem in good humor today. But you've been wanting to build this course for a long time and now, finally—" Marcus raised his glass in salute.

Sam smiled. "We'll have some championship golf in our own backyard."

"The boys are beginning to learn how to play with the clubs you had made for them."

"I'll come over tomorrow and give them some pointers," Sam offered. His nephews were a source of great pleasure to him.

"Evelina is having her reading group over tomorrow. You might prefer meeting us at the Blackheath course. Hedy Alworth will be at the house."

Sam dipped his head. "Thanks for the warning."

"She still thinks you're going to marry her someday."

"For no plausible reason."

"Her mother keeps telling her the Lennoxes and Alworths have always made marriage alliances."

Sam's brows rose. "Not in recent memory."

"Reason has nothing to do with female notions of romance and marriage."

Sam's gaze narrowed. "You and Evie are still getting along, aren't you?"

"Oh, perfectly. You know I adore her, and she's the sweetest of wives. Not to mention the best of mothers."

"Thinking of having more children, are we?"

His brother turned red. "Actually . . ."

"Congratulations!" Beaming, Sam rose from his chair and shook his brother's hand. "I'm pleased for you."

"I'm damned lucky. Especially after . . . well—"

Dropping back into his chair, Sam laughed. "You can say it. After my fiasco."

Marcus looked uncomfortable, but then, he always did when there was any mention of Sam's marriage. "Mother and Father shouldn't have insisted."

"And I shouldn't have married for no good reason. Or at least," Sam said with a fleeting smile, "I should have taken a better look at my fiancée."

"I'm not sure a closer look would have mattered. She was—"

"Deceitful . . . and manipulative?"

"So Evelina has always maintained."

"But Mother was looking at all those Sutherland acres with great longing, and Father, I believe, particularly liked Penelope's blond hair."

"Well, that's over with," Marcus said with feeling, the years of Penelope's presence in the family still a highly explosive subject.

"And now I'm depending on you and your boys to keep the title in the family."

"Surely you'll marry again someday."

Sam shrugged. "I doubt it. Although . . ."

Marcus smiled. "Does your 'although' pertain to Miss Ionides? Everyone saw you at Ascot and then not again last night."

Sam grimaced. "My Lord, this town is small."

"And you have a high profile for your—dare I say—profligacies?"

"They're no secret." The viscount's mouth curved faintly. "But Alex is very nice—very nice indeed."

"When will you be seeing her again?"

Sam shrugged. "Who knows?"

His brother scrutinized him for a moment. "Do I detect a female who isn't in hot pursuit?"

"We just politely said good-bye."

"For which you're no doubt grateful."

"Mostly."

"But not completely."

"Apparently, she's as casual as I about friendships."

"No, she isn't. No one's as casual about 'friendships,' as you so euphemistically put it, save you.

Evelina knows Miss Ionides and likes her. In fact"—
he pursed his mouth—"I *think* she's a member of
Evelina's reading group."

"You don't say?" Sam slid up from his lounging
sprawl. "Perhaps I'll come to the house to play golf
with the boys after all."

"Don't forget Hedy will be there."

"But more important, so might Miss Ionides."

"How important?" Marcus asked, enjoying the
spectacle of his prodigal brother intrigued enough by
a woman to brave an afternoon of female readings.

Sam grinned. "Tell Evie to set another place for
lunch."

Chapter 16

"Look what Sam brought us, Mama!" Six-year-old Jeremy Lennox waved his new golf club in a wide arc over his head, narrowly missing the Meissen shepherdess group on the drawing room table.

"And me too, Mama!" his four-year-old brother screamed, running in behind Jeremy, his club held high. "We been shooting golfs all morning."

The ladies sitting in a group around the tea table reacted in a variety of ways. Those who had children of their own smiled in understanding. Hedy Alworth drew back in distaste. Mariana Monteque said, "Not shooting golfs, playing golf, young Benjamin," because she ran a seminary for young ladies and prided herself on her scholarship. Alex smiled and held out her hand. "Show me your new clubs. I love golf."

"See!" Ben shrieked, smashing his club against the carpet. "It won't break no matter what!"

"They're from Watson's and made for us," the elder brother said, politely offering his club to Alex.

"He makes the very best, doesn't he?" Alex balanced the weight in her hand. "I think that might work for me."

"You could try our putting green in back." Jeremy spoke with a grown-up seriousness. He glanced at his mother. "Couldn't she, Mama?"

"Of course. Feel free, Alex. Perhaps after lunch," Evelina offered. "Now, you boys run along and wash your hands, because lunch will be served soon and you and your papa are going to join us."

"And Sam too!" Ben piped up. "He's sitting by me!" he proudly proclaimed.

As the boys ran from the room, Hedy Alworth leaned forward in her chair. "Sam is here?" she asked Evelina.

"Yes, he's been helping the boys with their golf this morning."

Alex could feel her cheeks become warm and eased back into her chair so no one would notice. But as quickly, she reminded herself that she was bound to meet Ranelagh on more than one social occasion and she would have to respond with suitable composure—not like some young girl just out of the schoolroom.

"Why didn't you say he was coming?" Hedy complained. "I would have worn something more fashionable."

"I'm sure your gown is quite lovely enough, Hedy," Evelina replied graciously. "And Marcus didn't mention Sam was coming over until this morning."

"Ranelagh's always had a tendre for me." Hedy touched her blond curls with a coquettish gesture.

"You and a thousand others," Susannah Dudley noted dryly.

"Well, he never looked at you at all."

Unlike Hedy, Susannah knew better than to throw herself at someone like Sam Lennox. She'd selected her husband for his wealth rather than his looks. "I'm happily married, Hedy."

Hedy sniffed and Evelina said diplomatically, "I'm sure lunch is nearly ready. Why don't we move into the dining room." Susannah and Hedy both considered themselves great beauties and their bickering rivalry could be trying. "And we have to decide what we're going to read for next week," she added, rising from her chair. "What does everyone think of Dostoyevsky's new *Diary of a Writer?*"

As the ladies moved down the corridor, they discussed various books while Alex wondered how she was going to deal with the sight of Ranelagh in so public a venue.

After last night.

A shiver raced down her spine at the recall of their heated passion.

But she forced her thoughts onto more temperate ground; it would never do to appear wistful or yearning or in full chase like Hedy. Ranelagh had enough females pursuing him. She had no wish to be added to those numbers.

She took a steadying breath, however, before entering the dining room. She experienced a moment of relief when she found the room unoccupied save for the servants. Maybe he wouldn't appear after all. And the quiver in the pit of her stomach would go away.

"We're informal, as you know," Evelina remarked, ushering her guests toward the table. "Please sit where you like." She waved toward one end of the table. "We'll save those chairs for the men."

Hedy insisted on taking her seat closest to the indicated chairs, as did Mariana Monteque, Alex noted with some surprise. Mariana wasn't a young woman, although the designation *spinster* had always annoyed Alex. It seemed an unfair label. Why shouldn't Mariana have an interest in Ranelagh if she wished, Alex charitably reflected. Surely she had as good a claim on him as anyone.

When the men and boys arrived, Sam and his brother greeted everyone in a general salutation and then seated themselves with a casualness that calmed Alex's apprehensions. Ranelagh had set the tone; surely she could be as blasé.

As it turned out, Mariana and Sam were friends of long standing, their common interest a marked enthusiasm for golf. Much to Hedy's annoyance, Sam and Mariana spent a considerable time discussing the game.

Sam was equally gracious to his nephews, who obviously worshiped him, Alex observed, surreptitiously watching their easy companionship. Who would have thought London's most celebrated libertine would turn out to be so warm-hearted toward children?

Of course, she'd had her own heady experience with his kindness.

He was the most unselfish of lovers.

"Really, Mariana!" Hedy exclaimed as dessert was being served, vexed at being so long ignored by the object of her pursuit. "You have completely monopolized Lord Ranelagh. There are those of us who have things to discuss with him as well!"

"Forgive us." Sam smiled politely. "Mariana's a better golfer than I, and I can always use some instruction."

"Me too!" Ben declared cheerfully through a mouthful of charlotte.

"Indeed," Hedy replied, casting an annoyed look at the boy before turning an expression of adoration on Sam. "Lord Ranelagh, let me congratulate you on your horse's win at Ascot. I couldn't help but notice, he was sired by Fernie Bey, who is related to my jumper. Have you had Invincible long?"

"Three years. And he's been a sweet goer from the beginning."

"Sam let me ride him, didn't you, Sam?" Ben cried. "And I went really, really fast on him, didn't I, Sam?"

"Faster than anyone," his uncle agreed pleasantly.

"Yes, I'm sure you did," Hedy noted curtly. "I was wondering, Lord Ranelagh, if you might ride in the park with us when my brother comes to town. Oliver has the most wonderful black out of Bright League." The Alworths were all first-rate riders, and Hedy wished to show off her equestrian skills.

"If my schedule allows," Sam replied politely.

Hedy offered him a winning smile. "I'll have Oliver send you a note."

Sam nodded in a clearly evasive way.

Coming to his brother's rescue, Marcus glanced down the table at his wife. "If you'll excuse us, Evie. Sam and I still have some work to do on our course plans."

Sam caught his brother's eye. "It can wait."

Hedy preened.

"Can we play some more golf after lunch, Sam?" Jeremy asked, not wishing to miss out on his uncle's time.

"In a few minutes," the viscount replied quietly, pushing his chair back and rising. As he walked down the length of the table, every luncheon guest followed his progress with rapt interest.

Alex stiffened at his approach.

He spoke very softly when he reached her, but the room was so expectantly quiet, his words were clearly audible to all. "Miss Ionides, might I impose on you for a moment?"

Uncomfortable as the center of attention, and uncertain how to deal with such brazenness, Alex glanced at her hostess.

After her husband's comments concerning Sam's interest in Alex, Evelina had anticipated something audacious from her brother-in-law and she quickly stepped into the breach. "Sam was hoping you could give him some information on Sir Leighton," she improvised.

"If you wouldn't mind, Miss Ionides." His voice was bland.

"No . . . of course not," Alex stammered.

He was already reaching for her hand as a footman leaped forward to pull out her chair. "Excuse us," the viscount said to the table at large, pulling Alex to her feet. Tucking her hand under his arm, he drew her away, the silence in the room so oppressive, even the boys fell mute.

Once the dining room door closed on them, Alex cast him a sardonic glance. "Hedy will be annoyed."

He gazed down at her. "You look wonderful in green and you were sitting too far away and Hedy Alworth is as insipid as usual, so please don't waste your breath."

"She said you have a tendre for her."

"But then, she's an idiot, as you must have noticed. This isn't your first time at the reading group, Marcus tells me."

"And what else did Marcus tell you?"

"He told me not to embarrass him, but then, I didn't care to sit through a long afternoon on the slim hope I might have a chance to talk to you alone, away from everyone."

"I see."

"I adore that prim tone."

"You're compromising me, Sam."

"You mean them?" He nodded back down the corridor.

"Of course them. Hedy has the biggest mouth in town, and she's not going to sit idle while I take away her beau."

"Is that what you're doing?"

She blushed. "I didn't mean it that way, and you know it."

Stopping, he backed her up against the wall gently, and bending low so their eyes were level, he whispered, "How *did* you mean it?"

"In the most generic, sensible way," she said, trying not to notice how his powerful body dwarfed hers, trying not to remember how exquisitely he utilized that brute strength. "Because Hedy's after you and not afraid to tell the world."

"You're not intimidated by Hedy Alworth, are you?"

"Only by her nasty tongue. There's my mother, if you recall, who has this misguided notion of what a lady should be. And"—Alex sighed—"much as I wish to ignore my family, there are limits to my indiscretions."

"And I'm the limit?"

"No, Hedy Alworth's malevolent interpretation of your actions toward me may be the limit. Not for me personally," she explained quickly. "But for my family."

He leaned closer, his eyes so near she could feel the heat. "So if I were to deal with . . . our friendship . . . with the utmost discretion," he softly suggested, "I could make love to you again?"

She shut her eyes against the wave of desire that flared through her body. "That's not fair," she breathed.

"I'm not interested in being fair." His voice was

velvety and low. "I'm interested in having you in my bed—just as soon as possible. Or better yet, we could go upstairs and find an empty room."

"Under other circumstances . . ." She looked at him from under her lashes, a feverish warmth in her eyes. "I might be willing."

"As I recall, you're always willing."

She shivered. "Don't do this to me. Not here. Not now."

"When . . . where? Tell me."

"Sam, please—what do you want me to say in this corridor where someone may intrude any second?"

"I don't know, but you've been on my mind constantly since you left me." He softly inhaled. "And I feel like carrying you away right now, and to hell with everything."

"Lord, no . . . ," she breathed. "You can't . . ."

"Tell me about it," he muttered.

"We have to be sensible." She was trembling.

"Or Hedy will be troublesome," he said with a sigh.

She nodded.

He bent to kiss her, his mouth gentle, lingering, reminding her of their first kiss at her garden gate. But then her lips parted beneath his, her passions immune to rational thought, and as his tongue slipped inside her mouth and the hard length of his erection pressed into her stomach, she gently sighed.

He growled low in his throat, pulling her closer so she felt the imprint of his arousal swell against her, his tongue exploring her mouth as though in prelude, and for a tenuous moment of unalloyed pleasure, they melted into each other.

Then with a soft groan he raised his head. "I think we've discussed Sir Leighton long enough, Miss Ionides," he said, half breathless with the fierceness of his need. Restraining his urges, he took a step backward. "May I escort you back before it's too late?"

"Thank you," she whispered, her pulses racing. "Because I'm not sure I had the resolve."

Running his hands through his dark hair, he exhaled softly. "No sense in letting Hedy Alworth eat you up." Smiling faintly, he ran his fingertip over the curve of her jaw. "I'm reserving that pleasure for myself. So send your carriage away. You're going home with me."

She nervously brushed his hand away. "Just make sure you don't sit anywhere near me. I'm not sure I can survive the afternoon if you do."

"Nor could I. I'll take the boys outside," he offered. "But once everyone leaves, you're coming home with me."

"If I could say no, I would."

"There's my girl."

"I'm not your girl." She grinned. "Hedy's your girl."

He winked. "Not likely, when I'm crazy for you. But, I warn you, my patience is limited."

"And I remind you, you don't want another note from my father tonight."

He grimaced. "I'll try to behave."

"And I'll endeavor to ignore Hedy's sniping remarks when I return."

"I'd be happy to put her in her place."

"But then that wouldn't be very useful to me."

He shut his eyes briefly. "I know. Lord almighty, discretion isn't my style."

"Then you'll have to learn."

"For you, I'll try."

When they reentered the luncheon room, conversation momentarily ceased and Alex was escorted back to her chair in a hush.

"Thank you, Miss Ionides, for your useful information." Sam bowed politely. Turning to Evelina, he said, "I'm taking the boys down to the lake if you don't mind."

Both boys uttered whoops of delight, leaped from their chairs, and raced toward their uncle, restoring a degree of normalcy to the scene.

But once the men and boys had gone, as expected Alex immediately faced Hedy's catechism.

"What did he want to know about Sir Leighton?" she asked sharply, leaning out over her plate to send a piercing glance Alex's way.

She wished to say "It's none of your affair," but said instead, with what politeness she could muster, "Ranelagh is thinking of buying a painting."

"Why would he ask you?" It was a blatantly rude query, since Alex's artistic talents were well known.

"Ranelagh knew Sir Leighton and I are old friends."

"He could have asked you his questions here, couldn't he?"

"I'm sure I don't know what motivates the viscount," Alex said as calmly as possible, considering Hedy was glaring at her.

"In any event, it doesn't matter," Evelina interjected. "You know Sam. He's always been brash and impulsive." She swept the table with a glance. "We're all finished here, aren't we? Why don't we go out on the terrace for a glass of champagne?"

"Well, that certainly was discreet," Marcus drawled as the men followed in the wake of the boys racing down to the lake.

"When I'm in this crazed mood, discretion isn't high on my list of priorities," Sam stated. "You're lucky I didn't carry her upstairs."

His brother scrutinized him with a small frown.

"And you needn't say anything about not hurting her, because I won't. In fact, if anyone gets hurt in this damnable relationship, it'll probably be me."

"You're serious."

"Hell yes. All I want to do is take her to bed and keep her there."

"What's so different about that?" his brother queried with a cynical gaze.

"Because it's one woman—the *same* woman, that's what's different. And I haven't even known her two days yet." The viscount sighed. "Lord, I hope this obsession is fleeting."

Marcus's voice was touched with sympathy. "This has to be a first for you."

"It's damned alarming." Sam's teeth flashed white in a grin. "When it's not damned sensational."

"I'm not sure how to put this tactfully, considering your past, but might this—er—sensational feeling be love?"

Ranelagh snorted. "God, no. You don't fall in love with someone so quickly."

"It happens."

"How would you know? You practically grew up with Evelina."

"But I fell in love with her at Christmas all those years ago—as we were singing 'God Rest Ye Merry Gentlemen.' "

Sam glared at his brother. "That's not real helpful."

"Think of all the women you'd leave pining," Marcus teased. "Should you be taken off the market, so to speak."

The viscount scowled. "This isn't a joke. I can't stay with *one* woman." He shook his head in bewilderment. "It's impossible."

"If you love her, it's not impossible."

"You're different, Marc. You've always been a better person than I, more conscientious, more exemplary in every way. I don't *want* to settle down."

"How do you know unless you try?"

"I did once—that was enough. And, Jesus, there are too many women in the world."

His brother shrugged. "Maybe it won't be a concern. You said Miss Ionides is as uninterested in permanence as you."

"Don't remind me," Sam scoffed.

"Oh, ho!" Marcus grinned. "A taste of your own medicine."

"I hope you're amused," Sam grumbled.

"Entertained, certainly. I didn't think I'd ever see the day."

"Well, you have, and I hope you're happy, because I'm hellishly cranky and bloody close to whisking Alex away, convention be damned."

"It shouldn't be long now," his brother said kindly. "The ladies generally leave soon after lunch."

But not everyone did. Hedy refused to depart.

Chapter 17

J'm not driving Hedy home," Sam said furiously. "I'll strangle her instead. Oliver, for one, will thank me. He can't stand her silly prattle."

"I'll go with you," his brother offered. "Together, we'll manage."

"What the hell's wrong with her?" Sam fumed. "I'm warning you. Keep her away from me. I can't guarantee I won't do her violence, the damned bitch. How long have we been waiting for her to leave?"

The two men had been standing outside the drawing room for the past hour, glancing from time to time through the partly opened door. And they'd just heard Hedy mention she'd sent her carriage home. "Poor old William was so tired, I just didn't have the heart to keep him waiting," she said with poignant drama. "I thought I might ride home with Sam."

"Or if Sam isn't leaving just yet, we'll send you home in our carriage." Evelina forced a smile, her own temper frayed after several hours of Hedy's irritating company. Her pregnancy made her tired, and she'd been hoping to go upstairs for a nap.

Alex had done her best to be courteous, but Hedy was bent on being malicious. Alex and Evelina exchanged long-suffering glances from time to time, neither able to bring about Hedy's departure.

Marcus, hearing the fatigue in his wife's voice, decided to intervene. Signaling his brother to stay behind, he walked into the drawing room. "Did I hear you say you needed the carriage brought around?"

"If you would, darling." Evelina's relief was apparent. "Hedy requires a ride home."

"Don't bother. I'll go with Sam," Hedy declared.

"He's still with the boys," Marcus lied.

Hedy folded her hands neatly in her lap. "I don't mind waiting."

Her emotions very near the surface in these early weeks of her pregnancy, tears sprang to Evelina's eyes. Marcus jumped forward to console her, but just then the drawing room door banged open and Sam stalked into the room. "My carriage is outside and I'm in a damned hurry. Come with me, Marcus, after you see Evelina upstairs. McClary wants to meet with us. Get your bonnet, Hedy." He paused for a second, and when he spoke, the anger had left his voice, but it was tightly curbed. "We'll drive you as well, Miss Ionides."

Hedy had leaped to her feet. "Thank you so much, Sam," she said, offering him a dazzling smile. "I *knew* I could count on you."

A tick appeared over Sam's cheekbone. "We're

driving right by your house. It's not a problem to drop you off."

Alex's nerves were on edge, and she almost begged off. But she wasn't so magnanimous as to give Hedy a clear field. Or perhaps she took pity on Sam, who appeared to be controlling his temper with difficulty.

While Marcus helped Evelina upstairs, Sam and the ladies walked outside to the waiting carriage. It was an awkward journey with Hedy brushing against Sam at every possible opportunity. If Sam hadn't looked so annoyed, Alex would have been inclined to giggle. One certainly couldn't accuse Hedy of shyness. Nor Sam of an inability to resist unwanted advances.

He was polite but always just out of reach. When they stood before the open carriage door, Sam said with a gruff bluntness, "You ladies sit together," and nodded to one of his grooms. The young man immediately stepped forward and offered his hand to Hedy. She had no choice short of making a scene, but her mouth was set as she stepped into the carriage. He winked at Alex. "I'll wait for Marcus outside."

"Coward," she murmured.

He grinned. "Pure survival."

Marcus soon appeared, and the brothers entered the carriage.

By this time it was becoming apparent even to Hedy where Sam Lennox's interest lay. Thoroughly vexed at the gross injustice of his preferences, she spent the whole of the drive into the City offering denigrating comments on women who chose to lead independent lives. "When it's perfectly well known," she declared, "that a woman's place is in the home and her God-given function that of a wife and mother." Glancing at Alex, she wrinkled her nose. "Of course," she said uncharitably, "not all women are able to have children. . . ."

"For God's sake, Hedy." Disgust vibrated in Sam's gruff voice. "What the hell do you know about anything?"

"I know, for instance," she said with soft venom, "your dear friend, Lady Denfield, is with child." She gazed at him, a look of triumph on her face. "Had you heard?"

Everyone knew Clara Bowdoin had several lovers. And he was always extremely cautious, so he knew the child wasn't his. But he couldn't reply, and Hedy knew it. "I'm sure Clara is pleased," he remarked politely.

"Are you?"

"Hedy, watch your step," Marcus warned, the fury in his brother's eyes barely suppressed. "Clara wouldn't appreciate your comments."

She bristled at his command. "It's common enough knowledge," she replied tartly. "Everyone isn't like you and Evelina, Marcus."

"Nor are they like you. And just a warning on that point, Hedy. If you upset Evelina again, I'll see that you're barred from my house. My wife's not required to listen to your nonsense." Marcus wasn't quick-tempered by nature, but his family was sacrosanct.

"My goodness, Marcus, aren't you the heroic figure!"

"One more word from you, Hedy, and I'll set you down in the street," Sam growled.

She opened her mouth but thought better of it when she saw the anger in Sam's eyes.

The remainder of the drive passed in silence.

Hedy was helped from the carriage by one of Sam's grooms, and when the door finally closed on her, Sam exhaled a long, low sigh.

"Trying not to strangle her, were you?" his brother remarked.

"It was a damned close thing. If anyone ever is so unlucky as to marry her, she won't last above a month."

"Not our problem."

"No, thank God. And I apologize, Alex, for her rudeness to you."

Alex smiled. "You're hours too late. I have been maligned for most of the afternoon. And educated as to the role of a woman with a great deal of arrogance and very little understanding."

"Luckily, she's out of our lives," Sam noted, moving over to sit beside Alex. "We'll give you a ride home, Marcus." He took Alex's hand in his and gently squeezed it. "Then we're going to find something better to do than think of Hedy."

But when Marcus left them and Sam and Alex were alone once again, Alex quietly said, "Tell me about Lady Denfield's child."

Sam half raised his hand in a dismissive gesture. "Hedy said that only to irritate me, antagonize you, and in general make mischief. Ignore her."

"Is the child yours?"

"No."

"Naturally, you'd say that."

Sam briefly pursed his mouth, debating how much he could disclose without slandering Clara. "I wasn't the only one, if that helps."

"So the child could be yours."

He shook his head. "I never take chances."

"You can be so certain."

He shifted uncomfortably, lifted his shoulder in the merest of shrugs. "I'm certain. Beyond that, I can't with courtesy say more."

It wasn't as though she was unaware of his reputation for sleeping with ladies of every description, but Hedy's comment forced her to face the reality of that conduct.

"At least she's not peeking in the windows," he offered.

She smiled. "So I shouldn't take issue with your other lovers."

"I'd rather you didn't."

"Because we're going to act like adults."

"After Hedy, it would be a great relief to at least try."

"You may remind me of Harry whenever I become difficult."

"You may not remind me of Clara," he said with a smile. "By the way, are you really going to see that young boy on Friday?"

"I don't have much choice."

"You always have choices," he said, struck by his displeasure at her seeing Harry again.

"Not in this case. He won't paint unless I see him occasionally."

"And you're his agent?"

"His friend. He's very good and, unfortunately, not disciplined."

"I see."

"That's not an adult scowl. And I'm sorry, but I've known you only a day. It would hardly be reasonable for me to discard my friends because of you."

"Friends?"

"Aren't your lovers friends?"

How to answer with any courtesy.

"Never mind, Ranelagh."

"I'm sorry." He didn't know what else to say.

"At least you're honest. So where are we going to make love tonight? Your place or mine?" she queried lightly.

"Since your parents know where you live—"

"And where you live, including the Strand."

"That leaves only my bachelor apartment in the Adelphi."

Lounging in his seat, Sam lightly brushed Alex's cheek with the back of his hand. "I haven't been this happy in ages."

She resisted the impulse to tell him she'd never been so happy either and said instead, simply, "I'm happy too."

"Claude will be thrilled you're back. I'll send for him."

"Don't bother. Perhaps tonight we can throw caution to the wind and I'll cook for you. Provided there are no carriages at my curb, I'd like to stop and gather a change of clothes."

"Fair enough. And if my home is equally quiet, I'll pick up my mail. I'm expecting some plans from a course near Aberdeen. They have the same water hazards we do."

"I think I'll stay in the carriage this time."

He smiled. "I don't blame you."

Chapter 18

As it turned out, however, Loucas was in wait for Alex in Park Lane. Though she stayed in the carriage, he found her.

"Beggin' your pardon, Miss Alex," he said through the half-open door of the carriage. Sam's hand was on the latch, his movement to descend arrested. "Tina's havin' her baby early and your ma wants you home."

"Oh, dear." She glanced at Sam. "My sister-in-law's not due until next month." Turning back to Loucas, she asked, "When did her labor start?"

"This mornin'. We couldn't find you, so here I am, beggin' your pardon, my lord," he said with an irony that made it plain he wasn't apologizing at all.

"I really have to go." Alex began to rise.

"I'll take you."

"No, please, that wouldn't be wise."

"The carriage is just around the corner, miss."

"I'm so sorry I have to leave," Alex apologized. "But Tina's last delivery was complicated and—"

"I understand." Pushing the door open, Sam stepped to the ground and then helped Alex descend. After escorting her to her carriage, he stood at the door. "Let me know if I can help in any way."

"Thank you," she said, distracted.

He shut the door and stepped back from the carriage. The driver's whip cracked.

As he watched her drive away, he felt a moment of anguish for Alex's distress, for her sister-in-law's travail . . . for his own profound sense of loss.

The moment the viscount stepped over his threshold, any further consideration of loss was eliminated by the sharp crack of his barrister's knuckles.

"Farris. What a surprise."

"It's a matter of some urgency, my lord," the elderly man declared, as though his presence in Sam's entrance hall weren't warning enough of disaster.

"Have you been waiting long?"

"Most of the day, sir."

At least he was aware now of the degree of misfortune. Farris didn't call on his clients as a rule. His offices in Piccadilly were sumptuous, centrally located, and staffed with enough underlings to run an extensive operation. "Follow me," Sam offered, moving down the corridor. "Coffee, Owens." He glanced at his butler. "In my study."

A few minutes later, Farris was seated, their coffee had been served, and Sam was lounging against the corner of his desk, too restless to sit. "Tell me everything,"

Sam charged. "You needn't spare me any details. I'm quite capable of withstanding shock."

"It's your—er—ex-mistress, my lord."

Which one? he thought, but said merely, "Ah."

"She intends to sell her story to the newspapers, sir."

"What story?"

"Of how you lured her from her home in Cairo, sir, with a promise of marriage and then"—the barrister flushed beet red—"mistreated her in a variety of ways." He wiped his forehead nervously. "She was quite specific, my lord."

"Farida," Sam whispered, his body gone rigid. "Bloody bitch." His gaze refocused on his barrister and he stood. "I'll talk to her and straighten this all out. There was no marriage proposal, and the question of luring is up to debate on several levels. She's been well compensated for her time. Did she tell you I bought her a house and paid off all her gambling debts? Along with those of her damned brother?"

"She did, my lord, but, of course, her interpretation of those gifts is—er—different perhaps from yours."

Sam glared at the elderly man in his morning suit. "Do you believe her?"

"It's not a question, sir, of whether I believe her or not," he answered as a barrister would. "It's a question of whether her story reaches the papers."

Sam drew in a deep breath because he knew what was coming next. "And what would you suggest I do?"

"I would suggest, sir, as a prudent measure, we offer her some settlement."

"Again? She already cost me more than she was worth."

Farris coughed discreetly. "That would be for you to say, of course, but should her account be published, the public would be treated to only her point of view."

"I want her silenced," Sam growled. At Farris's look of alarm, he quickly amended his statement. "Not literally, just in terms of her newsmongering. Good God, Farris, if I paid off every ex-mistress who threatened to spread gossip about me . . ." He shrugged.

"Yes, my lord. I understand."

"And now I've put you in a damned box, I suppose," Sam noted gruffly.

"One needs a certain degree of negotiating power, sir. She has Collins for her barrister."

Sam swore softly. Collins was celebrated for his notorious divorces. "Very well, what do you think would buy her silence? Be frank."

"Five thousand pounds."[6]

Sam's brows rose marginally. "For that kind of money, I want to be assured she's back in Egypt."

"It could be a nonnegotiable stipulation."

"It would have to be," the viscount said brusquely. "Tell them, otherwise they can publish and be damned."

"Yes, sir. I will convey your feelings to them most exactly."

"She receives no money until she reaches Egypt. If they agree, I want a detective on her trail and a report sent back to me that she has landed on her native soil." He blew out an explosive breath. "Do you know how much this adventuress has cost me?"

It wasn't a question he wished answered, Farris understood. "I'll speak to Collins personally, sir."

"Immediately."

"Of course."

Sam suddenly smiled. "Forgive my outrage, Farris. I know how hypocritical this must seem to you. But the woman's been very well treated."

"I know, sir. One of our agents has seen her house . . . and her jewelry."

Sam laughed. "Maybe I should think about settling down, eh, Farris? It would be considerably cheaper."

"Hardly a reason to marry, my lord." The elderly man had seen the misery of Sam's first marriage, and he genuinely liked his young client.

"You're right, Farris, as usual." His barrister had covered up with discretion all the lurid details of Penelope's death. "I defer to your advice on this matter as well. But keep me informed."

Farris rose from his chair. "I'm sorry to have delivered such odious news."

"Never mind," Sam replied kindly, reaching out to shake the man's hand. "It was my doing entirely."

"She's exceedingly greedy, my lord. Even Collins is surprised, I think."

"Really." Sam grinned. "Then I hope Collins gets

his money in advance. Otherwise, he's not likely to see it."

"I'll tell him, sir."

"Good luck, Farris." Sam pursed his mouth. "Perhaps I should consider celibacy for a time."

His barrister's eyes widened for the briefest instant. "Indeed," he affirmed, clearly at a loss for words.

Minutes after Farris left, Owens entered the study with a doleful expression on his face. Sam said, "Bring me a brandy before you speak."

Although Owens was tall and far from frail, he had the ability to melt into the background. For those few minutes in which Owens carried out his master's wishes, Sam was able to forget Farris's visit and dwell for brief moments on the pleasure he'd experienced with the beautiful Alex Ionides.

He was smiling faintly when Owens handed him his brandy. Immediately drinking it down, he handed the glass back to his butler. "Now that I'm fortified, tell me what has caused your woebegone look."

"Your father, sir."

"He's said something to disturb you?"

"He's here, sir."

"Bloody hell," Sam muttered. "Is this my day of penance?"

"He arrived before Farris left, so I put him in the back drawing room with a bottle of his favorite whiskey."

"Perhaps we could leave him there until he passes out."

"He seemed to be on a mission, sir. I doubt he'll stay quiet long."

"In that case, fill my glass up once more and then go fetch him," Sam said glumly. "And if anyone else comes calling, tell them I left the country."

"Very good, sir."

"You astonish me, Owens." He gazed at his butler's retreating back. "Do you ever lose your temper?"

"Not while I'm working, sir."

"Not even with my parents?"

Owens hesitated for the briefest moment before setting the decanter down and turning back to Sam with his drink. "They do try one's patience, sir."

"A true understatement. Thank you, Owens." Sam took the freshly filled glass from him. "Want to take any bets on my father's mission?"

"They're all the same, sir. I couldn't take your money. I believe the Thornton girl is on the agenda this time."

"So I thought. Mama has her eye on their York-shire acres."

"Begging your pardon, sir, but the countess is most persistent."

Sam smiled tightly. "No need to wonder why I drink."

The servants credited Sam's drinking to his intemperate amusements as well, but ever courteous to the well-loved master of Ranelagh House, Owens said only, "You do bear a certain burden, sir."

"Escort my latest burden in and then do me a favor and announce another visitor in, say, five minutes. I can listen to my father's admonishments for only a limited period of time."

When the Earl of Milburn appeared in the doorway, his habitual scowl in place, it took enormous effort for Sam to greet his father with courtesy.

"Do come in, Father. Forgive me for keeping you waiting. I had an earlier appointment."

"I hope not with that arriviste Miss Ionides. I heard you caused quite a stir leaving Wales's box beforetime day before yesterday."

He couldn't accuse only Alex's parents of undue surveillance, Sam thought with irritation. "Actually, no, Father, it wasn't Miss Ionides. Farris stopped by."

"Are you involved in some damned scandal again? Another whiskey, Owens," the earl barked.

"Nothing to concern yourself with, Father. I'll have a brandy, Owens." *Make it large,* he wished to say but stopped himself. He could deal with anything for five minutes. "And then you may leave, Owens."

His father sat down in the nearest chair. Sam glanced at the clock.

"Farris doesn't come calling for nothing," his father noted darkly.

For a flashing moment, Sam debated warning his father about the possible publication of Farida's accusations but decided it would be time enough if Farris's negotiations failed. "He had business concerning my railroad stock," Sam fabricated.

"You're wasting your money, my boy. Land—now, there's where you should be investing. It's the strength and backbone of this country."

"I'll tell Farris," he replied politely, watching his father take his whiskey from the silver salver Owens held out to him. With land prices falling steadily for decades, he wasn't likely to invest in property.

"Speaking of land . . ." The earl cleared his throat and Sam braced himself. "That Thornton gel has some damned good acreage in her dowry."

"I told Mother the other day, I wasn't interested, Father. Young girls fresh out of the schoolroom don't intrigue me." Taking his brandy from Owens, he quickly drained it.

"Don't know what intrigue has to do with those ten thousand acres in Yorkshire. It's a profitable connection, son. That's what matters."

"Not to me." Had the hands on the clock stopped moving? "If you're interested in Yorkshire land, Dudley has some for sale."

"If you marry the Thornton chit, it don't cost a thing."

"I'm not sure I'll marry again, Father. Marcus has two sons. I don't feel any pressure to provide a Lennox heir."

His father's brows drew together in a scowl. "You know how your mother feels about that."

"With great clarity. However, my feelings are in

opposition to hers." He glanced at the door, hoping to hear Owens's knock.

"Penelope was a bit of a trial, I admit, but—"

Sam's gaze returned to his father. "She was considerably more than that. She damned near put the Lennoxes on the front page of *The Times* more than once. Thanks to Farris, scandal was averted, but I'm not in the mood to marry now—perhaps never. So kindly tell Mother to desist from parading hopeful ingenues before me."

"You were too lenient with your wife."

"I didn't care to lock her in her room, and short of that, she was uncontrollable."

"Damned rocky patch you went through there, but it's over, and once you have time to lick your wounds, I don't doubt you'll find some young filly to marry."

"I don't have any wounds, Father. I never wanted to marry Penelope anyway. I don't like flighty young women."

"Then someone like Miss Ionides suits you better, doesn't she? A woman twice married." He winked. "She knows what she wants, eh, my boy?"

"I wouldn't know."

"Come, come, don't humbug me. We both know what young widows want. Hell, I remember when she married St. Albans. He was in a right fine frame of mind for the entire two years he was married . . . before he dropped dead. Probably too much of a good thing, if you know what I mean." The earl's smile was lecherous. "You can enjoy a dark-skinned beauty like that. Who wouldn't? But no need to get serious. Her family"—one brow arched upward—"merchantmen out of the Levant, you know."

By this time Sam was praying for the knock on the door, and when it came a second later, he practically leaped to his feet. As Owens entered the room, he moved toward him as though he were his savior.

"The Earl of Airlie, sir."

"Thank you, Owens." Turning back to his father, Sam said mendaciously, "I'm sorry, Father. Edward's here and we have an appointment at Tattersalls. If you'll excuse me."

"I thought we were going to Hattie's," Eddie remarked, appearing in the doorway.

Surprise registered on both men's faces.

Sam hadn't expected Edward in the flesh, while the Earl of Milburn always intimidated Eddie.

"Hello, sir." Eddie greeted the earl politely before half turning to Sam, his brows faintly lifted. "Meant to say Tattersalls," he said blandly.

"I'm sorry to take my leave so suddenly, Father, but there's a new hunter coming on the block this afternoon. And my stable master thinks it's worth looking at."

"I'll tell your mother we had a good talk." His father offered Sam a conspiratorial smile. "Calm her nerves for a time. You boys go off and enjoy yourselves."

"What the hell was that all about?" Eddie asked as the two men stood on the drive outside Ranelagh House, waiting for Sam's carriage to be brought up.

"My father came as emissary for Mother, who has decided Clarissa Thornton will suit as my next wife. I told him, as I did Mother, that I'm not interested. He thinks I need time to get over my wounds from Penelope. He also thinks Miss Ionides will serve in the interim as a suitable bed partner just so long as I don't entertain any notions about marrying her. Apparently, her skin is too dark," Sam finished sardonically.

"*Perfect* would more aptly describe it."

"Not when her family is made up of Levant merchantmen," Sam noted mockingly.

"Your *père* could, however, overlook Penelope's nymphomania because she was from good Anglo-Saxon stock."

Sam tipped his head faintly. "He called her a bit of a trial."

"He was lucky her escapades didn't *end* in a trial. That would have changed his notions about good Anglo-Saxon stock."

Sam exhaled. "Both my parents have descended on me in less than a week. Hopefully, I shall be free of them for at least another month now. And my thanks for appearing so opportunely, although I was quite willing to perjure myself to avoid listening to my father's views on the state of the country, the government and the rising tide of the bourgeoisie."

"Luckily, my *père* prefers the country. Not so many mushrooms,[7] he says."

"When so many country estates are being purchased by the new industrialists. Is he blind?"

"Conveniently blind. My mother keeps their social

circle small in order to forestall the inevitable shock when he discovers he's surrounded by new neighbors."

"Gentility is nothing more than ancient riches made by some tradesmen long ago. I was tempted to remind Father of our nabob ancestors."

"But you didn't wish to prolong the conversation."

"Exactly. I say as little as possible and leave as soon as possible when dealing with my parents."

"Thank God mine stay in the country. Now, are we really going to Tattersalls?"

"No, we're going to Aspreys. I need a present suitable for an infant."

Chapter 19

he clerk at Aspreys recognized Sam. The viscount was the envy of every young male who
aspired to status as a bon vivant. So his shock was
genuine when Sam said, "I am in need of a gift for a
newborn."

Though Eddie had had time to absorb his initial
surprise at Sam's aberrant behavior, he remained
mildly disconcerted. In his experience, Sam and babies didn't even have a nodding acquaintance no
matter gossip had tried to connect Sam with any
number of births in the years he'd been entertaining
himself in the boudoirs of society ladies. Perhaps it
was a joke.

But after viewing countless rattles and cups, dainty
jeweled picture frames and engraved spoons and por-
ringers, Eddie realized that Sam was perfectly serious.
Eddie burned with curiosity.

After a time, Sam decided on an antique silver rattle. It
was prettily wrapped, the clerk said, "Congratulations,

sir," with a degree of innuendo Sam ignored, and soon the men were standing outside Aspreys, their mission accomplished. "Now some flowers, I think," Sam said, looking across the street at a fashionable florist shop.

"For the baby?" Eddie inquired, his expertise in these matters nonexistent.

"No, for Alex." Sam pursed his mouth. "I hadn't thought about the baby—I suppose I should bring some for the child . . . and the mother as well."

"Do you even know the mother?"

"Of course I know her. She's Alex's sister-in-law," Sam said as though Eddie were dense. "I wonder where they live?" Apparently, he didn't perceive the two statements as incompatible.

In short order three bouquets were purchased, a small nosegay of white roses and two boxes of pink roses. Now the question remained—where to deliver them?

"Leighton will know," Sam decided.

When Sam asked Sir Leighton for Tina's address, the artist masked his surprise. Ranelagh had met Alex two days earlier and now he was bringing gifts to her relative? There were astonishing implications in this seemingly polite ritual.

But then, Alex *was* astonishing.

Sam, on the other hand, appeared unconscious of the wonder his actions provoked. After a few moments, he thanked Leighton for the address, declined his offer of a drink, and bid him good-bye with a marked casualness.

On reentering his carriage, Sam addressed Eddie. "I'll drop you off at the Marlborough Club if you like, or would you prefer Hattie's?"

"Don't I get to see the new baby?" Eddie looked pained.

"No. When did you begin to like babies anyway?"

"The same time you did. And you're not being very friendly," Eddie grumbled. "Didn't I just save you from your father?"

"I believe I've saved you a number of times as well, from circumstances a trifle more daunting than my father's visit. Like when I helped you out of the second-story window at Lady Waddell's, or that rather dicey incident when you needed me to back you up against Mordaunt's wrath when he found you with—"

"Point taken," Eddie conceded. "But if you won't let me watch this interesting spectacle unfold, tell me, at least, why the hell are you doing this?"

"Because I want to see her."

"Like you wanted to see the harem in Constantinople?"

Sam's expression was unreadable for a moment, and then he smiled. "Something like that."

The Ionideses lived south of the City, where the family had built a number of homes at Briana Hills. According to Leighton, the new mother resided in a Florentine-style villa just a stone's throw from the family mansion.

After reaching the appropriate house in a land-scape dotted with palatial homes, Sam descended from his carriage and stood for a moment on the gravel drive, surveying the beauty of the landscaped grounds. Flowers ran riot in a setting no doubt made to look natural by an army of gardeners, the colorful blossoms massed in a brilliant palette against the green of the hills. No wonder Alex's garden had been so lush, Sam thought.

A footman descended the long bank of steps and bowed before him. "Welcome to Briana Hills, sir."

"I've come to see Miss Alexandra Ionides. Is she here?"

"Yes, sir. Who shall I say is calling?"

"Viscount Ranelagh. I have some flowers in my carriage that should be brought inside."

"Very good, sir." The footman lifted his hand and a page boy came running out from behind a clipped boxwood hedge. After giving the boy instructions, he said, "This way, Lord Ranelagh. I'll see if Miss Alex is available."

A sense of excitement and bustle was immediately apparent as Sam stepped into a resplendent entrance hall of pink marble, jewel-encrusted icons, and plush Oriental carpets, adding an exotic splendor to the set-ting. Servants were running up and down the stairs, the sound of doors slamming and snatches of conver-sation echoed down the staircase from the floor above, and then suddenly the thin, high wail of a baby pierced the air.

Sam looked at the footman. "The child has arrived."

"Only minutes ago, sir. The household is in chaos.
If you'll wait in the drawing room"—the footman in-
dicated an open doorway to the left—"I'll find Miss
Alex."

"Don't impose on her if she's busy. I'm not in a
hurry."

"Very good, sir. I'll have tea brought in to you."

"That won't be necessary."

"Brandy, perhaps?"

Sam smiled. "Excellent." He waved the man away.
"I can find my way in." He could see the staff was in
disarray. No butler was in evidence. As he walked into
the sunny drawing room, he felt oddly pleased that the
child had arrived in apparently good health. A kind of
rare happiness overcame him, as though he were somehow involved in the joyful events of the day. A more
cynical person might credit his happiness to Miss
Ionides's imminent arrival. Not of an introspective nature, however, the viscount felt only unalloyed pleasure.

His brandy arrived in the care of another page boy,
who gazed at him with wide-eyed speculation. "Miss
Alex is still busy, sir. It might be some time till she can
see you."

"Tell her it's not a problem. My schedule is free."

"Yes, sir." But the boy continued to stare as though
Sam were an alien creature.

"Is there more?" Sam asked, entertained by the
young boy's inspection.

"They're arguing about you," the youngster replied artlessly.

"They?"

"Miss Alex's ma and her."

"Ah . . ." Apparently, not only his father was disturbed by their acquaintance. A hint of amusement shone in Sam's eyes. "Who do you suppose will win?"

"Miss Alex."

"No equivocation?"

The boy looked at him blankly.

"You're sure?" Sam translated his query into understandable English.

The boy's face lit up. "Oh, there ain't no question o' that. Miss Alex always gets what she wants."

Sam suppressed his urge to smile. He'd experienced that phenomenon firsthand. "In that case, please tell Miss Alex I await her convenience. And offer my congratulations on the new baby."

"Yes, sir. Everyone be right happy about the baby, what with it comin' early and all."

"I'm sure they are. Is it a boy or a girl?"

"A girl, and everyone's sayin' it's about time, seein' how they got four boys already."

"This is indeed a happy day, then." The viscount's well-being continued apace.

"It is fer sure. I'll go tell Miss Alex you be waitin' as long as it takes."

"Thank you." He handed the boy a sovereign.

"They said you was a rich cove."

Sam's brows rose.

"The footmens."

His brows lowered, mildly relieved. He preferred not being discussed in those terms by the delectable Miss Ionides.

"It's gonna take a while," the boy warned.

Sam smiled. "I don't care."

And he found he didn't, despite the fact he sat alone in the drawing room for a very long time. He had plenty of brandy, Alex was close, and sometime today he'd see her.

How simple life had become when pleasure was measured by the availability of an auburn-haired lady, when just knowing she was near brought a smile to his lips.

"You shouldn't have come here."

Alex's sharp voice shattered his blissful reverie. He looked up to see her closing the drawing room doors behind her, the rigidity of her spine matching the tartness of her tone.

"I know I shouldn't have," he said, rising from his chair. "I'm sorry."

She turned to him, her cheeks flushed, her gown rumpled, her hair tumbled down her shoulders.

"This is damnably awkward, Ranelagh." She ran a hand over her disheveled hair. She couldn't help noticing that he looked beautifully point-device in superbly tailored charcoal-gray superfine.

"My apologies again. Is the baby healthy?"

A smile warmed her expression. "Yes . . . thankfully. But you have to go."

"I know. I heard you and your mother were arguing about my presence."

"Fillippo told you, I suppose."

"If he's the blond page boy—yes. But I had to see you."

"My family doesn't approve. You know that. You're embarrassing me."

"Talk to me for five minutes and I'll leave."

"I don't need another Harry, Sam. I don't *want* one."

"Am I like him?" His dark gaze was bland, faintly mocking.

He was so damnably assured, she thought, the legions of women no doubt contributing to his confidence. "No, you're not," she said, peevish and ruffled, "and if you dare be smug, I'll hit you."

"You're not like any other woman I've ever known." His voice was ceremoniously polite. "And I wouldn't dream of being smug."

"I'm not sure I like the comparison."

"Truth to tell, neither do I. I wish you *were* like all the others. I'd be drinking at the club right now instead of chasing after you and feeling more like Harry than I'd wish."

"And I wish *you* were like Harry so I could deal with you in a rational way."

"Nothing about this is rational." He glanced around the room, as if in emphasis. "I had to get your direction from Leighton."

"Oh, good. Now everyone will know."

"They do already. My father called on me this afternoon and your name came up almost immediately."

"Maybe he and my mother could share their complaints."

Sam laughed and held open his arms. "Come here, darling. I have no complaints at all."

She didn't move. "Am I supposed to forgive your audacity and fall into your arms just like that?"

"I wish you would," he replied, letting his hands fall to his sides. "I feel strangely lost without you."

"Or perhaps you're only in your pursuit-of-pleasure mode."

He tipped his head faintly. "That wouldn't require a visit to your brother's house."

He was right, of course. Any number of amusements were available in London. She sighed softly.

"I brought the baby a present." He pulled the small gift from his pocket and smiled at her. "Does that help put me in your good graces?"

"You're too much in my good graces," she said. "That's the problem."

"It doesn't have to be a problem right now," he said, setting the gift down on a table. "Let me hold you for a moment. Please?"

"I shouldn't. Someone might come in."

"You can pretend you fainted in my arms," he said with a grin.

"I'm sure my family would accept that fiction," she replied, smiling back.

"Come," he cajoled, opening his arms again, and she went to him because she loved being held in his arms, as she loved everything about him. And as he enfolded her in an embrace, she leaned into his strong body, smiled up at him, and allowed herself to enjoy the pleasure. "Your flowers were beautiful," she said. "The nosegay is hanging from the baby's cradle and Tina is sure you're in love, but then, she loves love in any form whatsoever."

His glance was amused. "Ah . . . an advocate."

"I wouldn't normally bring up the subject of love with you, but I just finished arguing with my mother for the better part of an hour, and I'm no longer in the most civil mood, and *she* certainly would like to know. Mother's old-fashioned, and opposed to men like you, but then, you know that already." She blew out a large breath. "Forgive me . . . I'm tired and undone and maybe half sad because the baby's so beautiful and not mine and I shouldn't have asked you something so stupid. But what in the world *did* bring you here?"

"I wanted to see you."

She wrinkled her nose. "And it couldn't wait?"

"It didn't seem like it could wait."

Her gaze was direct. "You've lived too long without restraints."

He chuckled softly. "And you haven't?"

"I don't think I'd come calling at the house of my lover's brother, who, by the way, said pointedly that he's never met you and said more pointedly that he had no intention of meeting you today either."

"When can you leave?"

"Sam! Are you deaf? Don't you understand the damnable stir you've caused?"

"I understand. Really I do, but you have to sleep eventually, and I was thinking I could just wait for you outside in my carriage and when you finally feel the need to sleep, you could sleep with me."

"In your carriage?"

"In my carriage if you wish, but I was thinking possibly at the Adelphi, or if you need to be close by, at some inn."

"You'd wait?"

"Until hell freezes over."

The silence was so profound after his pronouncement, the ticking of the clock sounded like a hammer on an anvil.

"I mean it," he said softly.

"But you don't know why."

"Do I have to?"

Her mouth twitched into a half-smile. "I just thought one of us should."

"I don't think it's a requirement."

She took a deep breath and exhaled slowly, debating the ramifications if she did what he proposed. "I couldn't slip away until very late. And even then I'm not sure," she equivocated.

"I don't care how late it is."

"I won't have time to bathe."

"Lord, Alex." He was incredulous. "The clerk at Aspreys is even now spreading gossip about my purchase there today. Not to mention Eddie's at the

Marlborough Club, regaling my friends with the same story. Your servants are probably laying bets on whether I leave with or without my eyes scratched out, while your family is ready to pull up the drawbridge. Do you think I care whether you bathe or not?"

"How sweet," she said, smiling up at him. "I don't think the world realizes how sweet you are."

"I'm not sweet, darling. I'm obsessed." Lifting her away, he set her down at a safe distance. "Now go back upstairs before I do something rash; you'll be able to join me that much sooner."

"Did I say I'd join you?" she teased.

"Did you think I was giving you a choice?" he said, not teasing in the least.

Her eyes sparkled with mischief. "You're extremely brave in the midst of my family."

"I think the word is single-minded." His fleeting grin was constrained. "I'll be outside when you're ready."

"Around the curve of the drive, if you don't mind. Then I won't have to listen to my mother's exhortations. I'm going to tell her you left."

"Which I will have."

"Don't go too far." Alex arched one downy brow. "Stay within reach."

"Don't worry about that."

She looked so damned inviting, tousled and rosy-cheeked, like she'd just gotten out of bed, that suddenly his unnatural reserve snapped. He reached out and pulled her back and kissed her with a brute, fevered urgency that ignored the risk someone might walk in. Sliding his hands down her back, he cupped her bottom and hauled her into the rigid length of his arousal. "Let me lock the door," he whispered, lust drumming through his blood.

Wild desire flared through her body. How tempting he was, how impossibly tempting . . . his strong, muscled body pressed into hers, his erection rock hard and tantalizing, everyone upstairs . . . and for a fleeting moment she considered giving in to her scandalous need. But a modicum of reason still remained in the outland of her mind. Alecco's drawing room was the height of impropriety for a sexual interlude. Shoving hard against his chest, she breathlessly cried, "No!"

She didn't have the strength to hold him off if he wished to dispute her refusal. He knew he could have her if he really wished. "Are you sure?" His voice was taut with constraint; he'd not been obliged to curb his lust in recent memory.

"Go," she said. But her voice was tremulous with indecision.

"What if I don't?"

"Sam, please . . . I can't do this alone."

Feeling as though he couldn't breathe, he dragged air into his lungs. "How long," he asked on a suffocated breath.

"Soon . . . Lord, Sam, now—if I dared . . ."

He dared enough for both of them, but he could see the apprehension in her eyes. He forced himself away from her. "I'll wait . . . down the drive. You go first," he said, sheer will constraining him. "Get the hell out of here."

For a restless moment she hesitated, and his pulse leaped. Then she turned in a swirl of skirts and ran from the room.

Chapter 20

✧❦✧

Alex ran upstairs as though she were being pursued by demons. Dashing into an empty bedroom, she leaned back against the closed door and trembled. No previous measure existed for the violence of her feelings, for the insatiable need he inspired, and she wondered whether she was capable of dealing with such powerful desire. Although, if the past few minutes were any indication, the answer was no.

She understood why Sam had come. He wanted sex, not conversation or friendship, not even casual affection. And unless she was completely witless, she wouldn't forget that pertinent fact. Not that she wasn't similarly inclined; this wasn't a relationship of unrequited lust. It was passion pure and simple—or maybe not so simple after all, she decided with a small smile. She recalled his ability to bring her to consecutive orgasms. Sam's sexual repertoire was extraordinary.

Inspired by that delectable memory, she faced the dilemma before her with less equivocation. She went to the washstand, where she splashed water on her flushed face and arranged her hair into a semblance of order. She smoothed the wrinkles from her gown, then gazed at herself in the mirror, carefully surveying her image for any evidence of Sam's passionate embrace. Since there were sure to be questions from her family, her mother in particular, Alex would rather not give any clues that their meeting had been anything but decorous.

As if she had to explain herself to any of her family, she reflected disgruntledly, straightening the sleeves on her gown. She was financially independent, of age, and in charge of her own life. Their approval or disapproval should be irrelevant.

But unfortunately, she couldn't so cavalierly disregard their opinions. They were her family, after all, and more important, she detested conflict. With that thought in mind, she cautioned herself to prudence. Don't argue, she admonished herself silently as she exited her room. Be polite. She smiled as she moved down the hall. And escape as soon as courtesy allows.

"That rogue has nerve!" Euterpe cried the moment Alex entered Tina's bedchamber, where the family was assembled. "Has the man no sense of decency?"

Knowing her mother wasn't interested in a substantive answer, nor one that disputed her opinion,

Alex held out the package instead. "Ranelagh brought the baby a gift."

"Am I supposed to be impressed?" her mother snapped. "He can afford it with his millions."

"Mama Ionides, come," Tina implored, casting Alex an understanding glance. "It was very considerate of Ranelagh to bring a present."

Alex carried the package to Tina, who looked remarkably fresh considering she'd only just given birth. Attired in a fresh white linen nightgown, her hair tied with a pink silk ribbon, she lay back against a pile of lace-trimmed pillows.

"I hope he's gone." Euterpe scowled at Alex. "And I'd appreciate a little support, Pandias," she added, directing a scathing glance at her husband seated near the windows.

"Has Ranelagh left?" her father asked, his tone neutral.

"Yes, Father." Alex handed the present to Tina.

"He's gone, darling." Pandias offered his wife a smile. "The problem is solved."

"He's a rake and a rogue, Alex," her brother said. "Don't deceive yourself on that score."

"Alecco! Leave Alex alone," his wife chided, frowning at her husband. "Didn't the viscount drive all this way just to see your sister?"

The eldest Ionides son turned an affectionate gaze on his wife. He adored her today more than ever with their long-awaited daughter sleeping in the cradle near the bed. "I won't say another word, darling."

"Maybe she loves him as we love each other."

"Tina . . . you're much too romantic," Alex interposed. "I like Ranelagh and he likes me, but we're hardly in love."

"Well, it might come to that."

"And it might just as well not. Open his gift. I want to see what he brought. He said the clerk at Aspreys was surprised he was selecting a present for the baby."

"No doubt." Her mother snorted. "I imagine he's there more often buying some trinket for his ladyloves."

"Then I should ask for diamonds next time I see him."

"You needn't get smart with me, missy. Tell her, Pandias. Tell her the man is fickle as the breeze."

"I don't know him, my dear. I'd not wish to make pronouncements on his character."

"Well, all of London does. Why not you?"

"Because I don't know him. And until I do, I'll reserve judgment."

She sniffed. "Don't you care that people will talk about our daughter?"

"If people talk, I don't pay attention. If I did, I could take offense every day. You know we're not accepted at most of the better clubs, and any number of society engagements are closed to us. Bigotry exists, but I for one refuse to conduct myself in a similar fashion."

"Thank you, Papa," Alex said. "And, Mama, don't worry. Ranelagh's really very nice."

"Very nice, indeed. I'm not taking issue with his niceness, which is well known. It's the democratic expanse of his niceness that concerns me."

"I can take care of myself, Mother. Could we please not discuss this?"

Pandias shot a stern look at his wife, and with pursed lips, she fell silent.

"Look!" Tina exclaimed. "A silver rattle . . . a very old silver rattle. What do you think, Alex, is it Elizabethan or Jacobean?"

The baby chose that moment to wake with a howl, curtailing any discussion of stylistic differences in silver and instantly becoming the center of attention. She was fussed over, held by everyone, admired, and praised until no longer amused by her relatives, she screwed up her little face and set up a fresh wailing.

"She's hungry," Tina observed, "so if you'll excuse me . . ."

In short order, the room emptied of all save Alex, who remained at Tina's request.

Lounging in a chair near the bed, Alex gazed at the enchanting picture of mother and child. She felt left out, alone, as though she were outside looking in on an idyllic world beyond her reach.

"Do you ever wish for children?" Tina asked, taking note of Alex's pensive expression.

"I do right now. I envy you completely."

"Perhaps Ranelagh will be the one." Tina's voice held a teasing note.

"Not likely. He's the man least willing to have children, I suspect. Nor do I envision anything so outré."

Her mouth quirked in a rueful smile. "You know I go through this passing melancholy every time you have a baby."

"I have a feeling you just *might* consider Ranelagh as a possible father for your children," Tina speculated playfully. "In your current mood, I mean."

"He's soured on matrimony. I think we can scratch Ranelagh as a candidate." Alex's brows flickered. "Even if I were so inclined . . ."

"You never know," Tina observed.

"I wouldn't bet my fortune on his walking down the aisle again, and really, Tina," Alex said in a lighter tone of voice, "I adore my freedom. I don't wish to marry again."

"Someday you may fall deeply in love," her sister-in-law noted. "Not like the companionship of your marriages. But desperately in love. Then you may change your mind."

Alex smiled at her friend. "You're an incurable romantic, darling. But remember, I've never been as starry-eyed as you."

"Ranelagh's different though, isn't he, and don't tell me I'm wrong—and don't tell me it's been only a few days." She winked at Alex. "You're mad for him."

The two women had been confidantes since childhood, the London Greek community small and extremely close, their families neighbors. They'd shared girlhood wishes for knights in shining armor, blissful true love, and any number of other romantic ideals.

"I might be just a little mad for him," Alex admitted, grinning. "He's incredible in bed."

Tina giggled, the baby whimpered, and after calming her daughter, Tina returned her gaze to Alex. "I knew it the minute you walked in today. I could tell you were different. He's brought a new glow to your eyes."

"And my body too." Alex couldn't help but smile.

"Better yet. I hope he didn't really leave."

Alex shook her head. "He's waiting down the road." She sighed. "I feel like a schoolgirl waiting to sneak out of the house."

"You needn't wait. Go to him."

"I thought I'd stay with you until you fell asleep."

"Don't even consider it. There's absolutely no need for you to stay. I'm feeling fine, and the baby is a perfect darling, as you can see," she added, the pride in her voice unmistakable.

"Don't rub it in."

"Forgive me. I didn't mean to gloat. Go to Ranelagh now and have a baby of your own."

"Don't put any dangerous notions into my head." Alex grinned. "Especially when I'm feeling so deprived."

"That's why I said it." Tina wasn't above a little matchmaking for her friend, who, in her estimation, had married both times for all the wrong reasons. "I'm just saying *think* about a baby. You seem enraptured by the man—your excitement fairly glows. So go now, go to your Ranelagh. I'll make some excuse to your mother. I'll tell her I've sent you to the City on an errand for me. Don't I need that lace peignoir you and I saw in Westbourne Grove last week?"

"The lavender one? And Ranelagh's not mine, not in the remotest way."

"Yes, the lavender one, and he's yours right now, waiting for you because he wants to see you enough to drive all the way from London, knowing the entire family is in residence. You have to give him credit for courage," Tina said with a twinkle in her eye.

"Or foolhardiness."

"Not an altogether displeasing trait in this instance. I'd say he wants you badly. Now, go," Tina commanded. "I'll see you tomorrow."

"You're corrupting my nobler impulses."

"Good. It's about time. You have far too many noble causes and charities for a young woman. You spend half your time taking care of others, not to mention the years you tended your husbands. You're allowed to think of yourself, darling, and have a little fun. Now, if you aren't gone in two minutes, I'll call your mother back and make you both play bridge with me after the baby goes to sleep."

"Horrors!" Alex jumped to her feet. "I'd sooner walk over hot coals than play bridge with my mother."

"There," Tina replied brightly. "The very best incentive to go and see darling Ranelagh. Once I'm recuperated, promise to bring him out for tea so I can see the stunning legend for myself."

"Don't say that. I particularly dislike his legendary status."

"But you've brought him to his knees, haven't you, darling? Or at least a long, long way from London. That has to mean something."

"It means he likes sex."

Tina shook her head. "Sex with you, my sweet," she amended. "I doubt there's a dearth of women in town who would be willing. Now, bring the lovely man for tea someday soon."

"He doesn't drink tea."

"What man does? We'll ply him with ouzo."

"I'll extend your invitation. And thank you," Alex said softly, "for all your sensible advice. I really do like him."

"Think about that baby." Tina smiled at her friend.

"You're not exactly helping me to be virtuous."

"You could talk to him about it."

Alex laughed. "And watch him run."

Tina lifted her brows. "Maybe . . . maybe not."

Chapter 21

But Alex didn't have the opportunity to say more than yes to Sam's query about sleeping at the Adelphi before he kissed her hard and long and deeply.

Some minutes later, as they sat side by side, gently rocking to the rhythm of the carriage, their hands entwined, their smiles indication of their good spirits, she did mention Tina's facetious proposal.

Rather than shrink from her improbable comments, Ranelagh replied casually, "A baby—really. I haven't thought about it—for say—my entire life."

She punched him then because he was obviously mocking her. Once they were finished tussling, and once they'd stopped kissing again, he smiled at her in a particularly sensual way. "You know, maybe it's not such a bad idea after all."

Her gaze half narrowed. "You know it's ridiculous, and I'll sleep with you anyway, so you needn't be polite. I wouldn't have even mentioned it, except babies are on my mind." She smiled at him. "Tina's little girl is so soft and cuddly and adorable. I held her for the longest time, and she looked up at me with her big blue eyes and I think she even smiled once. I instantly melted in a puddle of love. So you see, I'm not exactly rational at the moment. You needn't take it personally."

"Maybe I don't mind taking it personally."

"Are you proposing?" She fluttered her lashes playfully.

"It depends."

"On what, pray tell?"

"Whether you become pregnant or not."

"Ah . . ."

"What the hell does that mean?"

"It means—never mind, Ranelagh, you wouldn't understand." She was about to take issue with his callousness and disinterest in love, until she remembered with whom she spoke.

"No, tell me." His gaze took on a challenging gleam. "I think my perspicacity is as good as anyone's."

"I don't want to argue and you don't seriously want a child, so let's change the subject."

"Maybe I like the subject."

"Until I mention marriage."

He tried to conceal his horror.

"There, you see." She grinned. "And I'm not perspicacious at all."

"I'm not completely averse to the idea of marriage," he said carefully.

"So long as it isn't yours."

He couldn't help but smile. "I suppose you're right."

"And I suppose if I'm looking for a father for my child, I should be sensible enough to look elsewhere."

It bothered him more than he thought to consider that alternative, and, conscious he was placing himself in serious jeopardy, he said, "Don't put me entirely out of the running."

"There are certain circumstances, then, in which fatherhood"—she lifted her brows—"and marriage wouldn't be completely anathema to you?"

He swallowed. "I'm thinking there might be."

She laughed. "You certainly know how to charm a lady."

He smiled back. "Consider, darling, I've never even thought of fatherhood until a few minutes ago. Give me a moment or so to adjust."

She glanced at the carriage clock and began silently counting.

"Bitch," he whispered with a grin.

"A very hot one," she whispered back with a delicious wink.

This time *he* glanced at the clock. "We've forty minutes before we reach the Adelphi."

"More than enough time," she replied cheerfully.

"I thought you'd never ask."

"I didn't know you ever waited to be asked."

"Sometimes I do."

"When ladies are talking about marriage?" she noted archly.

"No." He didn't say talk of marriage always fell on deaf ears. "When I'm not sure how much politesse is required."

"I'm not interested in politesse, darling. Only that." She pointed between his legs.

"Then I have only one question," he replied smoothly. "What do you want to do about a baby? Yes or no?"

She looked at him for a breath-held moment, began to answer, changed her mind, and finally said very, very softly, "Yes *and* no."

"That's not going to work."

"I know."

"So I should be careful."

"It probably would be best."

"Probably?"

"I want a baby too much right now to answer with any sanity."

"I could be sane for us both if you like."

"I'm not sure I do."

He took a small breath because he suddenly found her ambiguity tempting. When it never had been before. When he'd been scrupulously careful to leave no by-blows behind. When talk of babies in the past would have speedily sent him in the opposite direction. "Why don't I ask you later," he said mildly.

"Tina's little girl is so warm and soft," Alex went on as though he hadn't spoken. "With the sweetest little curls." Her voice went soft. "She has little, little dark ringlets . . ."

"If you want a baby with ringlets," he whispered,

kissing her temple, the pink flush of her cheek, "I could see what I could do." Gently turning her by the shoulders, he brushed her mouth with a smiling kiss. "You just have to put in your order."

A baby of her own—how unutterably priceless. Sam was fully capable of making good on his offer too. And she wasn't completely sure she didn't want him to. "What should I order?" Her voice was hushed; a small, exultant glow lit her eyes.

"Order twins—a boy and a girl and then we don't have to decide which to have first," he answered, confident and assured. He unclasped the pearl and amethyst brooch that secured the white collar of her gown.

"First?" A tiny frisson quickened her senses.

"Of course." He unhooked one of three concealed hooks under the tailored pleats that adorned the front of her green linen bodice. "Don't you want a large family?" A second hook came free.

"I don't know . . ." Her mind was racing, her pulse leaping at his touch, desire and extravagant hope running riot.

"You don't have to. I'll decide," he told her, unclasping the last hook, easing open her bodice. "All you have to do is nurse our babies with these luscious breasts," he whispered, sliding her chemise straps and gown from her shoulders. "I'll decide when to make you pregnant." He tugged away the silken wisp of underclothing caught on her nipples, brushed her garments down off her arms, gently cupped the fullness of her breasts. "And when our babies have drunk their fill, I'll take a taste for myself."

She glanced nervously out the window. "Sam . . . there are people on the road. We shouldn't."

But she was breathing hard and he'd been wanting her since he'd left London on his pilgrimage to Briana Hills. "I'll pull down the curtains." Quickly putting action to words, the interior was soon dimmed to a golden glow. "We're alone, darling. No one can see us, no one knows who's riding in my carriage." He gently lifted her chin and smiled. "There's no need for alarm."

"Easy for you to say," she replied, smiling faintly. "You're not lusting for a baby."

"I've lust enough for the baby's mother—enough to keep you in my bed forever, and as for these"—he ran his palm over her ripe, lavish breasts—"these pretty nipples obviously want to be sucked when they're jewel hard like this. We'll have to do something about that." He brushed his fingertips back and forth over the taut crests, and her concentration seemed to slip away.

Their predilection for sexual play was nicely matched, the reason perhaps he'd overcome his prejudice against drawing room visits, the driving impulse for his journey south, and he didn't care to have the lady's reservations get in the way. Sliding his hands under her plump breasts, he lifted them into high mounds, bent his head, and licked the tip of one nipple. "I won't drink much," he promised, his whisper warm on her skin. "Our babies need it more."

"Lord, Sam—don't . . . say that."

He ignored her protest because she'd sighed in a

particularly gratifying way the instant he'd touched his tongue to her nipple and languorously arched her back. It was acquiescence and consent; it was breathy longing. It also conveniently thrust her nipple into his mouth, and while he wasn't entirely sure she hadn't acted deliberately, he was currently undertaking to make one taut tip measurably longer.

"You're much too tempting . . ." she purred some moments later, hot desire shimmering through her senses, every tantalizing compression of his mouth sending fevered ripples down to her vagina.

The lush witchery in her voice contradicted her words, and he might argue degrees of temptation with her glorious breasts pressed into his face and his willingness to have a baby indication of her extraordinary charm. But examining his unease always fell just below staking himself to the cross in any list of priorities. "Let me tempt you a little more," he said instead, and he slowly drew her nipple taut, stretching it gently until she uttered a wild, frenzied cry.

Soul-stirring flame raced downward, and she felt herself open, unfurl; she could almost feel the mouth of her womb ready itself for conception, and rather than struggle to escape, she experienced instead an irresistible urge to mate. Squirming against a fanatical throbbing need, driven by primal longing, she grabbed his dark hair and held him captive at her breast, wanting the voluptuous sensations never to end, but more desperately wanting him deep inside her.

"Please, Sam, I can't wait!"

But he didn't stop sucking, ignoring her when she tried to lift him away, tightening his grip on her breasts instead. If someone had asked what was driving him, he wouldn't have known. He never even made love in carriages—or at least not in years. There wasn't room; he preferred comfort. As he preferred not being obsessed if he had the choice.

But lust inundated his soul and something more rare. And maybe he was fighting to save his soul. He'd do what *he* wanted, not she. He would decide where and when and how, as though physical command would prevail over the ravenous desire that had brought him here today, that kept him here even after talk of babies.

So he didn't stop. In some odd way, his freedom was at stake. He licked, teased, tasted, he devoured and manipulated. He tugged on her nipples with his teeth so she had to sit up straighter, moving from one to the other, sucking them in turn gently, thoroughly, punctiliously, until she was more than running wet with desire; she was sobbing frantically for him. Then he sucked harder, so sublimely hard, she braced her hands on her thighs and pressed her breasts into the exquisite, aching agony. He seemed not to notice, and when she should take offense, she found his indifference perfidiously arousing. As though she existed only for his pleasure and she was there to be used—no more than a receptacle for his passions and lust.

Sam's sexual faculties were, as ever, superb. He was consummately aware of Alex's level of arousal—of his. And he was fast moving into a rash, ungovernable mode, when delay and discipline had always been his strength. But nothing made sense today, nothing about his wanting her made sense.

Maybe he'd drunk too much brandy while waiting at the villa, or perhaps the lady's charms were too outrageous, or maybe his reckless impulse to make babies was a sign of some insanity. Whatever the cause, he was very near to mounting her, because he had this overwhelming need to be on top. When it would have been more reasonable in the confined space to have her sit on him. When if he was truly sensible, he'd run like hell.

"Sam, please, please—*please!*"

He covered her mouth with his hand. "Don't," he muttered against her breast, not wanting to hear the heated hysteria in her voice, not wanting to hear the echoing desperation in his brain.

He swore softly, shut his eyes, swore again—and then he gave in to lust, gave up any illusion of control, tumbled her back on the seat, tossed up her skirts, wrenched her drawers open, and gave her what she wanted—what he wanted, what some overriding spirit of begetting wanted.

He could barely stay on the seat, one leg on and the other braced with his foot against the door, but he met her frantic rhythm with his own pounding assault, and they pitched and rolled with the racing carriage and flung themselves at each other, delirious in their eagerness, furious, rampant, uncontrolled.

Until at the very last—when consummation was trembling on the brink—deep-seated duty clamored to be heard, the alarm finally breaching Alex's consciousness. "No!" she gasped, shoving hard against his chest. "I don't want a baby!"

He was already withdrawing as she spoke.

Although his deep-seated sensibilities had nothing to do with duty.

Freedom had been his spur.

While the lovers were struggling with radical notions like babies and marriage, a discussion was under way in the parlor of a small house Farris kept for unofficial meetings. He'd spoken with Collins after leaving Sam, and now the two barristers had been joined by Farida and her brother Mahmud to negotiate a settlement.

Farris had opened the conversation with a warning he'd already delivered to Collins: His client was willing to make a settlement, but only if he could be assured Farida and her brother returned to Egypt.

"Lord Ranelagh commissioned me to relay those stipulations to you," he finished, surveying the brother and sister seated across the table from him.

"First, tell me how much he'll pay me," Farida replied coolly.

"I'm afraid you would have to agree to leave the country first. Without that agreement, I can't begin negotiations."

Mahmud opened his mouth to speak but quickly shut it again as his sister shot him a stern look.

"Very well, I agree," she said, willing to say whatever

was necessary to get what she wanted. "What will he pay?"

"A thousand pounds."

"Surely you jest. The man is worth millions."

"He's already paid you a considerable sum."

"And well he should after what he did to me. I was an innocent when I met him, and now—" She affected an anguished look. She'd dressed today in a gown suitable to her virtuous pose, a white muslin buttoned to the neck.

"He paid your gambling debts as well," Farris said brusquely, not taken in by her false modesty.

Squeezing out a tear, she waited until it ran down her cheek for all to see. "I was only trying to raise enough money to support my dear brother and myself after we were cast out on the world by the infamous man."

"Considering the content of the accusations in question, perhaps the viscount would be willing to offer my client more than a thousand pounds," Collins interposed. He, too, knew what Ranelagh was worth. Although the viscount's disregard for scandal had to be taken into consideration as well.

"I could authorize another five hundred," Farris said. "But that would be my limit. The lady may not wish too-close scrutiny into her life as well. I suggest you take it."

"Surely you're not questioning my virtue," Farida retorted heatedly.

"I'm not, miss, but the viscount is. There's a possibility we could publish our own account of your relationship with Lord Ranelagh."

"But would you," she said with a degree of composure both barristers marveled at. Neither man had any illusions about the lady's character.

"If it were necessary."

"Farida!" Mahmud blurted out, his agitation plain.

"Leave the room!" she ordered, her voice sharp as a knife.

The young man jumped from his chair and immediately withdrew from the parlor.

"Now then," she said calmly as the door closed on her brother. She slowly surveyed the two lawyers. "Where were we?"

The brother had been frightened. Farris took the initiative. "Fifteen hundred is a very generous offer, miss. The sale of your house will bring you a goodly sum as well. Not to mention the jewelry Lord Ranelagh purchased for you."

"You don't understand. I want a *better* house in Cairo, and my brother wants his racehorses back, and none of that is possible on fifteen hundred. Perhaps Lord Ranelagh doesn't understand the explicit nature of my story."

"I must tell you, in all good conscience, that Lord Ranelagh is—how do I say this—rather indifferent to public opinion. Had you had a—er—relationship with some other member of the nobility, perhaps your accusations would have been more damning. But the viscount is immune to censure."

"Then, why are you here?"

"I'm here, young lady, to make an offer for you to

leave England because the viscount would like that. But if you chose not to or should you not agree to a reasonable sum, he is quite ready to have you publish whatever you wish. And I expect you know him well enough to understand that."

"I'd suggest you consider Mr. Farris's offer," Collins said. Ranelagh had lived with scandal much of his adult life. His offer was more than generous, and if the young lady doubted Ranelagh would say publish and be damned, he didn't.

"Double it and I'll agree."

Collins masked his surprise. Farris said, "Five hundred more."

"A thousand," she countered.

"Seven hundred fifty."

"Done. I'd like it in cash." She stood and smiled at the two men. "It was a pleasure, gentlemen."

"You won't receive your money until you reach Egypt," Farris reminded her.

She hesitated briefly. "Then I'll need three hundred for travel."

"Agreed."

"Three hundred *extra* if you're going to make me wait for my money."

This time Farris hesitated, concerned she would continue to have additional requests.

"You don't expect me to travel in steerage, do you?"

"The sale of your house should preclude that necessity."

"I was under the impression you wished me to leave

immediately. Collins will have to sell my house in my absence."

"Very well. Three hundred extra. A ship sails for Cairo next week."

"That should be time enough," she said ambiguously, and turned to leave.

"Collins will draw up the papers. Sign them before you leave."

She glanced back over her shoulder. "You English are always so precise. Of course, I'll sign any papers you like," she replied casually. "I wish you good fortune, gentlemen. This has been a very profitable afternoon."

Chapter 22

A note from Farris arrived at the apartment in the Adelphi as Sam and Alex were finishing Claude's excellent dinner.

"Something bad?" Alex queried, taking note of Sam's expression.

"Not anymore," he said, crumpling the paper. Although he wouldn't be entirely satisfied until he heard Farida had reached Egypt.

"That sounds ominous."

"I'm sorry. It isn't . . . just some unfinished business."

"Some woman is hounding you, I suppose." At his look of surprise, she realized her facetious remark had struck a nerve.

"Not anymore," he said again.

"It's none of my business, I'm sure."

"I'm sure it's not."

"What if I'm curious?"

He leaned back in his chair and gazed at her from under his lashes. "Too bad."

Resting her elbows on the table, she steepled her fingers under her chin and smiled at him. "Then maybe I might be inclined to say too bad to something you might like—later on. . . ."

"Are you threatening to withhold sex?" He grinned. "Is this the same woman who came four times on the drive into the City?"

"I could if I wanted to."

"No, you couldn't."

"Tell me anyway." She stuck her tongue out. "I want to know what's in the note."

"What do I get if I tell you?"

"My undying affection."

He smiled. "You'll have to do better than that."

"Something more tangible?"

"Tangible is fine."

"Something tangible and sexual?"

"There's a combination."

"I'll do it. Now tell me."

"Aren't you supposed to be coy and unwilling for an indeterminate time and then capitulate?"

"Aren't you interested in having sex with me ever again?" she replied pointedly.

"Then don't get angry with what I tell you."

"I won't."

His dark eyes took on a sardonic cast. "I didn't realize you were so impossibly curious."

"And I didn't realize you could be so impossibly difficult."

Inhaling slowly, he debated whether it would be wise to bring up Farida again.

"I'm waiting."

He mentally shrugged away his reservations. If she wanted to know, she wanted to know. "My barrister came to an agreement with the woman from Egypt. For a sum of money she has agreed to return home."

"She was blackmailing you?"

"Yes."

"How?"

"You don't want to know."

"Of course I do."

"She was threatening to send something to the newspapers."

"Something?"

"Look, I don't know what. She was going to make up some story that would discredit me. I told my lawyer to let her, and the hell with it, because I didn't do anything wrong, but of course lawyers are always more cautious. So I agreed to pay her if she left. That's all there is. It's over, and hopefully she'll soon be gone."

"I want to believe you."

He scowled. "Thank you for your confidence. And I want to believe you won't be seeing that young boy on Friday."

"You're changing the subject."

"No, I'm not. You don't like my women friends, and I use the term loosely with Farida, and I don't like your men friends."

"Since I've known you for only three days, my men friends are none of your concern."

"Nor should Farida be of interest to you."

"She isn't."

"Excuse me? I believe I was threatened with no sex because of her."

"My mistake."

"Then it doesn't matter whether I leave you now and go to another lady?"

"Would you really?"

"How late is it?" He glanced at the clock.

"You bastard." Pique tightened her mouth.

"Are we being concerned? Let me know, because I'm getting mixed signals."

"I *have* to see Harry. I promised him I would."

"I'd be happy to tell him you changed your mind."

"You don't understand. This has nothing to do with sex."

"I doubt Harry would agree with you. Should I come along on your visit?"

She had the grace to look disconcerted.

"I didn't think so."

"Are we going to be faithful to each other? I doubt it. Actually, I don't wish to."

"Why?"

"Why? Because I've known you three days. And more important, your record on exclusivity is nonexistent. Let's just say I'm skeptical."

"Would you otherwise?" The words were shocking even as he spoke them, and he wondered if he could be drunk on only one bottle of wine.

"You mean if you weren't the byword for vice and inconstancy?"

"I suppose that's what I mean."

"You might have denied it."

"It's rather hard to deny after fifteen years, but if you'd like me to, I will."

She surveyed him from under her lashes, a stubborn set to her expression. "Why are we even talking about this? It's ludicrous. Neither one of us is looking for love and marriage. We're interested in sex. You're the last person in the world to argue about that."

"You can be damned annoying." He pulled the cork from another bottle of wine and poured his glass full.

"I don't want to be annoying. I want to make mad, passionate love to you for another night"—she smiled faintly—"if I can stay awake two days in a row."

"I've never had anyone fall asleep on me," he said with a wicked grin.

"Screw you, Ranelagh."

"We'll do that as soon as I finish this bottle. Let me know how I compare to Harry."

"Suddenly, I've lost my appetite for sex," she snapped, rising from her chair. "Good night."

She'd not walked more than five steps when he caught her and pulled her to a stop.

"Not so fast, darling."

She hadn't heard his chair move, nor his footsteps on the floor, and the capacity for silence in so large a man was unnerving. "I'm not your darling."

"I beg to differ with you. At least tonight you are."

"I'm not staying."

"Of course you are."

"You can't keep me against my will."

"Why can't I?"

"Because I'll scream."

"And?"

"This isn't funny, Sam. I don't wish to stay. I'm angry with you."

"Maybe I can change your mind."

"Not unless you can erase fifteen years of your life."

"I can be very convincing." He pulled her closer so their bodies touched lightly, so she could feel the rampant extent of his desire.

"I'm not in the mood to be seduced, particularly by a man who finds women no more than a blur of selfish orgasms."

"Mutual orgasms, darling." He cupped her bottom, hauled her closer, gently moved his hips. "You remember those. . . ."

"I prefer not being the ten-thousandth woman in your life," she snapped, trying to push him away.

"*Au contraire* . . . you're the only one," he said, bending low to kiss her pursed mouth, the rigid length of his arousal iron hard against her stomach. "And I'd really like to make you come tonight—or all night . . . or all week if you prefer."

The words *all week* jolted her brain, settled flame hot in the damnable eager heat of her vagina, required a sustaining breath to tamp into submission. "Sorry, I'm not interested," she said tightly. "Now let me go and I'll bid you good night."

He heard the tautness in her voice, knew what it meant, knew more how little she could resist her desires and even better how their passions matched. "Stay a few minutes more. I promise to behave."

"You don't know how to behave. You've spent a lifetime misbehaving."

"You could show me how—a woman of your propriety and virtue."

"There's nothing I could show you, believe me."

Such a statement was difficult to ignore, almost impossible, but he resisted the impulse and said with exemplary courtesy, "I'm willing to learn."

The double entendre wasn't intentional, but it raced through her senses nonetheless, and she spoke in almost a whisper. "Let me go."

Something about her tone gave him pause, and he released her.

"Now step away from me."

"Yes, ma'am." And he did, deferential, polite, unequivocally beautiful at such close range—or any range. Maybe it was the candlelight or the room or the ghosts of Regency courtiers, but the viscount had never looked so darkly handsome or desirable or sweetly available.

"Have you thought any more about a baby?" His voice was like velvet, his dark eyes hauntingly seductive.

"Sam! Don't you dare!"

Her exclamation was answer enough. "We could talk about it."

"No."

But her voice was barely audible, her hands were clenched at her sides, and unless he missed his guess, her thighs were clenched as well against her sexual need.

"You liked Tina's new baby. You said she was all pink and cuddly." Moving forward, he took her in his arms and she didn't push him away this time. "We could think about it at least. . . ."

A much-longed-for baby would be heaven; how often had she wished for a child in her marriages, Alex thought, struggling to maintain her anger in the face of such blissful possibilities. She leaned a fraction closer to the man who could make her dreams come true—in terms of babies if nothing else. "You won't stay."

He didn't pretend not to understand. "I will." Even as he spoke, he questioned his sanity, but the words seemed right just then and true.

A warmth of longing, a glow of hope quite apart from reality, infused her body and soul, enveloped her—them, perhaps, she thought with roseate fondness. "I'd like to believe you."

He drew in a small breath against the shocking significance of what he was about to say. "Believe me."

She smiled. "Am I supposed to forget all the ladies?"

"At least I haven't been married twice, nor do I sleep with underage people."

"Harry's of age."

"By a day, maybe. But, look," Sam said quickly, "I don't want to argue about anything in our past. I don't want to argue at all. I want to make love to you. I even want to give you a baby if you want one, and just so you understand my amateur status in that regard, I'd like you to know I've never made that offer before."

"What if I accept your offer? What then?"

"We'll deal with it."

"It?"

"The baby."

Her brows rose.

"Our baby."

She suddenly laughed. "I believe that was terror I saw."

He smiled. "Only a transient uncertainty, darling."

"I do enjoy being your darling."

"Not as much as I. I hope we're done fighting."

"I seem to want you more than I don't want you."

"Thank God."

She shook her head. "My feelings are purely secular and explicit."

His smile was slow, unutterably sensual, and so beautiful, she knew she'd never forget it. "We're definitely in accord. Could I interest you in a too-small bed that I promise to replace tomorrow?" His bachelor apartment was austere.

"You could interest me in this carpet we're standing on."

"Ah." Knowing the particular style of her eagerness, he held out his hand. "Perhaps we should hurry."

"And I don't want a baby." Despite her unguarded passions, a particle of good judgment yet remained.

His hand closed over hers. "We'll see."

But elements of their discontent surfaced in the course of the night despite their mutual passions and lust. Alex couldn't forget how Sam had become so proficient at pleasing women. Meanwhile Sam found himself recalling her scheduled meeting with Harry tomorrow much too often for his peace of mind. Spurred by jealousy or bewitchment or rash impulse, Sam found himself forcing the issue of a child late that night when no more than a day ago, the subject alone would have driven him away from any woman so stupid as to mention it.

Alex resisted, a discretionary response that took every ounce of willpower she possessed when Sam was offering her the moon and it took several heated moments more before their emotions were restored to a semblance of calm. But passion ultimately prevailed, or carnal desire, or whatever strange attraction drew them to each other with such intensity and they agreed to agree and made up in each other's arms.

Chapter 23

When he woke in the morning, she was gone. Considering what a light sleeper he was, he gave her high marks for stealth.

After his initial surprise, his temper flared and he swore in a great number of languages. She hadn't been unhappy with the sex—her screams had been proof of that. And she hadn't taken issue with the number of times she'd climaxed—the bitch. But now that she'd had her night of sex, she could conveniently take affront once again.

It was Friday after all. She had to see her young friend Harry.

The viscount returned to Park Lane and spent the remainder of the morning closeted with Patrick McGuff, going over estate business. The men discussed the crop reports from all his properties. Sam's concentration was so unusual, Patrick said, "Are you feeling well, sir?" twice before Sam's heated glance cautioned him against further questions concerning his health. Once the crop reports had been perused, the men discussed the new wing that was planned for Sam's primary country house near Cambridge. Meetings were set up for the architect and builder for later in the week, a tentative construction schedule was established, and when Patrick asked whether Sam would be able to attend the commission on the new courthouse proposed for his parish, he shocked his employee by agreeing.

"The aldermen will be pleased, sir. Immensely pleased. They've been hoping to thank you in person for your generous donation to the building fund."

"It was your idea, Patrick. They should be thanking you."

"But your generosity made it possible, sir. Many of the nobles aren't so civic-minded."

"Our parish can use a new courthouse. The old one was falling down. The decision was simple enough. Now, what else do we have on the agenda?"

By this time, the estate manager was beginning to be genuinely concerned. Sam never spent more than an hour at a time in Patrick's office. "We could look at the reports on the parish schools, sir. There is some question of adding new teachers if the budget allows."

"Why wouldn't it allow? Show me the figures, Patrick. Let's see that we have enough teachers this year."

With both apprehension and elation, Patrick pulled the reports down from the shelf. If his lordship was ill, he hoped someone other than he would notice, too, and see that Lord Ranelagh received help.

"Perhaps we should order some food," Sam suggested, glancing at the clock. "It's well past luncheon. You must be hungry."

While Sam was astonishing his estate manager, Alex was at Harry's. And despite Sam's resentful speculation, she hadn't looked forward to the visit.

Harry was too possessive. If she hadn't already been uninterested in men of that ilk, she would have been after the evening with Sam.

But she tried to be courteous; Harry was so ingratiating and pleased to see her, she didn't have the heart to be cruel. He'd cleaned his studio, brought in enough roses to perfume the block, and had cooked a delicious-smelling stew, which was convenient because she'd forgotten to bring anything.

"Are you hungry?"

How did he know, she wondered, her night of sex having left her ravenous. "I am, just a little," she said.

"You looked like you were. You kept sniffing the air. It's almost ready. Sit down, take off your jacket, and I'll bring you something to eat. Look at my painting while I open some wine."

She should say no to the wine, because she didn't want to stay long, but a glass of wine sounded delicious just then, as the food did—as everything did with her senses still activated by the excesses of last night. Damn Ranelagh anyway. It wasn't fair that he was so extraordinarily good in bed. It made it that much more difficult to walk away from the pleasure. With effort, she forced her thoughts away from the previous night and concentrated on the issues at hand. Sitting down, she shrugged out of her jacket and surveyed Harry's seascape of Brighton. She would offer her encouragement to Harry—an easy enough prospect when his work was so good—eat quickly, and then leave.

Her obligation to visit him on Friday would be fulfilled, and she could return home and indulge in her sulks in peace. She'd already sent the peignoir to Tina with a note explaining her absence. In her discontent, she wasn't in the mood to spar with her mother.

"This is one of the bottles Beecher gave me when he sold my painting of the horse fair. I saved it for us." Harry poured the golden liquid into a goblet for her and filled one for himself. He lifted his glass to her. "To your beauty."

"Thank you. To your beauty *and* talent. The seascape is outstanding."

"I finished it last night because I knew you were coming."

"Beecher will be pleased."

"More important, are you pleased?"

"Of course I am. I love all of your work."

"Now, if you only loved me."

"Darling . . . don't, please. Let's just have a nice visit."

"Can you stay?"

She knew what he meant and immediately felt awkward.

"We can talk about it later," he said quickly, reading her expression. "I'm just glad you're here."

"Thank you." She lifted her glass to him and then drank a goodly portion of the wine. Other men didn't appeal to her anymore—not that Harry hadn't been sweet at one time. But she found herself thinking almost exclusively of Sam, of what he might say at a moment like this—or what he might be doing now, and she felt restless and desolate and angry all at once.

The stew was wonderful. Harry was an excellent cook, and he'd combined chicken and curry and an assortment of vegetables into a mélange of flavors so exquisite, Alex forgot her current obsession for a few moments. "You're as creative a cook as you are a painter. This is fabulous," she said, smiling.

"Everything's fabulous when you're here."

"Harry, you know how I feel about that."

"I won't ask you to do anything you don't want to do, Alex. I just like having you here. I wish you'd come over more often."

"Maybe I will if we can be friends."

"If you want to be friends, we'll be friends," he said in a very grown-up way. "But if you ever want to be more than friends"—he smiled—"keep me in mind."

She gazed at him fondly. "You're adorable."

"I know. You've told me so. And I'm thinking when you get tired of Ranelagh, maybe you'll come and see me again."

Was he prescient? She schooled her face to conceal her shock. "I'll keep that in mind," she said, keeping her voice carefully neutral.

"Make sure you do, because I'll always be here. I love you, Alex, even if you don't love me. And not just because you've helped me with my career." He smiled again. "I didn't even know painters had careers. I thought you painted because you had to."

"Talented people like you paint because they have to. Others wouldn't even know what you mean by that compulsion. You're so good, Harry, I want you to have everything you deserve. And I'll help you in any way I can."

"Except you won't marry me."

She couldn't help but smile. "You'd be tired of me within a month. I'm bossy and demanding, and when you saw me in the morning, you'd realize how old I really was."

"I have seen you in the morning, and you're beautiful. And you're only ten years older than I. That's not so much." His spirits were high because she hadn't said no and she hadn't left and he was never so happy as when he was with her. "And think . . . you like the way I cook. Wait until you try my plum tart with crème anglaise."

How could she refuse plum tart? She couldn't any more than she could refuse Harry's invitation to sketch with him that afternoon when he had a live model coming to his studio. "I know how much you like to draw from life," he went on to explain, "so when this man at the market said he'd pose anytime I wanted if I helped him with his watercolors, I wasn't about to argue. He's from Syria—Damascus, I think."

"You're spoiling me." She smiled at him, her mood

much improved after Beecher's fine wine, which she drank with the plum tart and crème anglaise.

"I want to spoil you. I want to do everything for you. I'd carry you everywhere if you'd let me."

The difference between Harry's devotion and Sam's profligate self-indulgence was profound. She wondered how she could be so irrational as to choose casual sex over ardent feeling.

But there it was. Without explanation or reason.

She couldn't get Sam out of her mind even while this young man was pouring his heart out to her.

Taking herself to task, she forced away her thoughts from the infamous viscount and concentrated on Harry's conversation.

"You always wanted to paint an exotic locale. Why don't we have Larry pose in desert garb. I had Chloe bring over some of the props from her studio."

"How is Chloe?" She was the painter Addison's beautiful daughter and had shown considerable interest in Harry.

"Chloe? Fine, I suppose. I didn't notice. Look what she brought us." And he went on to exhibit enthusiastically a full array of desert robes and weapons.

The model arrived soon thereafter. Harry introduced the young man, stumbling over his name.

"Just call me Ben," the model said kindly. "Everyone does." The handsome man bowed over Alex's hand with great courtesy and grace.

They briefly discussed Ben's homeland, how he'd come to London with the scholars who had been investigating Petra, how he'd been their guide, and once they decided on an appropriate robe and weapons, the afternoon of sketching began.

The work turned out to be just what Alex needed to take her mind from her unwanted fascination with Sam. For those hours while she and Harry worked busily, she didn't once think of him. Not until they began losing the sun did she even take note of the time.

She'd finished a pastel and a small oil study, both preliminary sketches possibly useful in a larger canvas.

Harry had concentrated on a portrait study in oil and had captured Ben's face with such vivid realism, the two-dimensional medium had taken on a sculptural quality.

Ben was pleased with the likenesses. While Alex rested, Harry gave the young model his watercolor lesson. She found herself in good humor; she always was when she was working. As she watched Harry help with the watercolor, she marveled at his talent. His hand moved with such sureness. He was kind and considerate in his instructions, always pointing out Ben's strengths rather than his weaknesses, generously offering praise. Harry really was a very nice young man, she thought warmly. She was glad she'd come to see him.

This very productive afternoon reminded her of what was truly important in her life. Not sex, nor transient pleasure, but her painting and charities, family and friends like Harry. She had so much to bring her satisfaction. While Sam had been a pleasant interlude, she needed to be sensible about their relationship. Passion alone wasn't enough for personal fulfillment, nor could she afford to let her infatuation overwhelm her life. More important, she refused to be so susceptible to his or any man's charm.

When she left, she thanked Harry with genuine warmth. "I so enjoyed myself today. I forget how pleasant it is to work with someone else."

"Come over and paint with me anytime." He smiled, then took her hand and shook it. "You see how well mannered I can be. I didn't try to kiss you once."

"I noticed," she replied, smiling too. "I appreciate your restraint."

He ran his fingers through his long, fair hair and then gently swung his arms and grinned. "Anytime you're in the mood, though, just let me know. I'm always available."

"I'll keep it in mind."

"I just thought I'd mention it. . . ."

"I might take you up on your offer sometime."

"Ben's coming over again on Monday—if you'd like to join us."

"Maybe I will." With a wave and a lighter heart, she left.

Chapter 24

O nce she was back in her studio, the memories came flooding back, and practical considerations gave way to emotion. Sam had stood right there, or lounged in that chair, kissed her there and there and there. No matter where she looked, she was reminded of him. She dreaded going into her bedroom, where the searing images would be all too intense.

She tried to paint for a time, but the unfinished garden landscape only escalated the level of her unease, the sunlit scene giving rise to lush memories of the wild, thrilling rapture they'd shared. She finally threw her brushes down, turned the canvas around, shut the door to the garden, and poured herself a brandy.

Slumped in a chair, her drink untouched at her side, she bemoaned the emotional turmoil that had plagued her since meeting Sam. It wasn't fair, she thought, that he'd entered her life and disrupted her hard-won contentment, nor, she reflected more bitterly, that he'd so easily changed her mind last night.

What really wasn't fair was that he could as easily change any woman's mind. For a jealous moment, she wished him and all his paramours to the devil.

Cooler counsel surfaced a moment later, and she reminded herself that she had been fully aware of his reputation before she embarked on that first fateful carriage ride. And his seduction last night had been delectable and enchanting as usual. So much as she'd like to blame him, she had no one to blame but herself.

Not a particularly consoling thought, nor one that brought her any measure of peace.

Damn him and his irresistible allure.

When Rosalind walked into Alex's studio that evening, Alex's mood hadn't improved. She'd actually drunk two brandies in an effort to mitigate the worst of her temper, canceled two appointments, tried to nap without success, dusted her entire studio, after which she made a note to increase her maid's wages or throw out some of the porcelain and artifacts littering her shelves and tables. And now she was seriously thinking about going to see Harry—as a diversion to her black mood.

"See Harry later," Rosalind suggested, standing in the doorway of the dust-free studio. "Right now you have to dress. Have you forgotten we're expected at Caroline's for dinner?"

Alex didn't move from her Empire chaise, her gaze, if not sullen, decidedly morose. "I'm not going."

Rosalind settled into a chair in a rustle of pale blue

silk, her matching pale blue gaze direct. "Ranelagh's not worth it," she said briskly.

A flash of surprise crossed Alex's face. "Is it that obvious?"

Leaning forward in a twinkle of sapphire ear drops, Rosalind patted Alex's hand. "He's the divine and glorious Ranelagh, darling. What did you expect?"

"Perhaps I didn't realize the full extent of his deification," Alex muttered.

"His godlike attributes are well known to anyone interested in dalliance. You've just never concerned yourself with amour before. If you want my advice, I'd suggest you get up, get dressed, go out tonight, and forget Ranelagh."

"Because he's sure to forget me, you mean."

Rosalind lifted one bare shoulder. "How blunt do you wish me to be?" And when Alex didn't answer, she said, "He leaves them all. But it's not as though you're looking for more." Her eyes narrowed slightly. "Are you?"

"No, of course not. In fact, I'm angry with him. Or, more aptly, resentful of his damned expertise— oh, hell . . . of all the women. I refuse to be another of the hundreds or thousands. I left him this morning while he was sleeping."

"Really. He must have been surprised when he woke. How clever of you to leave him guessing. I don't expect that ever happens to him."

"I wasn't intending to be clever. He annoyed me." But Rosalind's remark offered a new interpretation of

Sam's displeasure with her seeing Harry. Was his vanity involved rather than his feelings?

Rosalind leaned forward in her chair. "Tell me everything."

"Relax, Rosie. There's no juicy gossip to offer up. We just argued about my seeing Harry. For some reason, Ranelagh felt he could tell me what to do." She didn't mention their disagreement over the child because Rosalind wouldn't possibly understand.

"Do you think you were mistaken? It hardly seems like Ranelagh to restrict a woman's friendships."

"I could have been mistaken, I suppose."

"You're not in this mood just because Ranelagh didn't want you to see Harry?"

Alex shrugged. "No—I don't know; I'm not sure what I think. I'm trying to sort out my feelings."

"So you have feelings for him." Rosalind made a small moue. "I'm not sure that's wise, darling . . . considering—well, considering the sheer number of women who have passed through his life."

"Which is the pertinent point, is it not?" Alex sighed softly. "I'm trying to deal with this whole episode wisely."

"Good for you. We'll go to Caroline's tonight and you can show everyone your liaison with Ranelagh has not impaired your better judgment."

"But Caroline's." Alex wrinkled her nose. "It's sure to be boring."

"If you recall, she's invited the entire Russian ballet troupe currently onstage at the Apollo. It's their night off, and both Serge Voronkin and Nikki Linsky are enough to take anyone's mind off anything at all. . . ." Rosalind's pale brows rose and her smile was suggestive. "Just a passing thought to jog you out of that chaise."

"I suppose it's better than drowning my sorrows in vile brandy."

"You can drown your sorrows in Serge's soulful Slavic gaze instead. Or if you're not in the mood to throw yourself into another man's arms, maybe you could talk to Serge and Nikki about painting their portraits in their costumes from *Boris Godunov*. I adore those form-fitting ballet tights, and you might too"—her brows arched upward—"if you know what I mean."

Alex laughed. "Have you nothing better to do than suggest lovers for me?"

"But, darling, think how much more exciting my life has become now that you're a wicked widow."

"I wish I were a wicked widow; then I could cavalierly deal with men like Sam Lennox. Although if I'm to serve as surrogate for your virtuous life, kindly find me someone who will be enchanting but not *too* enchanting. I don't want to want a man like I want Sam."

"But it's his specialty, my dear. Why wouldn't he be a superb lover? A diversion will do you good. Wear your Indian silk tonight and those wonderful diamond earrings you bought in Paris, and I'll see that you meet Serge and Nikki." Rosalind smiled. "Would you like them both?"

"That certainly would be in the nature of a diversion," Alex noted sardonically. "If I felt like talking to a man—which I don't."

"Nonsense," Rosalind replied, not inclined to leave without her friend. "Wait until you meet Serge."

With Rosalind's nudging and cajoling, Alex was eventually dressed, the vivid gold-shot turquoise silk a resplendent foil for her auburn hair and creamy skin. The sheer silk overlay a crepe slip in a matching hue, the low décolletage and jeweled belt of flamboyant gems a lure to the eye. It was a dramatic gown. But in the mood she was in, Alex welcomed the drama. At least, it offered an alternative to her peevishness. It served as well to project a dégagé image that suggested she was perfectly fine without Ranelagh, because everyone at dinner would have heard of their liaison.

She wanted to show them she was in excellent spirits. See.

Dinner was less boring than she'd expected. The darkly handsome Serge sat beside her and flattered her with his attention. He had long black hair, Oriental eyes, high cheekbones, and a muscled body that was evident even beneath his superbly tailored evening clothes. She enjoyed their bantering conversation as much as she enjoyed his descriptions of his native country. But when he began to rub his foot against hers as they were finishing their desserts, she found herself profoundly indifferent—as though her brother might have accidentally touched her.

Was something wrong with her? she wondered. She glanced at him as though trying to find some reason to respond.

He smiled.

She smiled back.

"Would you like to dance?" he asked, soft suggestion in his voice.

She was about to refuse, when Caroline cried, "Sam, you darling! You came after all!"

Everyone's gaze turned to the door.

Dazzlingly handsome, resplendent in white tie and tails, his dark hair gleaming in the lamplight, the Viscount Ranelagh bestowed a smile on his hostess. "You're the only cousin I like," he drawled softly, but the room was so quiet, his voice carried to the farthest corner.

And the faint slur of intoxication couldn't be missed.

Caroline rose from her seat at the head of the table. "We were just finishing, darling. I don't expect you came to dine," she added, moving toward the man who could make any reception a success. It was a decided coup that Sam had come, although there was little doubt who had drawn him here. "Would you like to lead me out in the first dance?"

He bowed with exquisite finesse and offered her his hand.

Those gauging the degree of his drunkenness took note of his grace. Not too drunk, but then, when was he?

As Caroline and Sam entered the ballroom moments later, the orchestra began playing and most of the guests followed their hostess and Ranelagh onto the dance floor. The viscount partnered his cousin twice and then proceeded to systematically bestow his charm and waltzing skills on every female in the room. Save Alex. A fact noted by all.

Refusing to regard the curious looks and the occasional blunt query, Alex gave her attention to the inevitable array of suitors, entertaining them all with wit and charm. She danced almost every dance and never once looked in Sam's direction. But as midnight approached, the tension in her shoulders was becoming unbearable, while her splitting headache made it almost impossible to smile. Serge had taken his congé with good grace, and ever since, Alex had been looking for an opportunity to leave. When her most recent dance partner went to fetch her a lemonade, she found herself momentarily alone, and seizing the chance, she quickly slipped into a curtained alcove that opened onto a servants' passage.

In moments she found her way to the main corridor. She ran down the stairs, reaching the entrance hall without meeting anyone. After a footman brought out her wrap, she dismissed his offer to call her carriage. "My driver is just outside," she said. "I'm perfectly fine."

Which she wasn't. She had to get away from Sam and all the women fawning over him. She had to get a grip on her emotions.

Hurrying down the brick drive, she counted the

carriages as she passed, anticipating the moment of her deliverance. When she'd reach hers, climb in, and shut the door.

"How was Harry?"

The voice was familiar, close, scented with brandy.

But she didn't stop because she wasn't capable of being as casual as he when she would have much preferred hitting him or screaming at him or making love to him—or maybe all three together. When none were appropriate. When none would solve her dilemma.

Suddenly, she was lifted off her feet, spun around, and set down again, although the grip on her waist didn't loosen.

"How was Harry?" Sam repeated, his voice whisper soft, his dark gaze only inches away.

"I don't have to tell you." Even to her ears she sounded petulant.

"Are you a child or—"

"Are you?" she snapped. "You're not exactly acting like an adult. And you're drunk."

"I'm never drunk."

"Should we take a vote among the guests?"

"I don't give a damn about the guests. Tell me about Harry."

"Why don't you tell me about Adelaide or Charlotte or Helen, not to mention Tatiana, Barbara, Lydia, and Nadia. Have I left out anyone tonight?"

"They were all boring, if you must know. Now, about Harry. Did you fuck him?"

"Maybe I did and maybe I didn't. It's none of your business."

Tightening his grip, he jerked her hard against his body. "Perhaps I'm just a little drunk," he admitted, his gaze half lidded. "I suggest you answer me."

"If I scream, Sam, there are any number of drivers and retainers who will hear. We're not in the Adelphi, where your servants do what you wish. So it might be wise if you release me and I'll bid you good night."

"Do you think I care about the drivers and servants?" Abruptly lifting her into his arms, he protected her face with one hand and strode through the yew hedge bordering the drive. Coming out the other side, he glanced around, getting his bearings.

"I'm going to scream," she hissed, the scent of pine in her hair.

"Go ahead." He started walking.

Taking note of their isolation, she understood his indifference. "Sam, this is medieval," she said in what she hoped was a reasonable voice. "I'm already furious with you, and this is only—"

"*I've* been furious since you left this morning."

"I took issue with being seduced against my will last night," she said coolly.

He snorted.

"I *wanted* to leave."

"Sure you did. After which climax? The first or the tenth?"

"Fine. You're the quintessential stud. Is that what you want to hear?"

"What I want to hear is whether you fucked Harry today."

"No, I didn't. I know that might be hard for someone like you to fathom, but there it is. Welcome to the real world."

A smile appeared on his face. "Why didn't you say so before?"

"Because I didn't want to see you smile like that, that's why."

"You must have disappointed him."

"Yes, I'm sure I did. Just like you disappointed all the ladies at Caroline's who were hoping to share your bed tonight."

"The night's not over yet."

She slapped him so hard, the pain jarred her shoulder.

He grunted but didn't miss a stride. "I'll fuck you first, darling." His voice was silky. "So save your energy."

"No you won't," she said through gritted teeth.

"Allow me to disagree. With a hot little cunt like yours, you're always ready for fucking. All those old men made you hungry for cock."

"You—you . . . insolent, despicable, swaggering bastard! Put me down this instant!"

"I'll be putting you down in my bed, or if you really can't wait, we'll do it in my carriage on the way to my apartment."

"Sam!" She struggled against his hold. "I don't want this!" Kicking and twisting, she pummeled him with her fists. "I don't want you! I don't, I don't, I don't!"

Immune to her assault, he only tightened his hold and continued his progress through Caroline's moonlit garden.

The brute strength of his hard, muscled body, the effortless way in which he carried her, his purposeful lust, provoked a small, fevered intoxication . . . insidious, alarming—tantalizing. She steeled herself against the sensations, but the first tiny ripples irrepressibly cascaded down her vagina, the beginning pulse of arousal warmed her blood, a breathlessness quite apart from her struggles made itself known, and try as she might to ignore the piquant heat, she couldn't deny it. Horrified at her response, she went still, appalled to find herself no different from all the others.

Intuitively recognizing female willingness, he bent to gently kiss her forehead. "I missed you today," he whispered.

She'd missed him, but she couldn't dismiss her anger or admit to it. "You ruined my day completely," she replied, waspish and fretful.

"I'll apologize any way you wish."

The innuendo in his words, no matter how silken, further raised her ire. "I'm sure you will. But I'm not interested."

"Tell me what you want and I'll do it."

"I want you to set me down and go away."

"I wish I could." Each word was neutral, bland.

"Of course you can. You can do anything you want."

"If I weren't so selfish, I could. Ask me to do something more reasonable. Something we could do together," he added with a cheeky grin.

"You're so damned sure of yourself, aren't you?"

"Of course not," he lied.

She gazed at him for a speculative moment, his harsh features limned by moonlight, his beauty difficult to ignore, her ability to alter the balance of power restricted by his sheer size alone—not to mention any number of other more equivocal reasons. He wasn't going to release her. That much was plain. "What if we were to compromise?" she said, looking for advantage in this uneven contest.

"Then we'll compromise," he replied smoothly, knowing better, knowing more than she about what she was willing to do.

She glared at him. "How easily you agree."

"But then, I'm interested in being agreeable," he drawled softly, reaching the garden gate and pushing it open with his shoulder. He glanced down the narrow passage behind the house.

Following his gaze, she saw his waiting carriage. "You planned this!" Her voice was charged with affront.

"Not necessarily."

"So anyone would have served your purposes?"

"I didn't say that."

"Damn you, Sam, I'm not going to be your casual selection for the night! Put me down this instant!"

He set her down abruptly. "I'm not interested in playing some stupid little game where you pretend you don't want what you want and I'm supposed to be the big bad wolf," he growled.

"But you are." Her voice was bitter.

"And you want the big bad wolf," he said brusquely. "Admit it."

"Even if I did, I take issue with your arrogance," she said as brusquely as he. "Am I supposed to be thrilled that you're willing to make love to me? I can pick and choose like you. I refused a considerable number of men tonight. I don't need you."

He shifted his stance, restlessly clenched and unclenched his fists, then looked away for a moment before returning his gaze to her. "I apologize."

He was actually contrite. "My goodness," she whispered.

"I've been drinking all day. Would you consider that an excuse?"

"For last night as well?"

A tick appeared over his cheekbone. "Do you have to win every round?"

"I'm not sure I can win anything with you." She wished she weren't filled with longing the way she was.

"You could have fooled me."

They were both out of humor, or out of their depth in terms of desire, and he was right—she wanted the big bad wolf . . . in all his guises. "Perhaps we could begin this conversation again," she said softly.

He could smell, taste, feel her acquiescence, and maybe he had drunk too much, because he should have been more polite. "What if I don't want to talk?"

"What if I say you have to?"

"I'd have to say I can't guarantee anything right now."

She half smiled. "Have you reached your limit?"

"I did hours ago. This is restraint, sweetheart, on about a thousand different levels." He inhaled softly. "Could we talk in the morning? I promise to listen closely."

"When you're sober."

He shrugged. "When I'm not focused exclusively on fucking you." He lifted his hands quickly, palms out. "I apologize for my bluntness. And if you really want me to listen now, I'll try." His nostrils flared. "I think I could."

He looked so adorably sweet—if it was possible for someone as powerfully built and sinfully handsome to look adorable—and her last reservations melted away. "Morning will be fine."

His relief was apparent. "You can talk to me tonight, too, if you wish, but I can't guarantee I'll hear it all."

"Actually," she said with a smile, "I'm not really in the mood for talking right now."

He blew out a small breath. "Thank you."

Chapter 25

The sun barely intruded through the heavy velvet draperies in the Adelphi bedroom, but a thin sliver of light gave evidence that morning had come. It sliced through the dimness and lay golden and undulating on the rumpled covers at the foot of the bed.

The small brilliance jogged some part of her brain as Alex lay prone on the bed, her head turned toward the windows, and she opened one eye.

She half smiled, not at the sunlight, but in joyful memory of the night past. The heat of Sam's body lay against hers, his arm rested lightly on her back, and all was deliciously right with the world . . . until spontaneous emotion gave way to niggling reminders of her life beyond Sam Lennox. Her numerous appointments for the day leaped into her consciousness.

A heated tremor eddied deep in the pit of her stomach, reminding her of more pleasant activities. She shifted faintly to better absorb the luscious sensation.

At her movement, Sam tightened his hold and

pulled her closer. "I didn't know I could feel this good"—he nuzzled her neck—"are we in heaven?"

His erection nudged her bottom, and like an addict, she leaped in response. "It's heaven in the Adelphi," she whispered, wanting him again, always—when she shouldn't, when she should leave.

"Good, then, that I own." He adjusted himself against her bottom.

She shivered as the head of his erection nuzzled her labia.

And I'm going to own you, he wished to say, his sense of possession intense. But, circumspect, he said instead, "We still have time, don't we?" as though they woke up like this every day, in this ordinary way, and she was his. Without waiting for an answer, he eased his rigid length into her honeyed warmth in slow, rapturous degrees.

She uttered a breathy cry as he filled her, his invasion triggering rapture in every inch of ravished, susceptible tissue. Hypersensitive after hours of impassioned sex, overstimulated, her fevered senses quickened like wildfire, and she quickly climaxed. Aware of how insatiable her passions, he gave her more of what she wanted, what she needed, listened with a practiced ear to her heated breathing as a new orgasm began warming her blood. Consciously repressing his jealousy, he refused to speculate on how many other men had wakened with her and done what he was doing to her, how often she'd instantly responded like this. Instead, he focused on fucking the luscious Miss Ionides for purely selfish reasons.

Sometime later, when their selfishness was momentarily appeased, Sam lifted Alex from the bed and carried her to one of the armchairs. "Wait for me. I'll be right back."

Her smile was teasing as she leaned against the high-backed chair, her auburn curls gleaming. "How long do I have to wait?"

He looked up from pouring water into a basin. "How long would you wait for me?"

"For you?" She winked. "Indefinitely."

He chuckled. "As long as indefinitely is under five minutes, you mean." He dipped a washcloth into the water.

She cast him a playful glance. "That must be why we get along so well."

"Because I indulge you?"

"Is that what you call it?"

"I was being polite," he said, flashing her a grin.

"You would prefer a different word?"

"A blunter one." He began washing away the residue of their lovemaking. "But I'm content regardless of the semantics."

"Are you truly?"

She looked small in the large chair, innocent, when his life had been largely bereft of the quality, and a rare poignancy overcame him. "More than ever," he said softly.

"Me too," she said with charming honesty. "Do you think it's just because of the sex?"

More comfortable with talk of sex, he spoke with a

familiar drawl. "I don't know about 'just,' but sex is definitely a factor."

"How big a factor? Let me reword that," she said with a smile, her gaze on the object of his washing. "How much of a factor?"

"You tell me."

"Because this is a constant in your life."

"No." His dark gaze surveyed the room. "*This* is not."

"But sex is."

"Not this kind of sex."

"What kind?"

"The kind you like—constant, exclusive"—he shrugged—"personal."

"Personal?"

"Don't look at me like that. I just meant this is different."

"In contrast to your usual impersonal sex."

"It's no damned secret, if that's what you're implying." He came to stand before her, a fresh bowl of water and a washcloth in his hands. "Get up."

"I can wash myself."

"But I want to."

"That's not necessary." She knew where that would lead, and she was uncomfortably aware of the time.

"I didn't say it was necessary. Humor me."

"I've humored you sufficiently."

"And I you. Now do as you're told."

"Sam, I dislike commands."

"Not always." His smile was impudent.

"Don't remind me," she said with a grimace, "when I've spent so many years developing my independence."

"You can't always be independent."

"Easy for you to say. You don't take orders at all."

His dark brows rose in perfect arches. "Excuse me."

"Well . . . those weren't precisely orders."

"They sure sounded like it to me. I believe your exact words on more than one occasion last night were—"

"I concede, I concede," she interposed quickly. "Thank you, by the way."

"I'm sure I'll be amply repaid with—shall we say—a degree of ready compliance. . . ."

"I shouldn't."

"I shouldn't have last night, but I did."

"You weren't suffering."

"I can guarantee you won't either." He gestured with the bowl. "Up, darling."

"I want you to know, I'm doing this against my will." She came to her feet with a small, pouty moue.

"Now, if only I had a conscience," he said with a cheeky grin, "a comment like that might elicit some guilt."

"You're impossible." She smiled. "But very, very sexy. Although that shouldn't give you any leverage."

"You talk too much," he announced, pulling her forward, sinking to his knees before her.

"Maybe this won't be too difficult after all," she

observed, a mischievous light in her eyes. "You on your knees conjure a number of pleasant possibilities."

"There's a certain cachet to submission, I agree," he said blandly.

"I dislike the word submission."

He smiled. "I apologize." Inserting a hand between her legs, he eased them apart in a decidedly unapologetic way.

There was no point in being contentious over such a simple task, but when the damp cloth touched her sensitive cleft, she steeled herself to withstand the delectable sensation. She had no intention of submitting as Sam had so insolently suggested. But as he parted her swollen flesh and delicately slid the cool cloth over her throbbing tissue, she had to forcibly suppress her gasp. "This won't take long," he said as though he'd not seen her moment of constraint.

He shouldn't be kneeling at her feet, naked and aroused and much too close, when she should be thinking about leaving. But he was like forbidden fruit—intemperate, profligate, infinitely seductive. Instead of resisting temptation, she was literally trembling for him.

Undisturbed by moral issues, innately single-minded when it came to sex, Sam was aware of her arousal, taking note of her breathing, of the small rigidity in her spine. He took his time rinsing and squeezing out the cloth before brushing the cool linen over her inner thighs, deliberately prolonging the procedure, then finally touching her where she most wanted to be touched. Despite her efforts to resist, her body wouldn't cooperate—a pearly fluid diffused the pinkness of her labia. She was wet with desire.

"What am I going to do with you?" he asked, discarding the cloth, inserting one finger into the slickness of her vagina, gently stroking the sensitive flesh. "You're always ready for fucking." Reaching up, he stroked one of her nipples with his other hand, gripped it lightly, and tugged on it until she was forced to look at him. "Tell me, what am I going to do with you when all you want to do is fuck?"

She wouldn't answer save for the fevered look in her eyes, his touch inside and out kindling her ready sexual appetite.

"Just say the word and I'll give you cock," he whispered.

She glanced at his upthrust penis, turgid with pulsing veins, and drew in a sharp breath.

"You like it, don't you." Releasing her, he held his erection away from his body and ran the wetness from his finger around the swollen, gleaming head.

Only the sound of her agitated breathing broke the silence.

It was a contest of wills or willpower—mutual and perhaps more evenly matched than not, for the notorious Ranelagh had finally met a woman he couldn't ignore.

Headstrong, unfamiliar with restraint, he gave in to impulse first. Abruptly shoving the bowl aside, he surged to his feet and grasped Alex by the shoulders. Twirling her around, he placed her hands on the chair arms and pushed her over so her pink bottom was raised conveniently high—his for the taking.

Heedless of all but urgency, oblivious to issues of submission or command, he peremptorily entered her.

The swift, plunging invasion drew a shocked gasp of affront. "Damn you," she spat out, struggling to rise. "I hate you."

"Sure you do, and I hate fucking you too," he growled, holding her down with a firm grip, ramming in so hard, she was propelled forward by the force.

Abruptly grasping her hips, he jerked her back, the brute, unguarded impact buffeting their senses into a momentary breathlessness. When his brain began functioning again, he gruffly muttered, "Jesus, you feel . . . good."

"You're a bloody brute. . . ." But the rancor was modulated by a heated undertone.

"And I should cut and run while I can." The powerful muscles of his legs flexed, but he didn't leave. He held her motionless instead and deftly rotated his hips so they both felt a seething delirium in the pleasure centers of their minds.

"I don't know what to do," she breathed, half angry, conflicted, ravenous.

"Stay with me," he whispered, bending to kiss the velvety softness of her neck, the controversy of their mutual obsession muted by tumultuous sensation, the rhythm of their bodies exquisitely matched.

He continued to hold her captive, but she no longer decried her submission because carnal lust blurred her edgy discontent and orgasmic excess brought her to the verge of fainting. When he carried her back to the bed after a time and gently set her down, he settled lightly above her, overwhelmed by rare emotion. "Just one more time?" he breathed, feeling unquenchable.

"No . . . no . . . no."

"You always say no." He slid inside her, felt her welcoming flesh give way, and shut his eyes.

Lavish, soul-stirring ardor engulfed her. She was out of her depth, she realized, so far out of her depth she could no longer clearly distinguish the perimeters of the real world. It frightened her to be so enslaved to a man's touch. Could one become addicted to this glorious lust . . . to Ranelagh's inexhaustible stamina? Could she become servile to her inordinate need for orgasms?

But Sam moved just then in a particularly persuasive way, in a rare and refined demonstration of ultimate penetration, and raw, acute feeling washed over her in powerful waves, inundating apprehension.

Moments later, when she was able to breathe again, when she'd forcibly gathered her senses into a measure of order, she whispered, "I can't keep doing this—every day, every night—I'm feeling . . . out of control."

"I like . . . the way I feel." Lying beside her, his arms were flung over his head, his eyes half shut.

"We should take a small hiatus. . . ."

"No."

At the curtness of his tone, she turned her head on the pillow and looked at him. "No?"

"No, not now. No, not tomorrow. No, not next week." His eyes opened fully, he turned his head, held her gaze, and smiled. "And I mean that in the nicest way."

"Now, if only you had the power to enforce those pronouncements."

"I don't think it takes power." His voice was whisper soft. "Do you?"

She couldn't help but smile. "I concede on that count, my fine stud. However," she said with a new determination, well aware how predaceous his allure and how weak her defenses, "I can't just allow myself to be swept along on a tidal wave of lust. I have a very busy life." Her voice was brisk, as if her tone might bolster her resolve. "A life, I might add, composed of a multitude of activities other than making love."

"Why not take a hiatus from that instead of the other way around," he suggested calmly.

"I wish I could."

"Then, do it."

"It's not that easy."

"Of course it is. You're in charge of your own life."

"Sam, really, consider. I can't simply stay in bed with you until . . . when? Such a time as you become bored with me?"

"Is that what you're driving at? You don't bore me in the least. In fact, I'm perilously aware of my attraction to you. You have my full attention, darling. My word on it."

"You don't understand. Much as I love to make love to you, I can't devote my life to pleasure. It's too—too . . . frivolous, for one thing."

His dark brows rose in arched query. "Is life supposed to be unconditionally dutiful?"

"I hardly think you need worry about that."

Rising onto his elbows, he directed a skeptical gaze her way. "Are we comparing obligations in our lives?"

"No, of course not. I didn't mean to imply that."

"Do you think you perform more good deeds than I?"

"Outside of bed, you mean?"

"Very amusing. Why don't I have Patrick give you a list of my charities and the various boards I sit on, and you can relax."

Reaching up, she touched his cheek. "I'm not taking issue with your goodness—in any number of realms. I'm trying to deal with my own unease. I don't like to be so enamored. I don't like to think of you day and night. I don't want to want you every waking minute."

"Why not? I feel the same way."

"Because . . ." She hesitated, struggling to reconcile a level of wistful dreams with reality. "I haven't lived my life like you," she began to explain, trying to be diplomatic and honest at the same time. "I don't mean it in a pejorative way. I mean only, until I met you, I considered myself a rational person. I've never been impulsive or so . . . so—physically tempted. My decisions have been based on practicality and logic."

"Like marrying two old men."

"They were good men and very good to me."

"And I'm not?"

She smiled. "You're very good, darling. In a thousand different ways. In so many ways, I feel myself losing my perspective. And that loss and my loss of reason makes me uncomfortable. All I'm asking is for a brief hiatus from—"

"Fucking? I don't want to."

"But I do."

He sat up and scowled at her. "Jesus, Alex, you're asking a lot. How long a hiatus?"

"A few days, that's all."

"*Days!* I'll go crazy." The tacit exclusivity in his reply suddenly struck him, and he softly swore.

She lay very still. "I'm not asking."

He swore again, his brows drawn together in a frown, not sure he was willing to agree. After a small silence, he finally muttered, "Very well," because regardless of the unnerving implications in his need, he wanted her more. "But only for a day."

"Three days."

"I could lock you up here and no one would be the wiser." She looked so lush and inviting lying there, he was sorely tempted.

"My father and Loucas would be over by tomorrow."

"I could take you to my country house."

"I'm sure they know where that is as well."

"I'll take you abroad."

"Darling, please, don't be childish."

He grimaced. "I don't like this idea."

She smiled. "I'm not forcing *you* to do anything. I simply need some respite for myself."

"Don't split hairs," he grumbled. "Your respite becomes mine. Oh, hell—two days, then, but not a minute more. And don't try to tell me you're any less used to having your way."

She couldn't in good conscience disagree, when she'd been fiercely independent all her life. "Two days, then. Thank you for your understanding."

He gave her a black look. "It's going to be hell."

"It's an opportunity for us both to clear our heads."

"My head is *very* clear."

"Then, it's an opportunity for me."

"What the hell do you have to do?"

"Catch up on all the appointments I've missed since I met you."

"You needn't sound so cheerful." He was astonished at his discontent. As though he hadn't lived his entire adult life fleeing entanglements.

"I *will* miss you."

"You'd better not see Harry."

"I have no intention of seeing Harry. Does that mean you'll be celibate as well?"

It took a stunned moment to digest the word celibate, and then another moment to fully absorb it, and a moment more to persuade himself he could withstand the shock to his system. "I suppose if you can, I can."

"You sound unsure."

"Not *unsure* precisely."

"Unwilling?"

"I don't think so."

"How reassuring you are."

"Give me time to—"

"Fully understand what it means?"

"I suppose." His shoulder rose in an unconscious shrug. "It's in the way of an aberration for me, that's all. But I'll play golf while you're gone. That way I won't drink too much and, well, never mind. You did say two days."

"Just two days."

"No, it's two *whole* days," he countered. "What happens if I can't wait?"

"You have to wait."

He softly growled. "I wouldn't do this for anyone else, you know."

Her purple eyes held a gleam of amusement. "I'm flattered."

He suddenly grinned. "You should be. Now, when do these two days begin? I mean . . . would we have time now for—"

"I'd love to if I didn't have to meet my mother at our school's musical competition. And believe me," she said with a smile, "I'd much rather stay here with you than listen to her ring a peal over my head."

"I'll go with you. We can bend the rules if I don't touch you, can't we?"

"If you're interested in bending the rules," she suggested, "after we see my mother, we could have tea with *your* mother."

A low groan greeted her remark.

"That's what I thought," she said briskly, sitting up. "Why don't I meet you back here in two days."

"No Harry," he reminded her.

"No women."

He didn't answer, but then, he took orders poorly. He said instead, "If you leave now, the two days will begin that much sooner. I'll help you dress."

"Have you no patience?" she teased.

"Do I look like I have patience?"

"Actually, you look slightly *impatient*," she judged, her gaze on his beautiful erection.

"It wouldn't take long," he whispered.

"I don't know. . . ."

"Another few minutes won't matter. . . ."

But it turned out to be much longer, because pleasure wasn't so easily relinquished, nor desire curtailed, particularly in two people who had found a rare, enchanting Cytherea in a previously commonplace world. She said, "I have to go" twice, then twice more, to which the viscount always replied, "Yes" and then kissed her again. Or made love to her again . . . or made her laugh again.

She was very late leaving.

Chapter 26

I t's about time," her mother hissed as Alex slipped into the seat beside her.

"I'm sorry. I overslept."

Her mother's examining gaze swept her. "Overslept indeed," she said, tight-lipped. "I can still smell his cologne."

Already flushed from hurrying to dress and reach the school, Alex turned a deeper shade of red and quickly looked away, directing her attention to the stage. She tried to concentrate on the youngest children, who were lined up in two wobbly rows, singing. The sight of their scrubbed, cherubic faces brought an instant smile to her lips, and her mother's displeasure took second place in her thoughts. Before long she was humming along to the familiar tune.

As she watched the various classes perform, each child as familiar to her as any of those in her family, she realized how much the school meant to her, how her interest went well beyond charity. These wonderful children had come to fill a void in her life, brought her joy . . . gave her life meaning.

As a child of her own would.

She caught her breath at the astonishing thought. Did she truly want a child, or was this sudden perception predicated more on her reaction to the birth of Tina's baby? Or did her powerful new feelings for Sam prompt this shocking notion? Whatever the reason, it was impossible, of course. As impossible as were such wistful yearnings in relation to Sam Lennox, she firmly reminded herself. Turning her attention back to the stage, she listened to the children's clear, bright voices, their song one of joy and thanksgiving. How much she had to be thankful for herself, she realized, mindful of the great bounty in her life.

Even if she had no children of her own.

She'd been sensible to insist on this small hiatus, she decided. Two days without Sam was exactly what she needed to regain her equanimity.

After the program was over, in an effort to repress any further ill-starred fantasies, she threw herself into the reception as though she were personally responsible for everyone's good cheer. She spoke to each child and teacher, helped ladle out the punch, handed out cookies and sandwiches, gave a short speech before the prizes were awarded, and flitted from group to group with a nervous energy that didn't go unnoticed.

In search of normalcy, feeling the need to escape her thoughts, she immersed herself in the full gamut of activities.

Her mother remarked on her restlessness as they left the building. "I'm not sure you're required to bring happiness to every last person in that school. You looked positively giddy today."

"I like to make people happy. Is that a crime?" Alex's tone was defensive. "And if you don't mind, Mother, I'm not in the mood for chastisement."

Mrs. Ionides surveyed her daughter. "Did the viscount put you in poor humor?"

"No, Mother, he didn't. If you want to ask me something, just ask it. There's no need to beat about the bush."

The two women stood at the curb before their waiting carriages.

"He'll never take you home to meet his family."[8]

Her mother's remark struck a nerve regardless of the fact that Alex had no wish to meet Sam's parents. "It's not a problem for me," she said.

"They look down on families like ours."

"I understand; it's their loss. But you don't want to meet Ranelagh either, so you're hardly one to take offense."

"I never said that."

Alex softly exhaled. "If not precisely in those words, you've insinuated as much in every nuance of our conversations since I met him. Or would you like me to bring him to dinner?"

Her mother opened her mouth to speak, then shut it again.

"There, you see."

"Your father wouldn't allow it."

"Should I ask him?"

"He's very busy right now," Euterpe replied stiffly.

Alex smiled faintly. "Don't worry, Mother, I won't be bringing Sam to dinner. Now, if you'll excuse me, I have some work to do."

"With him, I suppose."

"No, alone. Does that make you happy?"

"If you married Constantine and gave me grandchildren, I'd be happy."

"How about just the grandchildren without the marriage?" Alex offered lightly. "How would that be?"

"How dare you even suggest such a thing! Your father will hear of this, young lady . . . such absolute foolishness! I'm going to pretend you never said anything so outrageous. I told your father his leniency toward you would—"

Her mother was still sputtering when Alex stepped into her carriage.

Alex went directly home, fatigued after her sleepless night, weary in spirit as well—totally unsure of what had been until yesterday clear and unequivocal goals in her life.

The moment she closed the front door, she began undressing, leaving a trail of clothing behind in her passage to her bedroom. When she reached her bed, she dropped onto the mattress in a sprawl, pulled a cover over her, and within seconds was fast asleep.

In the days since she'd met Ranelagh, she'd barely slept, and while he may have been accustomed to a schedule of continuous sex, she was not.

Chapter 27

*A*lready experiencing withdrawal symptoms, Sam couldn't have slept had a gun been put to his head, and knowing he had to keep busy if he were to last two days without Alex, he went to Eddie's house, dragged him out of bed, and insisted on his company.

They'd played eighteen holes under an overcast sky and, against Eddie's protests, began a second eighteen midafternoon, despite a light rain falling.

At the third hole, with the wind picking up, Eddie tossed his club at his caddy and hotly declared, "I'm done, Sam. If you have to keep your mind off the lovely widow by wearing yourself out on the golf course, I don't have to be part of your damned abuse. Not only did you wake me up at the crack of dawn—"

"It was eleven."

"As I was saying—the crack of dawn, not to mention you've dragged me up and down this damned course for hours without so much as a drink."

"I can't drink."

Eddie spun around, his gaze incredulous. "You're dying."

Sam handed his club to his caddy and waved the two lads away. "I'm not dying," he said calmly, "but I sort of promised Alex I wouldn't sleep with anyone for these two days, so I want to stay sober." He shrugged. "In the interests of caution."

Sam's explanation had done nothing to diminish Eddie's incredulity. Wide-eyed, he said, "You may not be dying, but you're obviously delirious. What do you mean, you promised her not to sleep with anyone?"

"Just that."

"You mean you're sleeping alone tonight?"

Sam nodded.

"And tomorrow night as well?"

"Yes."

Eddie softly whistled. "Damn, she must be good. How long has it been, Sammy, since you spent two nights alone?"

"Don't make it sound so unusual. I spend time at my country home and at my hunting lodge and I don't necessarily have female guests."

"But your pretty maidservants draw straws for you, if I recall. Or doesn't that count?"

The viscount had the grace to look disconcerted. "You've made your point. But I'll manage just fine for two days."

"Provided you don't drink and you wear yourself to exhaustion on the golf course."

"Something like that," Sam said with a grin.

"Well, I'm going to the clubhouse and get myself a brandy before I die of a chill." Eddie offered his friend a sardonic glance and began walking away. "Since you're in love, you may watch me drink."

Sam caught Eddie's arm and brought him to a standstill. "For the record," he said carefully, "I'm not in love."

"Good. Then you won't mind joining me at Hattie's tonight. She has a dozen new ladies in from Paris—your favorite type, as I recall."

"Maybe some other time."

"Bloody hell! I don't believe it!" Eddie made a cross with his forefingers as though warding off evil spirits. "I bloody hope whatever you have doesn't contaminate me."

"Alex is very nice. That's all."

"Really. Nice. I hadn't heard you refer to sex as nice before. Tell me how it's nice. Tell me what the hell she has, Sammy. Come, come, aren't we old friends? Describe this fucking rarity"—he grinned— "or rare fuck, because I'm all ears."

"Not a chance."

"Are we going to hear wedding bells?" Eddie mocked.

"What do you think," Sam said brusquely.

"Thank God. It would shake my principles to the core."

"You don't have any principles."

"Well, it would scare the hell out of me."

As it turned out, the men didn't stay long at the clubhouse. Eddie wasn't able to change Sam's mind, and after a period of cajoling and grumbling, he gave up trying to coax Sam into having a drink, and they returned to London.

"I hope you come to your senses," Eddie said as he exited Sam's carriage. "Do you think you should see a doctor?"

"I'm not sick, but thank you for your concern."

"It's not concern so much as a matter of survival. I don't want to think this could happen to me." He shuddered.

"I'll keep my distance," Sam promised with a faint smile. "Give my regards to the girls at Hattie's."

"I'll tell them you're in love."

"Tell them whatever you want."

And that casual reply more than anything alarmed Eddie.

Chapter 28

It wasn't a good night for Sam. He tossed and turned, rose a dozen times to have a drink, decided against it in each instance, finally dressed before dawn, and rode out to the site of his new golf course to keep his mind off what he couldn't have for two more days yet.

Watching the sun rise from the crest of a hill, he surveyed the broad green sweep of land that would one day be as perfect a course as man and nature could devise. But rather than the usual sense of satisfaction such contemplation provoked, he instead felt distrait and edgy.

He swore softly, and his mount turned its head in response. Sam stroked his horse's strong neck. "It's not you, Duff. I'm just losing my mind," he told the animal, a faint grimace lifting his mouth. "Over a damned woman." No matter the softness of his tone, the thought was staggering. He wondered how he was going to reclaim his life—or, more to the point, get through the next two days.

Alex had slept the sleep of exhaustion, and when she woke she was startled to see it was midmorning. Throwing off the covers, she quickly rose and dressed, keeping one eye on the clock. She had only minutes to spare before her first scheduled meeting at the Kensington Museum, where she was a member of the board. After that, she'd promised to listen to proposals for the new children's wing at St. Anne's Hospital.

Hurrying to her carriage house behind the garden, she felt a renewed sense of purpose in her return to the advocacy that was such a large part of her life. There was enormous satisfaction in helping others, in having her wealth serve the public good, and while the pleasure Sam offered couldn't be faulted, there was more to life than self-indulgence.

Especially with a man like Sam, whose self-indulgence was legend.

Breathing in the sweet-scented air of her garden, she looked forward to her responsibilities and obligations. Should she put all her diplomatic skills to use, she might convince old Mr. Tristam that buying the Courbet painting of two half-dressed women in a wooded landscape wouldn't condemn him to an eternity in hell. And with luck, the young architect of the new children's wing would have finished his drawings so she could finally move on to the building of it.

Since her trust fund was the principal financing behind the project, she had the last word. Something much less certain in her relationship with Sam. She smiled. Obviously, he didn't understand how often she exercised her authority in the world at large.

When she returned to her studio late that afternoon, the Courbet painting finally acquired and the children's wing scheduled for groundbreaking the following week, Alex was in fine spirits. She'd stopped for flowers to celebrate her successful day. Walking up the path to her front door, her arms full of delphiniums and white roses, she was surprised to see Ben seated on her doorstep.

"Harry sent me," he said quickly, rising to his feet. "I hope you don't mind. Harry said he'd meet me here."

Alex took note of the satchel at his feet. "He's coming here to paint?"

"He thought we could finish the sketches from yesterday. But if it's inconvenient . . ."

The young man looked embarrassed, his downcast gaze almost servile. Alex immediately attempted to put him at ease. "It's not inconvenient at all. I'm finished with my appointments for the day. Please, come in." She smiled. "I'd enjoy painting after a busy day."

"Harry should be here soon," the young man offered, picking up the satchel. "He asked me to bring some new robes."

After unlocking the door, Alex led the way into her

studio. "Let me put these flowers in water and I'll be right with you. If you'd like to change." She waved toward a doorway. "Use my study."

When she returned a few minutes later, Ben, garbed in a gleaming cerulean blue djellaba, was seated on a chair conveniently placed in front of her easel. It was impossible not to be impressed by the quality of the glamorous silk garment. Alex complimented him on his robe.

"My father gave me this before I left home. I think of him every time I wear it." Sadness overcame his features and tears welled in his eyes.

"You must miss your family," Alex said kindly.

He nodded. "After the earthquake I had to leave the village to help support them. London can be lonely."

"I imagine it can. Are you hoping to return soon?"

"Not soon, but eventually, God willing," he said. "Harry promised to find me more work modeling so I can earn extra money. Most of my pay from the museum goes directly home."

"Harry can be depended on, you can be sure. Would you like something to eat before we begin? I think I missed lunch." She hadn't, but the young man didn't look as though he had an abundance of food.

"If you don't mind, miss. I haven't eaten since yesterday."

"You poor man. Come to the kitchen. I'll find us something."

In short order, Ben was seated across from Alex at a large monk's table, an array of food before him.

While he ate, Alex kept him company with a slice of Madeira cake and a glass of hock, and between mouthfuls he gave an account of his family and the village poverty that had brought him to England.

It was a poignant tale typical of so many immigrants to the city, one she'd heard many times before. As the story of his plight unfolded, Alex offered not only sympathy but in the end also a well-paying job at her father's warehouse. "You could still help at the museum. I'm sure my father would allow you flexibility in your hours, and you'd be able to send more help home to your family."

Ben's eyes filled with tears again. "Thank you, thank you, kind lady." His voice vibrated with emotion. "It was the most fortunate of days when I met young Harry and you."

"We're more than happy to help. Once Harry arrives, he'll tell you himself."

"Bless you, my lady." Ben's bottom lip trembled. "You are our benevolent angel."

"Well, well, well . . . ," a lazy voice intoned. "What do we have here?"

Alex spun around at the low drawl, saw Sam looming large in the doorway, and immediately frowned. "What are *you* doing here?"

"You probably should run along." Sam gestured at the man seated across from Alex. "And tell your sister to stay out of my life."

Alex's gaze swiveled to Ben and then back to Sam. "What's going on here?" A hint of temper vibrated in her voice. "What sister? Ben's modeling for me."

"I'll bet he is."

"You know him?"

"You might say so. And I doubt Mahmud's up to any good."

"His name is Ben."

"Today maybe." Sam snapped his fingers at the young man and indicated the door with a jerk of his thumb. "Get out, Mahmud."

As the young man scrambled to his feet, Alex put up her hand to stop him. "You needn't leave," she said, taking issue with Sam's peremptory commands. "I won't let Lord Ranelagh hurt you."

"You decide, Mahmud," Sam gritted out, soft menace in his tone. "Do you think this lady can save you?"

Slipping around the end of the table, Mahmud bolted for the back door, and a moment later silence filled the kitchen.

Alex rose and faced Sam, her annoyance plain. "Would you care to tell me what that was all about?"

"Would you care to tell me what you were doing with him?" Sam returned, a minute edge to his voice.

He filled the doorway, his broad shoulders brushing the jambs. Resentful of this unwanted intervention, she said, "You're not my keeper. You have no right to question me, and I *don't* like you barging into my house. I particularly don't like you frightening my friends away."

"He's not your friend. He's Farida's brother and he's not here because he likes the color of your eyes. Let me rephrase that. If he likes the color of your eyes, you're damned lucky I showed up when I did."

"He was modeling for Harry. He's perfectly benign, and don't think just because your liaisons come to disastrous ends that Ben, or Mahmud, or whatever his name was, would necessarily be a danger to me."

Sam blew out an impatient breath. "That brother-and-sister duet are predators, and danger follows in their wake as sure as the sun rises in the east."

"I beg to differ with you. He's not a predator. For your information, he comes from a village near Damascus that was nearly destroyed by an earthquake and he's working very hard to support his entire family on very little money, and—"

"He was born and raised in Cairo."

"How do you know?"

"I know because Farris had them investigated. They're thieves. They have been most of their lives, and while I don't question the motives behind their life of crime, I'm done paying for it. They have orders to leave London by week's end or lose the settlement I've agreed to give them. Is that a clear enough picture?"

He took a step into the room. Alex unconsciously braced herself. "Very clear," she replied stiffly, irritated to have been momentarily intimidated. "But it still doesn't give you the right to intrude into my house and life. This is *my* home, Sam, and even if you hadn't disregarded our agreement, I don't appreciate your barging in."

"I saved you from a thief, possibly more. Most would thank me."

"Thank you," she said coolly. "Now, I'd appreciate it if you'd leave."

"What if I said I didn't want to?"

"Then, you'd be no better than he. I don't want anyone taking advantage of me."

"Am I taking advantage of you?" His voice had suddenly gone soft.

"Yes." She steeled herself against the silken accents, against potent memory, against his seductive gaze. "Yes, you are. I prefer my privacy."

"What the hell does that mean?"

She straightened her shoulders. "It means I can't—I won't allow you to take over my life."

"And I've done that?"

"Completely. Since I met you, I haven't done anything but—"

"Make love?"

She flushed crimson, but her voice, when she spoke, was firm. "I can't afford to keep doing that."

"Why not? You liked it."

"It's not enough. Don't you understand?"

"No, I don't. Explain to me why you won't do something you like."

"Explain to me why making love is all you do."

"It's not all I do."

Her brows rose. "You're simply misunderstood by the world at large. Is that it?"

"I don't care what the world thinks."

"Obviously. And perhaps there's where our visions differ. I do care—"

This time his brows rose. "Really. I don't know too many ladies who pose nude."

"Let's just say I care in my own way," she said,

impassioned about her freedom. "And I also care about a great number of things other than my own pleasure."

"Don't suddenly turn Puritan on me. I know you better."

"You couldn't wait even two days."

"Waiting somehow makes me a better person?"

"You could have done it for me. Instead, you chose to indulge yourself as usual—as always."

"Look, I don't want to fight," he said quietly.

"And I don't want to give up my life." She lifted her chin. "I've come too far to relinquish my independence for—what? Your capricious desires?"

His eyes suddenly turned chill. "Nobody asked you to give up your life," he said curtly. "And pleasure isn't necessarily evil, despite your newfound virtue. You're reading way the hell too much into this, sweetheart." He nodded, a brisk, dismissive gesture. "It's been interesting." His cool gaze raked her from head to foot. "I'll give you that." And then he turned and walked away.

When the door shut a moment later, the soft sound was utterly final.

Chapter 29

*W*ell, that little scene demonstrated how useless it was to try to please a woman, Sam decided angrily, striding away from Alex's studio. He hadn't even had a drink since last he saw her—not with Eddie, not the previous night, nor had he considered seeing another woman, all in an effort to meet some damned exacting standard of some dutiful bitch who had just told him she wasn't changing her life for him.

As if he *wanted* her to change her life for him!

As if he wanted more than the pleasure of her damned hot body!

Standing at the curb, he surveyed the empty street, begrudging his stupidity in sending his carriage away. Who would think she didn't want to have sex when she'd been having sex with him for nearly a week now. Silly him. He should have known she was in a new celibate phase. If he was a fortune-teller, maybe he might have known, he fumed, turning toward the park. Well, he wished her pleasure in her cold, chaste bed. There were plenty of other women in London who were more than willing.

But he'd not walked far before he found himself wondering just how long her bed *would* remain chaste, and considering the passionate nature of their relationship the last few days, that disastrous thought refused to be dislodged from his brain. She didn't seem like the type who would go long without sex and, of course, there was always damned Harry with his soulful eyes just waiting to console her. *Merde* and damn and bloody hell. It wasn't a pleasing prospect. Especially knowing how unbelievably hot she could be. Especially after having screwed her almost constantly the past week. Dammit, he didn't like to think of her with Harry—or whomever—and for a flashing moment he considered pirating her away to some distant place where he could keep her for himself. Cooler reason almost immediately put period to such a ludicrous notion, and he instead surveyed the street ahead, looking for a pub.

He needed a drink badly.

Alex was equally distrait, but in a less predaceous way. She didn't distribute blame or wish to spirit him away for herself alone. Instead, she wished it were possible to have him without compromising her entire life. It wasn't, of course. Men like Sam were used to making demands, used to having their wishes fulfilled, familiar only with compliance. She couldn't so easily acquiesce, although she realistically understood he hadn't asked her for anything more than the pleasure of her company.

Perhaps *she* was the one who wanted more, and for a contemplative moment she considered the astonishing thought.

Did she want him for more than sex?

Did it matter if she did, she sensibly posed a second later, considering his manner of living?

The answer to that question was negative in the extreme, and setting aside any further flights of fancy, she decided what she needed was a good book, her own company, and an evening of quiet to bring her life back into balance. She glanced at the clock. Four-thirty. It was going to be a long night.

It turned out to be an equally long night for Sam. He sat alone in his study, making Owens extremely nervous because he stopped drinking before nine, refused food or visitors, even turning Eddie away, and when Owens peeked in from time to time, his master was busy writing at his desk until well past midnight.

It was enough to cause alarm.

"I told you it wouldn't work," Mahmud said for the tenth time that night, still frightened by his narrow escape. "I wish you'd stop scheming and let us go home to Egypt."

"We will just as soon as I exact a last measure of revenge, dear brother," Farida insisted, lying beside him with her arms crossed under her head. "We still have two days before we have to leave, and I want to make Ranelagh miserable. And don't say taking his money will bother him, because he'll hardly notice so small a sum. In fact, he won't notice it at all!"

"If you think my sleeping with Miss Ionides would have made him angry, I think you're mistaken. Anyway," he muttered, "they were fighting when I left."

"Of course it would have made him angry, you stupid fool. He would have been humiliated to find you in her bed."

"I wonder if you're deluding yourself. I doubt the man can be humiliated by a woman. He's indifferent to them, if you ask me."

"I would have found it a charming fillip, if nothing else—a little frosting on the cake of vengeance, but since the ruse is exposed—"

"I don't know why you thought it wouldn't be if he's been sleeping with her all week. . . ."

"Darling"—she turned to him with a feline smile—"you simply don't understand where best to prick a man's pride. Nevertheless," she added, a new briskness to her voice, "since we can't mortify him with his newest bit of fluff, I was thinking, maybe we could take that gold Ptolemy necklace he has in his collection. I always wanted it anyway."

"Lord, Fari! Your greed is going to land you in jail."

"I think you've lost your nerve, darling," she replied, one dark brow arched in mockery.

"You didn't have him look at you the way I did. He's very, very large."

"I'll just do it myself," she said. "As usual."

"If you think to shame me," Mahmud said with a grin, "you're years too late. I wish you luck, sweet sister. And if you end up in prison, don't expect me to visit you."

"I have no intention of going to prison. Ranelagh's Egyptian collection isn't even locked up. He keeps it in his study, for heaven's sake. And the terrace doors are very convenient."

"You're mad even to consider going to his house."

"He owes me," Farida stated. "I intend to collect."

Chapter 30

The next morning Sam emerged from his study at six, called for breakfast, handed three notes to Owens to have delivered, and went upstairs to bathe and change.

The names on the envelopes caused a deal of gossip below stairs, and various possibilities were bruted about concerning the viscount's intent. Farris arrived first, only minutes after seven, and was ushered into the breakfast room, where Sam was well into his morning repast. The servants were dismissed, and try as they could, the conversation inside was too muted to be heard through the door. But Farris was beaming when he left an hour later and, for that matter, so was the master.

Owens was instructed to see that the cook prepared an opulent tea for ten o'clock. "And I want flowers in the reception rooms," Sam added. "Something summery."

"Summery?" Owens wondered with raised brows

as he related the orders to those below stairs a short time later. "Have you ever heard the master so much as mention flowers before?"

"He don't seem even to notice them," the housekeeper said. "Except that once when he accidentally knocked over the vase in the hall with his walking stick."

"Did he say who were coming to tea?" the cook asked.

"No, but Farris has already come and gone, and since the other two notes were to Mr. Ionides and the Archbishop of London, it's either one or the other or both."

"The archbishop. I hope he ain't dying," one of the footmen repeated, his concern having been expressed in their earlier conversation about Sam's letters.

"He's healthy as an ox," Owens replied, although the butler had reservations about the viscount's mental health after his unusual behavior last night. "But we haven't much time to put the reception rooms in readiness." He surveyed the servants. "His lordship said opulent, and opulent he shall have."

Pandias Ionides, accompanied by his wife, arrived at Ranelagh House precisely at ten. Although Sam's note had been addressed only to him, Euterpe had said, "I'm coming with you whether you like it or not, whether Lord Ranelagh likes it or not, and don't look at me like that, Pandias. Whatever he has to say, I want to hear."

Sam entered the drawing room, where his guests had been ushered only minutes after their arrival. He apologized for having kept them waiting, wished them good morning with a winning smile, and with considerable graciousness and charm offered the hospitality of his house.

Euterpe had had every intention of expressing her displeasure with the viscount but found herself instead captivated by his extraordinary warmth, his smile, the very personal way he immediately engaged everyone in conversation. Soon she found herself telling him about the Camden Street School as if they were friends of long acquaintance. When Owens arrived with the tea tray and Sam asked whether she would pour, she preened and said, "I'd be delighted."

It required great restraint for her husband to observe his wife's abrupt volte-face without breaking into a grin, but he managed. And when Sam declared after tea had been poured, "I've asked you here for a reason," Pandias presented an equally bland countenance.

"I rather thought you had," he replied.

"I'm afraid it's a presumptuous request, but one I've mulled over all night and feel compelled to make. You know, Alex and I have been spending time together."

As Greek consul, Pandias had spent a lifetime in diplomacy, and his aplomb was well honed, but he was hard pressed to resist choking at the viscount's bluntness. "We were aware of it," he finally said in a near-normal tone.

"And while we haven't known each other for long—scarce a week—I find myself deeply attached to her."

Euterpe set down her teacup with a clang.

"The fact is," Sam went on quickly, as though he might change his mind if he didn't forge ahead, "I'd like to ask for your daughter's hand in marriage."

Euterpe gasped.

Sam smiled at her. "I realize it's unexpected."

"Have you spoken to Alex about this?" Pandias asked, concealing his surprise.

"No. I wished to respect the formalities. Alex has a sense of—er—decorum that I didn't want to offend."

"While I would willingly give you my permission, my Lord Ranelagh, there's no guarantee my daughter will agree with me. As you may know, she has a mind of her own."

"I'll speak to her," Mrs. Ionides interposed sharply. "Indeed, it's about time she listened to someone." She surveyed Sam with a critical eye. "At least you're not old."

Sam smiled. "I assume that's an asset?"

Euterpe sniffed. "Indeed it is."

"Then, I have your permission to present my suit to your daughter?"

"Of course." Pandias smiled. "Although this *is* sudden."

"I'm thirty-three. I don't consider it sudden at all."

The unspoken implication hung in the air, all the decades of women instantly springing to mind.

"If I may inquire," Euterpe said, impelled by more

significant considerations. "What do your parents think of your proposal?"

"I thought I'd speak with you first. And with all due respect, I'm well past the age when my parents have any say in my life."

Pandias frowned. "I gather they won't approve."

"I'm sorry. They may not. I hope that won't alter your opinion of me. I'm quite independent of my family. We don't get along as a rule."

"There you are, my darling boy!"

The Countess of Milburn sailed into the drawing room with Clarissa Thornton and Hedy Alworth in tow. "We were out to do a bit of shopping and decided to stop by for a moment and visit with—" Her eyes widened, she came to an abrupt stop, and stood gape-mouthed.

"Mother, may I introduce Mr. and Mrs. Ionides. Mr. and Mrs. Ionides, my mother, the Countess of Milburn, Lady Clarissa Thornton, and Miss Alworth," Sam offered calmly. "We were just having tea, Mother. Would you care to join us?"

She most certainly did not, but all her marriage plans for her son were clearly in jeopardy, so she quickly reconsidered. "Yes, certainly. You sit beside Sam, Clarissa," she ordered. "Clarissa tells me she has learned one of your favorite songs, dear," the countess added, smiling at her son. "She most particularly wishes to play it for you, so when your guests have left," she went on pointedly, "we can enjoy her superior talent."

"I didn't know you played the piano," Hedy said uncharitably, moving quickly toward the seat beside Sam, not about to allow Clarissa a prominent position or proximity to the man she coveted.

"I'm afraid the piano is in disrepair in any event," Sam lied, moving to the far side of the sofa as Hedy sat down. "A shame . . . dry rot, I believe."

"It's much too early for piano music anyway—" Hedy inched closer to him and smiled. "Don't you agree, my lord?"

Sam quickly rose. "Owens forgot the scones, when I particularly asked for them. Mrs. Ionides, would you do the honors?" He pushed the tea tray a fraction closer to her. "Owens!" And he moved toward his majordomo as Hedy's mouth settled into a pout.

Never say Euterpe was intimidated by anyone, regardless of their rank, and at that moment the feelings of a mother lioness were swelling in her breast. As if those insipid young ladies with blond curls and over-ruffled bonnets and gowns the countess was parading before her son were going to take the place of *her* daughter! She didn't care how blue the chits' blood; the young ladies plainly didn't hold a candle to her Alexandra. It was a completely partisan observation but deeply felt, and when Euterpe said in the warmest of accents, "I'd be honored, Lord Ranelagh," he understood even from the small distance that separated them that his suit for Alex's hand had met with favor.

The countess's fury showed in the high color on her cheeks. It was all she could do to keep from storming out of the room. But Clarissa Thornton had a dowry that would add considerably to the Lennox wealth, and even Hedy Alworth, although of lesser estate, would be preferable to a twice-married Greek vixen. The countess had every intention of seeing her son married to a suitable lady, and for that purpose she would stomach even foreign upstarts like the Ionideses.

"Apparently, I misunderstood about the scones," Sam prevaricated, returning to the group with a plate of small pastries. "Cakes anyone?" he offered, playing host as though he were familiar with the role, as though he handed cake plates around the table every day of his life.

"Oh, goody!" Clarissa squealed, reaching for a pastry.

Sam's wince wasn't visible, although the tick over his cheekbone came into play.

"I just love cakes anytime at all," Clarissa cooed, putting a second on her plate. "And chocolate icing! My favorite!"

Sam glanced at the clock on the mantel, wondering how soon he could send his mother and her friends away.

Taking note of Sam's reaction, Hedy said, "No, thank you," when she was offered the sweets. "I prefer more wholesome treats."

"Now you must promise to come up to Milburn Grange," the countess interposed, taking advantage of the public occasion to force her son's acquiescence. "Our midsummer ball will have any number of your old friends in attendance. Sam loves the country," she added, surveying the Ionideses with a smug smile. "You people prefer the City, I'm sure."

"We live in the country," Pandias replied quietly, restraining his wife with a hand on hers.

"The Ionideses have a lovely estate, Mother." Sam set the plate down and pulled up a chair beside Pandias. "I was there the other day to bring a gift to their new granddaughter."

Hedy gasped, the countess turned beet red, and Clarissa even stopped eating, recognizing the seriousness of such a visit.

A sudden hush filled the room.

"What the hell—is this a wake?" The Earl of Milburn stood on the threshold, his gaze sweeping the odd assortment of silent people in his son's drawing room, the most curious sight that of his son with a teacup in his hand.

"Good morning, Father. It's not a wake. We're having tea. Would you like to join us?"

"For tea? Are you daft?"

"Then, I'll wish you good morning."

"Not so fast, my boy. I'm here on an errand." He cast a disparaging eye on his wife. "Seems I'm not the only one."

"If you're staying, Father, may I introduce Mr. and Mrs. Ionides. I invited them over for tea."

"You don't say. Then, Eddie's story's true." The earl moved into the room, his gaze half narrowed as he surveyed the Ionideses. "Pleased to meet you," he said bluffly and jerked a small bow in their direction. "Seems my boy here has a tendre for your daughter.

That's what I came to find out, and there you have it." The earl turned his critical gaze on Sam. "Don't say you're marrying the gel?"

"If she'll have me."

Hedy spilled her cup of tea down her dress front.

The earl's brows flew up into his receding hairline.

"That's impossible," the countess bit off, tight-lipped and furious.

"Not at all."

"Of course it is. Our family has always—"

"I'm not concerned with what the family has done, Mother. My mind is made up."

"But what about me?" Clarissa wailed.

The earl rolled his eyes.

"I'm sure you'll find some young man who will better suit you," Sam asserted.

"But you're so very rich!"

Sam glanced at his mother and his mouth twitched, but he managed to keep from laughing. "Perhaps Mother can find you someone equally wealthy."

"I doubt that very much," Clarissa replied pettishly. "Everyone knows you have the most money."

"Damn you all to hell! Get your hands off me! I was just coming to say good-bye to the viscount!"

The woman's high-pitched screams echoed down the hall and into the drawing room, the cries not only near but notoriously familiar to Sam. He'd braced himself before Owens appeared in the doorway with Farida's wrists in a viselike grip.

Her shrieks came to a sudden stop when she saw

Sam. "I just came to say good-bye," she muttered sullenly. "This, this vicious *person* assaulted me."

"She was stealing your Egyptian necklace, sir. The gardener saw her enter your study and came to tell me."

"I wasn't stealing anything. I was *looking* at it."

"Thank you, Owens. Would you escort the lady out? And lock the study doors."

"Very good, sir."

"May you burn in hell, Ranelagh," Farida spat out. "May your flesh fall from your bones, may all the fiends of—"

Sam nodded at Owens to take her away, wondering as his majordomo pulled her screaming from the room how he was going to explain this to Alex's parents.

"Here's the bitch now! He'll leave you just like all the rest! Don't think you have what it takes to hold him, you redheaded witch—"

Farida's shrill voice echoed down the corridor and into the drawing room, precipitating a round of gasps. A second later Alex stopped in the doorway as so many before her had.

"Oh, my God," she whispered, her soft exclamation ringing out like a clarion call in the stillness of the room.

"Alex, come in!" her mother cried.

"Don't leave me! Don't do this! You know what he's like!" The unseen male voice interposed another level of shock until Harry suddenly appeared on the threshold and gave form to speculation.

Alex glanced at him, dumbfounded. Then her gaze swung back to her parents and she was almost paralyzed by the sight of so many unexpected people. She didn't know whether to run or take her chances where she stood.

Sam had jumped to his feet the moment he saw her and, undeterred even by Harry's arrival, he was at her side before she could make up her mind. "I know this looks daunting." He took her hand.

"A true understatement," she whispered.

"Alex, please—"

"You stay out of this," Sam ordered, scowling at Harry.

"Sam, be nice to him."

"I love her, so go home," Sam said to Harry, and turned back to Alex. "Is that nice enough?"

"You do?"

"Very much."

"Really?"

"Really."

"Alexandra!" Her mother beckoned her with a smile, a very smug smile that she bestowed in turn on each and every one at the tea table.

"Why are my parents—"

"I invited them . . . actually, I invited your father, but your mother came too; we're getting along very well."

Alex stared at him as though he'd suddenly sprouted a second head.

His brows flickered in sportive response. "Really, we are. Do you want to meet my parents? I wouldn't necessarily wish them on anyone, but since they're here and you're here"—he shrugged—"maybe we should get it over with."

"I'd rather hide."

"You have to meet them eventually."

"No I don't."

"You do if you're to be my wife."

"Obviously, this craziness has infected you."

He shook his head, glanced around at all the gawking faces, said, "If you'll excuse us a minute." Then he turned to Harry because Alex wished him to be nice and said politely, "We'll be right back." Tightening his grip on Alex's hand, he pulled her out into the corridor. "I was hoping to make this more romantic, but under the circumstances"—he nodded in the direction of the drawing room—"I'm afraid any romance is out of the question. Will you marry me? I have already asked your parents' permission." He grinned. "Please, just say yes and put me out of my misery."

She smiled. "I came over to apologize to you. To thank you for saving me from—whoever Ben was."

"I don't want an apology. I want you to answer my question. I've never really asked anyone to marry me before; I haven't slept all night for thinking of this."

"Do you actually know what you're doing? You don't have to marry me to sleep with me because I missed you dreadfully last night and I decided my pride could be sacrificed to pleasure."

"You *do* like pleasure."

"*Your* kind of pleasure."

"Good. Now, I'm going to need some kind of

commitment here, because I'm not the kind of man who deals with amour in a casual way."

She snorted.

"Not anymore anyway."

"Allow me to be skeptical."

"I swear, my word on it. Last night was the longest night of my life. You have to marry me."

"What about those little pink and white misses in your drawing room?"

"They're interested only in my bank account."

"They don't know what they're missing."

He grinned. "And you do."

"Which is my dilemma. I'm not sure I want to give it up."

"Good." His mouth twitched into a smile. "I'm waiting."

With a man like Ranelagh, every rational impulse urged her to say no. "Yes," she heard herself say.

"That's the nicest thing anyone's ever said to me," he breathed. "And I promise to say yes to you anytime you want."

Such delectable motivation was impossible to ignore. Whatever remaining caution she possessed fell away. "Do you think they might leave soon?"

"I can assure you they will," Sam said firmly. "Come, darling, let's make our announcement. And then I'll tell them we have to make our wedding arrangements and we need privacy."

"I don't want a big wedding." Someone else seemed to be speaking for her, each new statement more astonishing than the last.

"I have the archbishop waiting down the hall. Is that small enough?"

Suddenly her head was clear, and her gaze turned challenging. "You were pretty sure of yourself."

"Just hopeful. If you didn't say yes immediately, I was going to seduce you into saying yes."

"Do you think that would have worked?"

"Well," he said calmly, repressing his grin, "based on past experience . . ."

"Don't be smug."

"Never. I apologize. Please, can we get these people to leave? We can argue the nuances later. Please . . ."

He looked so contrite, it was impossible to refuse. Then he kissed her gently and said thank you with such unutterable sweetness that she was lost.

Chapter 31

*Once Sam made his marriage plans plain to his parents, they did what was required of them and acquiesced—with politesse if not grace.

Clarissa, Hedy, and Harry each took their congé with varying degrees of civility, or in Hedy's case with no civility at all. "Don't you care about Clara Bowdoin and her coming child?" she inquired spitefully. "Poor Clara will be heartbroken if you marry."

"Miss Alworth is leaving, Owens," Sam said grimly. "See her out."

Everyone pretended not to hear Hedy's continuing vituperation as she was pushed out of the room by Sam's butler. Clarissa and Harry abruptly took their leave, the two handsome blond youngsters deep in conversation as they left.

"Now then," Sam said into the awkward silence.

"Sam, perhaps we should wait," Alex suggested. "How can it matter if—"

"No."

She shot him a fractious glance. "Pardon me?"

"I meant, please . . . I'd rather not wait if you don't mind, darling." Ignoring their audience, he smiled for her alone. He pulled her aside, and said in the merest breath of sound, "I'm thirty-three, I love you, and I don't want to wait."

"What will people say?"

"Since when did you begin to care what people said?"

"Since I found myself in the middle of this scandalous occasion."

"What's scandalous? Your parents are here; my parents are"—he grinned—"unfortunately, also here. It's broad daylight in my drawing room and I'm offering you my heart, my name, my title, my life."

"I don't know," she equivocated. "Everything's so sudden. We met only a short while ago."

"You mean, we *finally* met. And need I remind you, I've never offered a woman what I just offered you, so consider not only the signal honor I've afforded you, but my consequence," he said with a grin. "Furthermore, if you're concerned about scandal, think how it will look if I pick you up, carry you down the hall to the archbishop, and *force* you to marry me."

"I'm well aware of your consequence, my lord, in any number of areas," she added with a half smile. "And you wouldn't dare force me."

"Knowing you"—his lashes drifted downward in suggestion—"I'm not so sure I'd have to, but if I did, I rather think your mother might help me."

Alex took momentary pause. "That in itself is terrifying, over and above any concern with scandal."

"This won't be scandalous in the least, darling. Our sudden marriage will be considered the most captivating of love matches." He winked. "I've been very hard to land, you know."

She made a moue. "How can I even be thinking of this when I said I'd never marry again?"

"Because you love me and can't live without me."

The simplicity of his reply couldn't be faulted, no more than its veracity. "I do love you," she replied softly, "and last night was the longest night of *my* life too."

Sam smiled faintly. "Then let's make your mother happy."

"And give yours an apoplexy."

He shrugged. "You can't please everyone."

A mischievous light brightened her eyes. "I suppose as long as I am . . ."

"And I . . ."

He bowed gracefully, offered her his arm, and turned to the remaining guests. "If you'd care to join us in our wedding . . ."

But Sam was no more tolerant of delay in his wedding ceremony than he was in any other particular of his life. As the archbishop droned on, Sam said, "Just move along to the end, if you please."

The clergyman's astonishment lasted only a second—the viscount's expression was clearly one of impatience. He quickly pronounced the couple before him man and wife.

Ignoring the archbishop's stern look, Sam thanked him warmly, lifted Alex into his arms, and turned to their parents. "If you'll excuse us now, we'll have you all to dinner once we return from our honeymoon."

"Honeymoon?" Alex blurted out. "I have appointments all week that—"

"Can be canceled." He was walking toward the door.

"Not all of them."

"Then, I'll let you out of bed occasionally to attend them," he said, exiting into the quiet of the hall.

"Don't think you can just—"

"Make love to you day and night?"

"No . . . I mean"—she took a small breath—"did you say day and night?"

He smiled. "And anytime in between . . ."

Her answering smile was instant. "With such cogent argument, how can I refuse?"

"How indeed, considering I'm so much larger than you—which you like, as I recall. Also, I'm intent on having my way with you—which you also like, *and* aside from all this talk of sex, I'm thinking at my age we really should seriously contemplate having a child right away. So you see, making love becomes not only a pleasure but a duty. Are you interested in being a dutiful wife?" he inquired, a wicked gleam in his dark gaze, his deep voice lush with suggestion.

"If you agree to be a dutiful husband."

"You have my word on it, Lady Ranelagh." He smiled. "I'll be diligent in my duty, zealous even."

"How nice."

"Almost as nice as my finding you," he replied, gracefully descending the main staircase as though she were weightless in his arms. "I bought Leighton's painting, by the way."

"Knowing him, it cost you dearly once he knew you wanted it."

"It was worth every shilling. I prefer my wife not be naked on the walls of Grosvenor House. And Cassels turned out to be cooperative too."

Her gaze took on a new directness. "I hope you're not implying censure of any kind."

"Not in the least, darling. Pose nude all you wish." He nodded at the footman opening the front door. "I'm not averse to having a very large personal collection of your modeling."

"Would you buy them all?"

"I already have." His shoes crunched on the gravel of the drive as he moved toward his waiting carriage.

Her eyes widened. "You're going to be very hard to handle."

Leaning through the open carriage door, he deposited her on the seat. "So will you."

She grinned. "It should be interesting."

"It'll be more than that, darling." His smile was tantalizingly close as he sat down beside her, his voice heated, low. "It will be pure, undiluted pleasure. . . ."

Epilogue

The viscount's family enlarged apace, with a baby born in each of the first three years of their marriage. The two boys and a girl brought enormous joy to Sam, who had given up the hope of ever having children. While Alex found that happiness wasn't so much in independence as in the heart of the whirlwind that made up her life as wife and mother. Her golf improved as Sam designed more courses; their children turned into youthful prodigies on the Lennox fairways. And the parents who had questioned the suitability of the match came to be the most partial advocates of the union—not to mention the most adoring of grandparents.

As a great admirer of his wife's artistic talents, Sam encouraged Alex to open a gallery of her own, and in the bargain he had his own private gallery of all her portraits he'd purchased. And now when Alex chose to sit as subject, in deference to the man she loved she posed in a modicum of clothing.

They would remark from time to time, with loving glances, how lucky they were to have run into each other that day at Leighton's. In the interests of harmony, Sam always refrained from mentioning he would have found her wherever she was. In those days, he'd been single-minded in pursuit.

With marriage, his former amusements were no longer of interest. He'd found love and contentment in full measure, and even the most skeptical in society were silenced. The Viscount and Viscountess of Ranelagh, despite the brevity of their courtship, were truly a love match.

It just went to show, the gossips would say—not without a certain incredulity—even the most unbridled libertine could be tamed.

NOTES

[1.]My heroine, Alex, is a combination of various women from history, but one of them was Angela Burdett-Coutts (1814–1906), the granddaughter of Thomas Coutts (1735–1822), who brought the banking house of Coutts and Co. to prominence and fortune in London. Thomas Coutts was married for almost forty years to Elizabeth Starkey, who bore him three daughters. But when Mrs. Coutts died in 1815, Thomas married the popular actress Harriet Mellon and left her the whole of his immense fortune and the directorship of his bank when he died in 1822. Harriet Mellon married in turn the Ninth Duke of St. Albans in 1827 and died ten years later. Harriet left the duke a modest fortune, but the bulk of her vast wealth and property went to Thomas Coutts's granddaughter, Angela Burdett, who then assumed the additional name and arms of Coutts.

Angela gave away immense sums of money to charities ranging from the endowment of colonial bishoprics to prizes for costermongers' donkeys; from the construction of model dwellings in the East End of London to the provision of drinking fountains for dogs. She was particularly concerned with the welfare of women and girls and established and maintained schools for them, as well as providing improved facilities for the training of girls in the national schools. For her wide-ranging philanthropies, she was created a baroness in her own right.

[2.]Princess Louise, the only one of Queen Victoria's daughters to be considered anything near a beauty, first met Joseph Edgar Boehm, a Hungarian born in Vienna who had been living in London for six years, when she started classes at the

National Art Training School. Fourteen years older than Princess Louise, married with a young family, the blue-eyed, curly-haired, tall, slim, and wiry-like "a battered soldier," sculptor-in-ordinary to the queen, had achieved fame in English court circles with his statue of Queen Victoria, unveiled at Windsor Castle in 1869.

Princess Louise was already involved with Boehm at this time, and their relationship was of such concern to the queen that she deliberately sought out an appropriate husband for her daughter. Eventually, the Marquess of Lorne, son of the Duke of Argyll, was chosen, because Louise very much wanted to live in Britain, she said, and the fact that Lorne was homosexual may have been an asset. Louise spent very little time with Lorne before they were married on March 21, 1871, at Windsor. Evidence from Louise's writings suggests that the couple did engage in physical marital relations, although according to some sources the physical relationship ended soon after the honeymoon.

Two years after their marriage, Princess Louise and the Marquess of Lorne moved into an apartment in Kensington Palace, which happened to be close to both Boehm's studio and his home. Princess Louise continued to practice sculpture, working in Boehm's studio. In 1878, shortly after her old teacher Mary Thornycroft moved to Melbury Road, Louise had a studio built on the grounds of Kensington Palace. Godwin was her architect, and he explained the task to his architectural students: "I built the studio 17 feet high and put over it a kind of Mansard roof, with windows looking into the garden. The walls are of red brick, there are green slates on the roof to match the old house . . . and all the light is reflected so as to reduce the horizontal ceiling as much as possible. This studio seems perfectly satisfactory to the Princess, to Mr. Boehm, the sculptor (for it is a sculptor's studio) and also to myself."

The princess's relationship with Boehm continued throughout the 1880s, and the circumstances of Boehm's death in his studio in the company of Princess Louise on December 12, 1890, provided the press with much speculation. Wilfrid Scawen Blunt's version from his diaries is generally believed:

It was during one of these visits [of the princess to Boehm's studio] that while he was making love to her Boehm broke a blood-vessel and died actually in the Princess's arms. There was nobody else in the studio or anywhere about ... and the Princess had the courage to take the key of the studio out of the dead man's pocket, and covered with blood as she was and locking the door behind her, got a cab and drove to Laking's [the Queen's physician], whom she found at home and took back with her to the studio. Boehm was dead and they made up a story between them to the effect that it had been while lifting or trying to lift one of the Statues that the accident occurred.

The sculptor Alfred Gilbert, who occupied a studio in the same premises, became an accomplice to their concocted story by taking responsibility for finding the body. Princess Louise championed him for the rest of his life, provided him with accommodations at Kensington Palace in later years, and saw that his ashes were buried at St. Paul's Cathedral when he died.

[3.]I'm always interested when I run across another mention of Queen Victoria's personal servant, John Brown. I mentioned him in the notes for *Brazen,* and when I was reading about the queen's daughter, Princess Louise, his name emerged once again because Louise's lover, Edgar Boehm, was sculpting a bust of John Brown for the queen. (A movie of the relationship between this Scotsman and Queen Victoria, titled *Mrs. Brown,* starring Judi Dench, was made several years ago.)

According to Queen Victoria's journal (parts of which were copied by her youngest daughter, Princess Beatrice, before the original was destroyed—not an unusual circumstance in Victorian times, when appearances counted more than the truth), John Brown in October 1850 was "a good looking, tall lad of twenty-three with fair curly hair, so very good humoured and willing,—always ready to do whatever is asked, and always with a smile on his face." An indiscreet comment, of course, immediately comes to mind.

John Brown was a gillie at Balmoral from 1849 and in charge of the ponies there from 1855. Three years later the queen appointed him her personal servant in Scotland, to wait upon her at all times. At the end of 1864 (Prince Albert had died in 1861) Brown went south to be on duty at Osborne, too, and in February 1865 he was appointed her personal servant wherever she was, not only in Scotland. She described him to her eldest daughter as "so quiet, has such an excellent head and memory, and is besides so devoted, and attached and clever and so wonderfully able to interpret one's wishes."

When Queen Victoria made him her personal servant outside Scotland in 1865, he was thirty-seven and she thirty-nine.

The queen and Prince Albert had a small hut at Balmoral, where they could escape from the formality of life. At her husband's death, this property went to the Prince of Wales. Now Victoria needed once more "some little Spot" to go occasionally for a night or two of quiet and seclusion. In 1866 she began planning additions to a small lodge at Glasallt Shiel, and on October 1, 1868, she slept there for the first time. Sir Henry Ponsonby felt that she always returned "much the better and livelier" for her visits to the shiel, although he wouldn't himself have chosen so lonely a spot. On March 29, 1883, John Brown died, leaving the house the queen was building for him at Baile-na-Coille incomplete. The Glasallt became, according to her journal, "now most terrible for her to visit—it is like death, far more than the peaceful Kirkyard . . . The Queen can never live at the Glasallt again. The whole thing was planned and arranged by him. He meant everything there. That bright Chapter in her saddened life is closed forever!"

In 1865, Victoria had published a small number of copies of *Leaves from the Journal of Our Life in the Highlands.* It was so well received, she was encouraged to publish another edition that would reach a broader audience and this "people's" edition sold thirty thousand copies. In 1884, a further volume was published, *More Leaves from the Journal of a Life in the Highlands,* which continued the story from the death of the prince consort to 1882. It was dedicated, not as the *Leaves* had been to the memory of her husband ("him who made the life of the writer bright and happy"), but to her "Loyal Highlanders" and especially to "my devoted personal attendant and faithful friend John Brown," who had recently died. A tribute to him concludes the book. Wise advisers prevented the queen from publishing a memoir of Brown, which would have surely been misconstrued, they suggested. No doubt.

[4.]During the second half of the nineteenth century, the most desirable locations in London for artists' colonies were St. John's Wood, Hampstead, Chelsea, and Kensington; the most prestigious address was Holland Park, home to the celebrated artists George Frederic Watts and Frederic Leighton, and to lesser lights such as Marcus Stone, Colin Hunter, Hamo Thornycroft, and Luke Fildes. The royal family were patrons of these artists, as were some members of the aristocracy, but their main supporters were the newly rich middle classes. Large fortunes were being made in Birmingham, Manchester, Liverpool, and London, and these industrialists wanted the "genuine article and fresh paint" rather than a spurious "Old Master." And they were willing to pay well for what they wanted.

During a period when the average annual income was about one hundred pounds, many artists were earning in excess of five thousand pounds (roughly half a million pounds today). In the year Leighton commissioned his house in Holland Park, his receipts from sales of paintings and investments exceeded twenty-one thousand pounds. Leighton was the model for Disraeli's Mr. Phoebus in *Lothair* and Henry James's Lord Mellifont in *The Private Life,* and nowhere was his personal success more apparent than in the palace he created in Holland Park Road.

The houses commissioned by the artists in Holland Park now sell for several million pounds—a one-bedroom apartment carved out of Marcus Stone's large studio house sold in 1999 for over one million pounds.

The mid-quarter of the nineteenth century was the zenith of the artists and millionaire-princes in their palaces of art. The collapse in the value of Victorian art was well under way before the end of the century and the individual wealth and social status achieved by the artist in the Holland Park Circle was sustained only during their lifetimes. Only recently are Watts, Leighton, and Albert Moore regaining some of their former status.

[5.]Regardless of the origins of golf, it was the Scots who gave the game its unique character. It was already known as a national pastime before King James II's abortive efforts to ban it by Act of Parliament in 1457. By 1552, January 15 precisely, the citizens of the town of St. Andrews were given, by charter right, the use of the links for "golf, futball, shuteing at all times with all other manners of pastime." The game of golf as we know it today didn't emerge from its crude beginnings on the east coast of Scotland until it began to become organized about the middle of the eighteenth century. The first golf club for which there is definite proof of origin is the Gentlemen Golfers of Leith, instituted in 1744.

There have been claims from other clubs that they are older than the Leith club, for example the Royal Burgess in Edinburgh and the Royal Blackheath in England, but no evidence to substantiate their claims has been found.

Among those instrumental in drawing up the first set of rules was John Rattray, an Edinburgh surgeon who won the first Silver Club in 1744. His golf was interrupted when he was called from his bed to act as surgeon to Bonnie Prince Charlie's troops at the Battle of Prestonpans.

He followed the prince, some say reluctantly, on his march to Derby and thereafter to the defeat at Culloden, where he was taken prisoner. It was only the intervention of his fellow Leith member, Duncan Forbes, that saved him from the gallows and allowed him to resume his duties as captain of the club in 1747.

The game witnessed some early movement out of Scotland to other golfing outposts. It was taken by royalty to England as far back as 1608, by Scottish merchants to India, where the Royal Calcutta Golf Club dates back to 1829, and by the armed forces to South Carolina, where golf was played long before the Apple Tree Gang founded the first American golf club at Yonkers in 1888.

However, by the middle of the nineteenth century, professional golf was still very much in its infancy. Money matches became the forerunners of the tournaments of the present day, and it was as a result of these matches that professional players came into being. The oldest championship in the world is the Open, first played at Prestwick, Scotland, in 1860. For the first thirty years of the Open, none but a Scot took the title. Not until the great English amateur John Ball from Hoylake won the Open in 1890 did the Scottish stranglehold on the famous claret jug loosen.

The rise of the gentleman amateur and the golf boom of the 1880s was a result of the same emerging, wealthy middle class that was so drastically altering the fabric of society. More people had more money and leisure time, and a measure of the demand for new courses is indicated by the number built in the last two decades of the nineteenth century. In 1864 there were about thirty golf clubs in Scotland, while England had only three. By 1880 it is estimated that there were sixty clubs in Britain. The British Amateur Championship was inaugurated at Hoylake in 1885 by the Royal Liverpool Golf Club and the number of golf clubs continued to increase. By 1890 there were 387 and by 1900, Britain had 2,330 golf clubs.

Perhaps the biggest appeal about golf is that when brought right down to its basics, it's between you and your golf ball. Courses have changed over the centuries, as have innovations in equipment, but the skill of the player still matters most. The story of the devout Catholic golfer who crossed himself before he putted and holed his putts every time is a case in point. His opponent asked him, "Does it help?" and the Catholic replied, "No. Not if you can't putt."

[6.]Five thousand pounds is equal to approximately five hundred thousand pounds today, or $785,000.

[7.]In the early Victorian era, *Punch* magazine humorously discussed the meaning of the aspersion "mushroom" that denoted someone newly arrived:

> *A sister of Mrs [Spangle] Lacquer's married a gentleman of property, and resides in the country. Her name is Mrs Champignon Stiffback ... In company with their London relatives [they] ... partake largely of the nature of mushrooms, in as much as they have not only sprung up with great rapidity ... but have also risen from a mould of questionable delicacy ...*

Society looked askance at the nouveaux riches or arrivistes, although in the end, new money talked. When H. G.

Well's fictional uncle, Edward Ponderevo, exchanged his chemist's shop for a lordship, he found the local vicar a useful bridge into country society.

> The vicar ... was an Oxford man ... with ... a general air of accommodation to the new order of things. These Oxford men are the Greeks of our plutocratic empire. He was a Tory in spirit, and what one may call an adapted Tory by stress of circumstances, that is to say he was no longer a legitimist, he was prepared for the substitution of new lords for old. We were pill vendors, he knew, and no doubt horribly vulgar in soul ... but we were English and neither Dissenters nor Socialists, and he was cheerfully prepared to do what he could to make gentlemen of us.

[8.]By the late Victorian period, the process of assimilation—the marriage of land and capital, gentry and haute bourgeoisie—was clear for all to see and new money was calling the shots. "Nowadays," observed the Countess of Cardigan, "money shouts and birth and breeding whisper!"

But of the three props that supported the ruling elite—money, land, and title—it was the possession of a hereditary peerage that was the clearest determinant of class and the most obvious focus of ambition. In the mid-Victorian period, the House of Lords remained a difficult hurdle for new money. Not until the 1880s did both Liberal and Tory governments surrender their patronage to the market. By 1890 the proportion of business and commercial families achieving peerages was twenty-five percent and rising. Between 1886 and 1914 about two hundred new peers were created, at least half from nonlanded backgrounds.

This rise of the bourgeoisie to titled status did not occur without resistance. Many of those in power were offended by "the rustle of banknotes," and native English gentry took affront that social control of London "is now divided between the Semite and the Yankee." Anti-Semitism ran high, as did mockery of the "trans-Atlantic Midases," referred to as peltry or pork kings. But by 1899, the peerage included fifty American ladies; by 1914 seventeen percent of the peerage and twelve percent of the baronetcy had an American connection, frequently through marriage to an heiress. "Failing the dowries of Israel and the plums of the United States," noted Escott with realism, "the British peerage would go to pieces tomorrow."

I became aware of the disdain directed toward American heiresses not only in the memoirs of numerous heiresses who had been treated abominably by their husbands' families, but in particular while touring the Duke of Roxburghe's family seat in Kelso, Scotland, when I was researching *Outlaw*. In 1902, May Goelet of New York, co-heir to a twenty-five-million-dollar fortune, noted that Captain George Holford had hopes of marrying her: "Dorchester House, of course, would be delightful and I believe he has two charming places [Westonbirt and Lasborough, Gloucestershire]. Unfortunately, the dear man has no title . . ." She settled for the Duke of Roxburghe. And apparently he settled for her as well, because in the Roxburghe palatial home in Kelso, as we walked through room after room adorned with priceless antiques, exquisite furniture, carpets, and beautiful paintings, we eventually came to a kitchen hallway, where a collection of fishing gear was displayed on the walls—along with the full-length portrait of the American duchess. Her rating in the hierarchy of the Roxburghe family was eminently clear.

Be sure to look for the next sizzling
SUSAN JOHNSON novel from Bantam Books,
on sale in Summer 2002.

ABOUT THE AUTHOR

SUSAN JOHNSON, award-winning author of nationally bestselling novels, lives in the country near North Branch, Minnesota. A former art historian, she considers the life of a writer the best of all possible worlds.

Researching her novels takes her to past and distant places, and bringing characters to life allows her imagination full rein, while the creative process offers occasional fascinating glimpses into the complicated machinery of the mind.

But perhaps most important . . . writing stories is fun.